COOPER

RILEY EDWARDS

BE A REBEL
Riley Edwards Romance

Cooper
Blue Team 5

Cover design: Lori Jackson Designs

Written by: Riley Edwards

Published by: Riley Edwards/Rebels Romance

Edited by: Rebecca Hodgkins

Proofreader: Julie Deaton

Cooper

Paperback ISBN: 978-1-951567-27-9

First edition: June 28, 2022

To my family - my team – my tribe.
This is for you.

1

"SO LET ME GET THIS STRAIGHT." Kira's pale green eyes danced with humor as she glanced between Gabe and me. "You want me to sit in a chair in the middle of the dance floor, and you want Cooper to put *that* on me."

"Yes."

"I think you forgot the part where Evette tosses—"

"Okay," Kira chirped.

"Great."

Gabe's slap on my shoulder before he went in search of his new wife to tell her the good news that he'd found two suckers to embarrass, was a warning. I might've no longer been the "new guy" seeing as the teams now had five new guys to haze, but I was still the newest member of my team, and being that, I was still subjected to their foolishness.

Unfortunately for them, I didn't embarrass easily. Unfortunately for me, Kira Winters struck me as a woman who was up for anything. And the wicked smile she was aiming my way told me I was in for a world of hurt. The kind of hurt that was going to start in my balls but eventually, the pain would travel to my chest when she ripped my heart out and stomped on it.

Kira was the kind of woman a man fell for. It wasn't her extreme beauty, it wasn't her shiny blonde hair, it wasn't her eyes that resembled pastel jade ice crystals, it wasn't her body that had mine aching every time I saw her. It was all of it, what those eyes said when she looked at me. It was her fun, flirty, outgoing, up-for-anything personality. It was how gracefully she moved. The promise of all that was her. She'd be down to lounge around in sweats all day in front of the TV. She'd be happy going skydiving. She'd let me fuck her breathless on the hood of my GTO. She'd let me tie her up and smack her ass, or she'd ride me slow and sweet.

Anything.

Absolutely anything.

And I knew this because she'd camped out on my couch all day watching old sitcoms with me more than a few times over the last five months, and she did it looking sexy as all-fuck. She ate popcorn by the handfuls, and she drank whiskey on the rocks. She wore ratty sweats paired with tight tank tops that showed off her flat stomach. She laughed like she didn't give a single fuck what anyone thought about her. She grabbed life by the balls and did whatever the hell she wanted to when the spirit moved her to do it. Including calling me at midnight to tell me she'd made reservations for the next day for us to go skydiving. And when she jumped out of the plane, she yelled with wild abandon all the way back to the ground. But when the mood hit her, she could be quiet and thoughtful.

The woman drove me to the brink of insanity.

"You're looking a little scared, my friend."

Scared was the last thing I was. On the verge of taking

her home and putting us both out of our misery was more like it. Ending the five months of foreplay that she'd instigated and that I'd been doing my best to ignore.

"How'd you get here?"

A slow sexy smile pulled at her lips. It was no less effective at making my cock jump in my slacks than the wickedness of her previous grin.

"Kevin and Layla."

"After this, I'm taking you home."

A perfectly manicured eyebrow arched, and yeah, that, too, made my cock twitch.

"You are?" she asked under the pretense she was pondering my statement.

"I am," I confirmed.

"And will you be walking me to my front door like a gentleman, so I can ask you in for a drink?"

Brink. Of. Insanity.

I heard the music change then the MC called our names over the opening electric guitar riff of an old, familiar Guns N' Roses song.

"Shall we?" Kira laughed and offered me her elbow to escort her to the dance floor.

Fuck that.

I stepped closer, tagged her around the waist, and dropped my mouth to her ear.

"There's not gonna be one thing gentlemanly about tonight, baby."

"Thank God. I was starting to get worried you were a prude."

I dragged Kira out onto the dance floor, deposited her in the chair that had been set out for this purpose, and dropped to my knees in front of her. Without a word, I pulled the ugly-as-fuck hot pink satin garter belt out of my pocket, then lifted her right foot.

In the background, "Welcome to the Jungle" barely drowned out all the hoots and hollers of our teammates. I was sure I was supposed to put on a show, go slow and drag out the spectacle of a wedding tradition I had no interest in participating in. But when my fingertips glided up Kira's silky-smooth skin, all thoughts except one vanished. I shoved the garter over her knee and my hands dipped beneath her skirt.

Now that my hands were no longer in view of the guests, it was time to educate Miss Winters.

My right hand continued to maneuver the garter into place while my left went higher, and I watched those sexy eyes get hazy when my fingers brushed over her wet panties.

Kira looked down at me and tilted her head in a taunt that made my cock jerk. She was calling me out, knowing I wouldn't go any further with everyone watching.

The woman was crazy.

I yanked my hands free, helped her stand, and paused just long enough to take in her triumphant smile.

I could look at that smile every day for the rest of my life, and it wouldn't be enough. I'd still want more of it.

"You think you won," I noted.

"I did."

"Game's not over, sweetheart."

———

FIVE MINUTES LATER—PARKING *lot behind Gabe and Evette's wedding reception.*

"This still feels like winning," Kira panted.

My fingers dug into her hips, the material of her skirt bunched under my hands, my seat pushed back as far as it would go, not giving her much room to move. But she didn't need space, not when the feel of her slick, tight pussy was enough to send me over the edge. The swivel of her hips only intensified the pleasure.

I slipped one of my hands down between us and my thumb instantly found my target. I gave her a few slow circles.

"That feel like winning, baby?"

"Yes," she moaned.

Fuck, yeah, it did.

"Harder, Kira."

I let go of her dress, slid my hand around to her ass, and groaned when she slammed down on my cock, hard.

"So good. I'm close, honey."

Her back arched, her drives became uncoordinated, and I felt her pussy clench.

And there I sat, Kira riding my cock with wild abandon just like I knew she would, fucking me hard and fast until she was breathless. The feel of her so goddamn good I saw stars. She fucked me through her orgasm, she fucked me through mine, she threw her head back and moaned her pleasure like she didn't give a fuck who heard. The woman was out of this world. Best sex of my life, bar none. I never had better, and I knew with my cock planted deep in her sleek, wet pussy I never would. No one would ever compare to Kira Winters. Not in any way.

She'd be the woman who ruined me.

She'd take what I could give and then demand more.

She'd take and steal until she had all of me.

The fuck of it was, I knew how it would end. I knew

she'd spent ten years working in the dark, and she was ready to live her life again. She was ready to drink it in and drown in as many experiences as she could. She'd use me until she was full, then she'd move on.

And I was going to let her.

2

"DIE, SUCKA, DIE!"

Kira's voice carried down the hall and I quickened my step. As soon as I rounded the corner, I saw it. Lincoln and Jasmin Parker's twin sons Robbie and Asher fully kitted out —wrist bands loaded with ammo, tactical vests with more ammo tucked into slots, and magazines secured in pouches. Both boys holding long rifles, pistols secured in thigh rigs.

Then there was Kira.

Beautiful, sexy, funny Kira. Long blonde hair pulled up into a ponytail, tight faded jeans, a hideous lime-green t-shirt with bright white, bold letters that declared her a "Nerd". Yet as ugly as the shirt was, the color managed to highlight her gemstone eyes. She was geared up like the boys with the addition of a second rig on her left thigh. The sight in front of me stole my breath. A reminder I was in love with a woman who was going to break my heart, but I lacked the willpower to let her go.

Robbie lifted his rifle, took aim, and pulled the trigger.

"Bang! Bang!" the kid shouted.

Kira dove behind a chair narrowly escaping the whistling bullet.

Not to be outdone, Asher pulled his pistol from the holster, dropped to his knees, and repeatedly shot his brother.

"Got you!" Asher yelled.

"Stop, Ash, you're on my team!"

"I'm my own team," Asher announced.

"You can't do that," his brother argued.

The situation deteriorated from there into total mayhem. Blue and orange darts haphazardly flew around the room, hitting the wall-mounted screens, the whiteboard in the corner, and the windows more than they hit the individuals who were engaged in battle.

"What's going on in here?" Zane boomed from behind me.

I stepped aside to give him a better view of his conference room which now looked like a daycare war zone.

"Lincoln!" Zane bellowed. "Come get your semen demons."

Kira's gaze sliced to the doorway and her eyes found mine.

They were alight with mischief.

She also had a big, broad smile on her face.

Goddamn, she was gorgeous.

That was Kira. She was always smiling, always happy, always up for fun. And when there was none to be had, say like now while she was supposed to be working, she'd create it.

Whether it be Nerf gun wars with Lincoln's twins or waiting for Garrett to leave for lunch then going into his office and rearranging his desk, to leaving Slim Jims on Owen's desk, Kira was always up for a good time.

In the five months I'd known her, except for when our boss Zane and our teammates Kevin and Theo had been held captive, I'd never seen her not smiling.

She played video games like a teenager, jumped out of planes like a pro, cracked jokes like it was her job, and she fucked like the world was ending and it was morally imperative to get in one more orgasm before she bit the dust.

I'd never met a woman who was on a mission to suck life dry. Her sense of adventure was intoxicating. She pulled you into her orbit and took you along for the ride. She was addicting.

And that was the problem—I was hooked.

She'd spent ten years stuck behind her keyboard with very little social interaction. Hidden away running an off-the-books operation that required twenty-four-seven attention. Now she had her life back and I was convenient. But when she got her fill and was ready, she'd move on.

I wouldn't.

I'd turn into my teammate Garrett and spend goddamn eternity knowing I lost my one.

I needed to end the madness, but I knew I wouldn't. I needed to protect myself, but I was too far gone.

Kira's gaze darted to Zane, her smile widened, and it was then I learned something new about the woman who'd been in my bed the last few weeks—she was totally insane. She drew her Nerf rifle up, aimed, and peppered Zane Lewis in the face with darts.

The man didn't flinch at the barrage of rubber-tipped bullets as they nailed him in the face.

"Uncle Zane!" Robbie yelled and threw a pistol in the general vicinity of his uncle. "Catch."

Zane's hand shot out. He nabbed the gun out of the air and returned fire on Kira.

"Frag out!" Asher screamed.

"Not yet," Robbie returned. "I need cover fire."

Christ, who raised these kids, Rambo?

"What the hell's going on?"

Zane shifted and I ducked just as a dart whistled by my head, hitting Lincoln.

"Goddamn, I almost lost an eye." Linc's hand came up to cover his face. "What'd I say about shooting guns indoors?"

"Daddy said goddamn!" Robbie shouted.

"Good Lord, do your children ever not yell?" I asked.

All three statements were said simultaneously.

Kira belted out a laugh, the sound of it so damn captivating I missed her reloading. Which meant I was so taken in by all that was her I missed her taking aim.

"Tango, one o'clock," Asher called out. "Take cover."

The boys didn't take cover; they threw themselves on the floor near my feet.

"Brother, you need to teach your boys the definition of cover." I heard Zane tell Linc as bullets pelted my chest.

Kira wanted to play—we'd play.

I knelt, tagged Asher's discarded rifle, and returned fire.

"No fair." Kira laughed. "I'm out of ammo."

"Shoulda thought about that before you shot me, KK," I suggested.

"Mercy," she called out.

But instead of surrendering, the crazy woman rushed forward, and with no signs of her stopping, I had no choice but to lower the big plastic rifle before she impaled herself. Then in true Kira fashion, she leaped—her legs went around my waist, her arms over my shoulders, and I felt her lips brush my throat as she tucked her face into my neck. My hands automatically went to her ass to hold her up. The weight of her in my arms was so familiar it felt natural. Everything about her felt intuitive, inherent, easy. In only a few short months Kira had become a fundamental part of my life. Right down to the mundane, the everyday minutia that could bog life down, but with her the trivial became significant.

I didn't have to lower my head far before I caught a whiff of her unique scent—grapefruit and mint. And just as easily as the fragrance filled my nostrils, I could picture her orange bottle of shampoo that sat on the shelf in my shower next to mine. Along with her shampoo were her conditioner and razor and some poofy ball she used to "exfoliate" with. I was unclear why a woman needed to exfoliate but I couldn't deny the outcome—soft, smooth skin that felt fucking fantastic bare and pressed against me. Another thing I was well acquainted with. Something I'd never been fond of in the past but something I couldn't get enough of with Kira. Since the night she started to stay over she slept close. Always. Tucked into my side, or she'd crush her chest to my back, cheek to my shoulder, arm around my middle. All that sleek skin pressed tight—yeah, I fucking loved it. Couldn't get enough. So much so, that I was willing to bear the consequences of heartbreak to get my fill.

"Baby, you're a cheat," I murmured.

"It's not cheating if you're winning."

"Not sure how you think you won, KK, you dropped your gun."

"Your hands are on my ass, aren't they?"

Hell, yeah, they were.

And just to punctuate how much I enjoyed having her ass where it was, I gave it a squeeze.

"You know there are children present," I reminded her.

"Incorrect. They are not children, they are Viking Spawn."

"That might be the case, but I still don't think Linc would appreciate where this is gonna go if you don't drop down."

Kira lifted her head and blinded me with a smirk that set my chest on fire and had my cock jumping to life.

"I reckon he'd like that less—"

"You'd be right," Linc cut her off.

"I'm a Viking," one of the boys called out.

"No, I'm a Viking," the other argued.

"You're demons," Zane corrected. "Now clean up this mess."

Fortunately, that was Kira's cue to unwrap her legs and jump down.

"Uncle," Robbie whined. "We were training."

"Training for what, the *Army*?" Zane spat like the word Army tasted bad.

Seeing as he and his brother Lincoln were both former SEALs but Linc's wife Jasmin was former Army, this was an ongoing argument around the office. Sometimes my brother Jaxon jumped in the fray and suggested Robbie and Asher join the Air Force. Unfortunately for him, he was outnumbered. The majority of our teammates were former Navy. Jasmin, Colin, and Myles were the only three that came from the Army. And I was the odd man out with no prior military experience. Zane took me on after I quit the LAPD and moved to Maryland.

"Go Army. Sink Navy," Asher belted out the motto.

"Your mother's brainwashed you," Zane said before his gaze went from his nephews and paused on me. "You're fired."

"Why am I fired?"

"Breach of contract."

"Maybe can we have this conversation when my boys aren't within earshot?" Linc jumped in. "And, boys, the saying is, Go Navy. Kick Army's butt."

"Is this what the world's come to?" Zane questioned. "Nerf guns and *butts*. What happened to the good old days when actual bullets rang out? Now you people are shooting rubber darts that don't even leave a mark. Next thing, you're gonna be loading your magazines with blanks whining about dispatching scumbags to hell."

"Brother," Linc drawled and swept his hand in the direction of his twins. "Proof I don't shoot blanks. I got two in one go."

I watched Kira's lips turn up into a smile before her throaty laughter filled the room.

Yep. I was totally fucked.

In way too deep with a woman who would never be mine.

"Daddy, what are blanks?" Asher asked and Zane joined Kira. Only his laughter wasn't smooth like silk, it was obnoxious.

"Yeah, *Daddy*, what are blanks?" Zane echoed.

"You're a dick," Linc mumbled to his brother.

"Ohh. Daddy called Uncle Zane a dick," Robbie chanted.

"So? A dick is a penis and Uncle Zane's a boy, so that means he has one," Asher proudly declared.

I glanced around, taking in Linc's twins, then at Zane smiling down at his nephews, then over to Linc who was trying his best not to smile at his boys, and finally I stopped on Kira.

This was my new life.

Family and laughter.

My boss was mostly a sarcastic ass but under his rough exterior was a man who'd give his life for his family. His loyalty was second to none. He was skilled in the art of war —deadly, ruthless, merciless. Yet, the man had more compassion than anyone I'd ever met. He'd heard I quit the LAPD, he heard why, and within twenty-four hours of me handing in my resignation, Zane was in California. I couldn't say his attempt to set me straight was a hundred percent successful, but he was there. That was Zane Lewis. And more proof Zane was who he was, he wouldn't leave until I agreed to move to Maryland and take the job he'd offered me. The man wasn't worried about my unemployment. He wasn't thinking about my financial stability. He wasn't so much offering me a job—he was offering me a family. A group of brothers who wouldn't let me sink under the mounting guilt. He gave me an opportunity to be close to my older brother Jaxon, his family, and my parents.

If it had not been for Zane, I would've stayed in California.

If he hadn't reached out, I wouldn't have this.

I would never have admitted how lonely I was living in California. I'd had friends, men and women I'd worked with. But it wasn't a brotherhood. I had women, but none of them had sparked anything beyond physical attraction and that attraction fizzled out fast. I would've stayed where I was, buried under the guilt of the five lives I couldn't save. Not that I didn't still feel that guilt, it was just somehow easier to manage.

Then there was Kira.

I wouldn't have her for however long I was going to have her if Zane hadn't dragged my ass to Maryland.

I wasn't sure if I was grateful for the time or if she was my biggest regret.

I already knew she'd be my downfall, the woman who ruined me, the one who shattered my soul. No one would ever fill the void she'd leave.

Yeah, Kira Winters was my biggest regret and my greatest love.

This was gonna hurt like a motherfucker.

3

"GOT A SECOND, KIRA?"

I looked up from my tablet and over at my office door to find Garrett. He wasn't looking at me, he was taking in my space which was nowhere near as awesome as his glass enclosure right smack dab in the middle of the main office area.

I'd been stuck in a corner office. Not that I should complain; it was a corner office with two walls full of windows with an awesome view. Plus it was much better than my previous workstation, otherwise known as my spare bedroom. Or, if I felt like venturing out—which I rarely did —Patheon had an office in a high-rise. Top floor penthouse, fully furnished. The views didn't suck but they weren't of the Severn River and the Naval Academy.

But more than that, I used to work alone. I had no co-workers who I interacted with daily in person. I spoke to my boss, Layla Cunnings-soon-to-be-Monroe every day, sometimes multiple times a day. I saw her occasionally, but my other teammates—Theo, Easton, Smith, Jonas, and Cash—

never. That was, I never saw them or spoke to them on the phone. Our communication had been limited to encrypted electronic mail. That had lasted ten, long, lonely years. I'd given up my twenties to help Layla run an off-the-books black ops team. I'd done this gladly. I'd happily given up what I'd heard called the best years of a young person's life to avenge my brother's murder.

Maybe avenge wasn't the right word; the terrorist who had beheaded my beloved brother was dead. His brothers-in-arms had seen to that. So perhaps I agreed to help Layla and the guys because I had nothing else. My parents had been murdered the summer I'd graduated from high school and two years later, Finn was taken from me.

So much death.

No, not death, murder.

My brother. My mother. My father.

All gone. All killed in the most horrific of ways.

I'd been all alone in the world, hellbent on finding every detail I could about my brother. Hacking the CIA to get that information was how Layla had found me. At the time, I gave zero fucks to getting caught, all I wanted was answers. Regrettably, I got the answers I was after, now I wished I didn't know. There were some things in life that once you knew them changed your perception of humanity. Now I knew too much. The blinders had been removed and I fully understood evil.

"Kira?" Garrett called, pulling me back to the room.

"Sorry. What's up?"

"Where are you on the Langford file?"

"I finished the searches," I told Garrett.

"And?"

"Let me ask you something. Did you give me this

because you're still testing my skills? Which I've proven are just as good as yours. Or did you know I'd find things you couldn't? Or alternately, does Z Corps have nothing better to do than run traces on a novelist with questionable Google searches?"

"That's what you think this is about, an author with questionable Google searches?"

"No, I think Kingston Langford is a bullshit artist pretending to be a former spy. But the other name you sent me to look into is indeed a fiction writer. Next time you want me to look into some harmless author please choose a genre I at least enjoy."

Garrett's gaze intensified and he leaned against the door frame as he studied me.

Did he think I couldn't perform the remedial task of tracking back freaking Google searches and connecting a few dots? I could hack into the most secure locations within an hour. Give me twenty-four hours and I could override security protocols and redirect satellites. So, obviously, I was smart enough to weed through Google searches and find Whitmore's pseudonym all in under ten minutes. Kingston Langford took me a bit longer to suss out but not by much.

"Why do you think Langford's a bullshit artist and not the spy he claims he is?"

"Would you like to come in and sit down or do you prefer to lurk in doorways?"

Garrett didn't hide his smile when he said, "I think I'll stand. I heard you're strapped, and I don't wanna take a dart to the face."

Yes, I indeed did have two fully loaded Nerf guns nearby. One could never be too careful when there were two rug rats running around the office with shockingly good aim. Though I shouldn't have been surprised considering the boys' mother was a badass chick and the DNA they'd inherited from their father was exceptional. If those two boys didn't grow up to be tall, good-looking commandos seeing as they were already tall (for their ages), cute, mini-commandos, I'd eat a dirty sock. They also liked to attack, and they did it as a pair, thus I was always armed.

"I only shoot the Viking's offspring."

"And Zane," he reminded me.

"Only when the Dimple King interrupts an epic battle."

"Right." Garrett chuckled. "And Cooper? What'd he do?"

Ah, yes, Cooper. The real question was, what *didn't* he do?

The man was the epitome of perfect. He indulged me in every way. I'd yet to find anything he'd say no to. He'd take me to an indoor rock wall and climb with me for hours. He'd chill on his couch with me and binge crappy TV. He'd go skydiving with me. He'd take me to a club and dance. He'd eat greasy fast food and not complain. He'd fuck me so hard I couldn't breathe. He'd make out with me. He'd give me slow and sweet.

But above all else, he let me be me.

At work, he respected me and my opinions.

Outside of work he treated me like I was a queen.

Cooper Cain was the man I was going to marry. I felt it down to my soul. I also knew he didn't believe it. Not that I'd told him I wanted to marry him, nor had any avows of love been exchanged. We hadn't even defined our relationship. We hung out all the time. I spent the night at his place more than I slept at my apartment. We were damn near inseparable, but I knew—not because he said it but because

I could feel his hesitancy. This was not a deterrent, nor did it make me question my feelings.

Cooper had yet to learn something about me—I was a fighter.

I did not quit.

So what if I had to work extra hard to prove to him there was no other man for me?

"Cooper didn't do anything," I admitted. "I just didn't want him to feel left out."

Garrett shook his head as he walked into my office. His gaze didn't leave mine until he took a seat across from me and his eyes dropped to my desk.

"Clean, isn't it?" I asked.

"Smartass," he mumbled but I didn't miss the smile in his voice.

"No, really. See the nice wood? This is what a desk looks like. I'm sure if you moved all the files and clutter off yours and found some Pledge it would be just as pretty."

"Move my files and die."

Garrett was full of shit. I moved his files all the time and in turn, he threatened my life frequently, yet I was still breathing.

"Here." I grabbed the folder I'd made especially for Garrett and handed it to him. "Under extreme protest, I printed everything out for you."

Garrett leaned forward, took the folder, and when he sat back, he asked, "Extreme protest? Not slight protest?"

"I shudder to think of the trees who died so you could have a paper trail."

"Who died? You mean *that* died," he corrected.

"And that's your problem. You're a tree killer. I think you spend too much time behind a computer screen and you need to get out in nature. Appreciate the sights and sounds. Maybe hug a tree or two. The flip side is you'd save Zane a whack if you went digital."

"Says the hacker who knows how easy it is to wipe a database."

"I thought your system was the best. Totally impregnable."

"There's no such thing and you know it."

He was correct of course. Someone or a group of people with the right skills, motivation, and given enough time could defeat any system.

"Damn, One, here I thought you were the master of cyber security."

As soon as Garrett's old nickname left my mouth I felt like a bitch. And watching his smile die was akin to feeling a knife inserted into my belly.

Clearly, Garrett still had some issues to work out, and who wouldn't after what he'd been through. Honestly, I was a little surprised he interacted with me at all. After all, I was the little sister of the man who ended his career. Not because Finn had done something to end it, but when Garrett's team received bad intel—bad as in, a traitor in the CIA had purposely given Garrett the wrong intel—which led to my brother being murdered and Garrett erroneously blaming himself. And that ended Garrett's career. He quit his team and disappeared. The whole situation was as screwed up as any situation could get.

Totally FUBAR as Finn would say.

And ten years after my brother's murder it was still fucked-up but I was holding out hope it wasn't beyond all repair. Garrett deserved to find peace.

"Damn, Garrett. I'm sorry. Sometimes I forget."

"There's nothing to be sorry for."

His deadened, flat tone told a different tale, but I'd never call him out on it.

I watched him open the file, leaf through papers until he found what he was looking for, then waited for him to scan the page. I did this silently wishing I had the right words to take away Garrett's pain.

I'd lost my brother.

Garrett was just lost.

And I hated that for him.

"Tell me about Langford," Garrett prompted.

"Kingston Langford spends more time behind a computer screen than you do. Social media groups, good old-fashioned message boards, Reddit, Quora, Ask, and he even has penned entries on Wikipedia. He spends roughly nineteen hours a day online. He's fifty-one, divorced, I found no sign of a current girlfriend, and with the amount of time he spends trolling the internet, I think it's safe to assume that's correct. No kids. He likes Doritos and is seriously lacking fruits and vegetables in his diet if his weekly grocery delivery is anything to go by. No employment but his bank accounts are healthy. Disability and a workers' compensation settlement are what he lives on. He has no debt. His two-bedroom home is paid off. He drives a twenty-year-old Honda—again paid off. His life is boring as hell."

"And Whitmore?"

"Whitmore is a legit political thriller author."

"Know that, Kira. What about his personal life?"

"He's boring, too. Divorced, sixty, no kids. He's a full-time self-published author, has been for five years. He quit his job as an advertising specialist a year into his writing career. He lives in a one-bedroom apartment. Credit history is good. Carries minimal debt. His biggest expense is rent and his car payment. See? Boring."

"What else?"

"What do you mean what else? His Google searches would flag him, but I cross-referenced them to the content he writes and they're on par with book research. He asks a lot of questions on different information-sharing sites, especially Quora. That's where Whitmore found Langford. Whitmore asked the community about the White House gates and what kind of barricades and checkpoints there are to enter. Langford directed him to Google Images, then took the conversation to direct message where he provided detail about the entry points."

"What's Langford getting out of these exchanges? We've got thirty weeks of emails. That's a long-ass time for Langford to engage. What's his game?"

What *was* his game?

I didn't analyze intel. I collected it and passed it on to Layla.

"How the hell should I know?"

To his credit, Garrett didn't express his impatience even though I was fairly certain he was getting fed up with me.

"You're smart. Very smart. Think about what you found then ask yourself why would Langford continue to engage with Whitmore for over six months? Is this normal behavior? Are there others? If not, why Whitmore? And who else is Whitmore getting his information from? Has his online interaction changed? Is he asking more or fewer questions on these forums?"

"One." *Damn.* "Sorry, Garrett, I'm a hacker. I don't know why people do the things they do. I have no idea what Langford is getting out of exchanging emails with an author.

The only thing I know is James Whitmore is nosy as hell and asks a lot of questions. I have no idea how much research goes into writing a book, so maybe his questions are normal."

"What kind of books?"

"Political thrillers," I reminded him.

"Did you look into what kind of political thrillers?"

I should've been offended he asked. Just because I didn't understand why people did the things they did, didn't mean I wasn't thorough.

"Of course I did. His latest series is about a man fed up with the government. Books one and two were about the man taking aim at different high-profile figures in Washington. Whitmore's next release..." I trailed off.

"Keep going," Garrett instructed.

"The book's about the man assassinating the President."

"Right. So think—"

"Wait," I interrupted Garrett. "You don't think this fiction author is actually planning a real-life assassination attempt, do you?"

"I'm not thinking anything. Right now, we're gathering pieces of information and seeing if we can fit them together into a clear picture. It would help us do that if we understood what Langford's motives were. Maybe he is just some bored dude who gets off pretending to be some big shot and keeping someone on the hook, especially an author who is gaging for information. Maybe Whitmore's just a writer who wants the details of his book to be authentic. Or maybe he's looking for intel for a different reason."

I might not have been versed in book writing or the research that goes into these books, but I wasn't stupid enough to think that Z Corps would have any interest in investigating someone's internet searches.

"Why is Z Corps looking into this?"

"Why not?" Garrett quipped.

"Why not? Is business so slow that Zane has nothing better to pay me to investigate? Really, Garrett, Google searches?"

"And emails."

"Yes, emails that are from some kook who's lying about being a spy."

I was trying my hardest to rein in my attitude, but I didn't sign on to investigate authors and fake internet profiles unless those profiles belonged to terrorists. And Kingston Langford was no terrorist. He was some bored middle-aged guy with nothing better to do than email with a stranger and discuss hypothetical White House protocol.

Wait.

I swiveled my chair, woke up my computer, and clicked the folder that contained the files from Langford's computer.

"Langford's ex-wife works for General Motors," I said and continued to scroll through the documents until I found the automotive drawings I was looking for. "The drawings aren't labeled but that's a limo for sure."

I enlarged one of the images and sat back. When I glanced at Garrett, he was leaning forward studying my computer screen.

"Go on," he encouraged.

"GM makes Cadillac," I told him.

"What else?"

"The presidential limo is a Cadillac."

"What else?"

Garrett was no longer looking at my computer; he was staring at me expectantly.

"I don't know what else. Caroline Langford works for GM. Kingston has drawings for a limo on his computer.

GM makes Cadillac. And The Beast is a Cadillac. But there's no date on these plans and I don't know how to read automotive plans, so I don't know what I'm looking at."

"But you remembered them," Garrett pointed out. "Something triggered you to pull them up. What made you think about the drawings?"

"You should ask Layla to—"

"I'm asking you," Garrett interrupted. "You're a scarily good hacker. You have great instincts. You know what threads to pull. You know which leads to chase. You already analyze data, you just don't see it that way. You didn't have Layla sitting next to you when you were tracking five men, shifting through their intel. You instinctively knew what information to follow up on. You unconsciously keyed in to what was important and what wasn't."

I thought perhaps Garrett was giving me more credit than I was due.

"Theo, Easton, Cash, Smith, and Jonas sent me the reports. All I'd had to do was dig deeper into what they'd found. The guys and Layla did all the heavy lifting."

Garrett settled back in the chair and something amazing happened—amazingly beautiful. Everything about the man softened—his eyes, his mouth, his shoulders. It reminded me of how my brother used to look at me, and just the thought of that and how many years it had been since I'd seen my big brother made my stomach somersault and my heart hurt.

"That's not true, Kira. Layla gave me access to everything. I read every SITREP, every email, every note you made. You have it, you just have to hone in the skill."

That was a lot of reading. Over ten years, I'd collected a lot of mission data and written thousands of situation reports. And there had to be thousands of pages of notes I'd made over the years.

"I have what?"

Garrett didn't answer. Instead, he said, "There's a saying in basketball; you can't teach height."

I thought that was pretty obvious, but I had no idea what it had to do with me or what we were talking about.

"Okay."

"A coach can teach the game—the rules, how to shoot, how to dribble. The same as I can teach anyone how to break code, how to get into a system, how to install a virus. But I can't teach instinct. And that's what you have. It just needs to be sharpened."

"You think so?" I whispered, not trusting my voice.

"I know so."

When my parents were alive, they were proud of me. They told me and Finn all the time how blessed they were to have us. I knew Finn loved me, I knew he thought I was smart, I knew because he told me all the time. Every time he called me to check in, he told me. Every. Time. He never missed an opportunity to tell me how proud he was of me.

Had I told him how proud I was of him?

Had I told him how scared I was to lose him?

Had I told him how lost I would be without him?

But now he was gone, and I'd been alone for so long I'd forgotten how good it felt to have someone believe in me. Layla relied on me, and so did the guys. They trusted me. And she'd been a good friend to me. A mentor. Someone I looked up to. My years with Patheon felt like one big trial by fire. There was no room for error when five lives were on the line. But Garrett sitting across from me, telling me he thought I had good instincts and wanting to help me refine my skills, felt different.

"I miss—" I stopped mid-thought and shook my head.

"You miss what?"

Shit.

I took in the man before me, the man who'd been sent to rescue my brother, the man who, when the mission failed felt it was his fault so deeply, he'd quit his team and gone underground. The man who felt guilt for something that was not his fault. That guilt cost him ten years of no contact with men who had thought of him as a brother.

There was no way I was finishing my thought. Not because I didn't miss Finn. Not because I didn't want to talk about him. But to save Garrett the reminder he was gone.

"Nothing," I muttered, and Garrett's eyes narrowed the same way Finn's always had when I tried to pull a fast one. "Should I look deeper into Caroline Langford?"

Garrett was staring at me intently, and since I was fixated on him, I saw the muscle in his cheek jump. He looked like he was getting ready to call me out when he changed his mind and closed the file.

"Go with your gut," he told me and stood. "We'll talk in the morning before you present the case to the team."

Say what?

"Wait. What do you mean, I'm presenting the case?"

"You're presenting," he mostly repeated and started for the door.

"I don't know how to do that."

Garrett's eyes went around my office before they landed on me. My breath seized in my lungs at the sadness I saw.

"You've been presenting intel for ten years. You know how to do it. And if you trip up, I'll be there with you."

With that, he left.

Out of all the men I worked with, Garrett was the hardest to read. He was close to his teammates, all nineteen of them. He was friendly and outgoing but there was an underlying melancholy. An emptiness he couldn't hide. I didn't know him well enough to know if the despondency I saw was due to my presence, or maybe it was Easton, Smith, Jonas, and Cash being around that brought up bad memories. Or maybe it was something else entirely. But whatever it was, it hurt to see.

Looking at Garrett was like looking in a mirror—pain lingered just under the surface. A longing so deep, nothing would ever quench the ache. There was a piece missing. I knew that feeling well. I knew what it meant to have a hole in your heart that was so big, if you gave in to the pain you'd drown in sorrow. I had three of them. Three big, huge, giant, gaping holes that would never be filled.

I turned back to my computer and pushed Garrett out of my mind. I focused on the automobile plans that were still on my screen, but my attention was elsewhere.

In less than half a year my whole life had been uprooted, turned upside down, and changed completely. Eight months ago, I was living a life of ambiguity. I was isolated and alone. Now I lived open. I was making friends. I was falling in love with a group of people who were loyal, protective, and honest to God, besides my own team, the best people I'd ever met. Finn would've loved them. He would've jackassed around the guys, he would've matched Zane's sarcasm and wit, and he would've loved Cooper for me. But mostly, he'd loathe Garrett's sadness.

However, with all the changes that had happened, I was still me. I was the woman who'd lost everything and through that, I lived the lessons my parents had taught me. I vividly remembered my brother's commitment, his sacrifices, his love for me, and I worked my ass off to be the woman he told me I was.

I was kickass behind a keyboard. I was a damn good hacker. There was nothing I couldn't do. There was nothing that would stop me from being the best.

Focus, Kira.

I minimized the image and went back to the report I'd typed up for Garrett. I'd missed something and I was damn well going to find it.

4

IT WAS NEARING nine o'clock by the time I finished my workout, showered, changed, and made my way to Kira's office. When I got to her door I paused just outside. She was so focused on what she was reading she hadn't noticed me standing there. Which worked for me, it gave me time to drink her in. Even only having her in profile she was outright stunning. There were times when it took me by surprise—like now, having seen her a few hours ago before I went to the basement gym, having memorized every inch of her body, having tasted and touched and kissed every part of her—it still rendered me stupid. She managed to keep the girl-next-door sweetness when she was anything but. Despite the losses she'd suffered, the things she'd seen over the last ten years, the evil she knew to be out in the world, she'd somehow maintained an innocence that was immensely attractive. Couple that with her inner strength and fortitude and her appeal was off the charts. But her beauty was breath-stealing—always. Whether it had been hours or minutes since I'd seen her, she never failed to stun me.

But tonight, she looked tired. And she would—she'd been at her desk going on thirteen hours.

Too long.

I stepped into the room and asked, "Ready to call it a night?"

"Damn," she gasped and covered her heart with her right hand. "You scared the hell out of me."

I bet I did.

Before I could apologize, she continued, "Go on without me. I have a few more hours of work."

That wasn't going to happen.

I took a seat in one of the chairs in front of her desk and she again spoke before I could.

"You don't have to wait."

I ignored the silliness of her comment.

"Langford case?"

That got her attention.

"Have you read the file?"

I had and I'd been instructed not to give Kira my opinion. But that didn't mean I couldn't discuss it with her.

"Yep."

Her brow crinkled and she frowned when she inquired, "Has everyone?"

"I doubt everyone has. But Kevin, Owen, Myles, and Gabe have."

"So Garrett *is* testing me."

She wasn't asking, it was a statement. And since she didn't need my confirmation, I said nothing, but she did.

"Garrett told me I'm presenting the case to the team in the morning."

I knew that, too. I also knew she'd do well.

Beyond her beauty, her resilience, her sense of humor,

the woman was smart—exceptionally so. Before things between us had progressed to where they were now—which was confusing as all fuck, but exclusive—I'd read the dossier Garrett had put together. I knew she dropped out of college when Layla recruited her. I knew she went back and finished her degree online. I knew she taught herself programming. And not how to code websites—she taught herself how to code a facial rec program so sophisticated Garrett along with hundreds if not thousands of other security experts used it, including the U.S. government. That didn't say impressive, that was downright astonishing.

"And you're worried, because?"

Kira blinked and for the first time since I met her blatant doubt crossed her face that normally held a healthy dose of attitude, so much of it I could describe her as cocky. She knew she was intelligent; not that she made those around her feel less than, but she also didn't hide it. And she knew she was damn good at her job and didn't hide that either. And since it was only Garrett who could match her skill she got in her good-natured digs when she could.

But never had I seen Kira unsure of herself.

"Because I'm presenting a case."

"Baby, you're the smartest person in the office. I don't understand why that would worry you."

I watched her body jerk and her lips turned down.

What the fuck?

"I'm not the smartest," she denied. "And I've never analyzed data like this. I've never presented a case. I have no idea what I'm doing. Layla or Violet or Garrett should be doing this. I collect intel, I don't present it."

Layla was a damn good team leader and I had to admit, she was also good at analyzing data. So was my sister-in-law

Violet. She was CIA-trained and very little got past her. And there was no doubt Garrett was a master at both collecting and evaluating intel. But Kira was selling herself short.

And I was going to prove it to her.

"What's your take?"

"I don't..." she abruptly stopped and switched gears. "You've read the case, what's *your* take?"

"Don't have one yet."

"Did Garrett give you my intel?"

Again with the sheepish, unsure tone.

Garrett had indeed told the team Kira's report was ready and it was thorough. And I had read it. But what I wouldn't tell her was she'd found more than Garrett had during his searches, I'd wait for Garrett to tell her tomorrow at the meeting.

"I went over the files you uploaded onto the server."

"So? What do you think?"

"I told you what I thought."

"No, you didn't."

"KK, I told you that you're the smartest person in the office. That's what I think."

"Why are you being evasive, Cain?"

She only used my last name when she was being sassy, something I enjoyed a hell of a lot more than the hesitant tone she'd been using.

"I'm not, *Winters*. Now stop dallying and tell me your take."

"Who says dally?"

"I do. Now, tell me," I demanded.

I saw her eyes spark with irritation.

Fucking cute.

"I don't want to tell you."

"Why not?"

Kira sat back in her chair and I lost her eyes when they slid to the side.

Not once in the months I'd known her had she ever broken eye contact first. Not with me, not with anyone. I'd seen her stare down Zane, who was the master of the evil eye.

Seriously, what the hell was going on?

"Kira?"

"Listen, I'm gonna be here for a while. You should go home."

That was something that hadn't happened since the first night I'd spent with her. Most of the time she stayed at my house, but there were times I went to her apartment. But whichever bed I was in, she was in it with me. And I wasn't breaking that streak now.

"What's really going on?"

"Nothing. I just have a lot of work to do."

"Bullshit. I read your report hours ago—your completed report. And your notes."

"I need more time."

"Again, bullshit. You're overthinking this."

"You don't know what I'm doing," she snapped.

"I sure as fuck do. You're all wound up for no reason. You've been at it for thirteen hours today, and I know you spent at least ten hours on it yesterday. Baby, you're presenting the preliminary intel, you're not single-handedly solving the case."

"See, that right there, I don't know what the case is. I don't understand what I'm supposed to be trying to solve and I don't want to embarrass myself by not knowing."

There it was.

"Do you think Garrett would embarrass you? Fuck, Kira, do you think *I'd* let you go in blind? And you know the team, would any of them do anything to make you uncomfortable? Here's the deal; you're not supposed to *know*. You're supposed to be *learning*. You're no longer a one-woman show, you have a whole team to bounce ideas off of. That's how this works. That's how *we* work. Especially with something like this."

"And what *is* this?" she asked.

"Your first lesson in real teamwork. You and Garrett will take the lead, we'll give our input, but we'll take direction from you. And, Kira, you got this."

"How do you know?"

Since she hadn't listened to me the first two times I'd reminded her she was smart, I tried a new tactic.

"Because I believe in you."

I watched her green eyes go soft, but before I could fully appreciate the look, her computer chimed and her gaze slid to one of the screens. Much like Garrett, she had a full setup—a laptop and multiple desktop machines. The difference was I could see Kira's desk.

"What if Kingston Langford is a real spy?" she asked.

That was highly unlikely. So unlikely, I had to bite back a laugh.

"Wouldn't you have found a trace—"

"Not a CIA officer, but a real spy," Kira went on like I hadn't spoken. "What if he's a foreign spy or a corporate spy?"

Kira was going down the what-if rabbit hole. Typically, when it wasn't after nine at night, I was all for a good what-if session. Sometimes throwing out *all* the ideas, even the farfetched ones, helped bring an investigation into focus.

"I'll make you a deal," I started. "I'm all-in to talk this out with you, listen to all your theories, but only after I get some food in you."

Her computer chimed again and she frowned.

"Problem?" I asked.

"Yes. My squad is down to third place."

I glanced at her screen and saw an instant messenger box open.

"Your squad?"

"You know, the IC Mafia. I haven't been on to play in forever and my team's slippin' in the ranks."

Ah, yes, her video game. End of World.

If someone had asked me six months ago if I'd ever date a thirty-something-year-old woman who played video games, I would've said absolutely not. I didn't understand the appeal, and furthermore, I thought they were a waste of time and brainpower. But watching Kira play End of World was hilarious.

"Tragic," I muttered.

"It is. The world championships are coming up and only the top two compete," she huffed. "We have a title to defend."

"Then we better get you home and fed so you can jump online and geek out with your squad," I told her.

"I can't play video games when I have work!" she exclaimed, going as far as narrowing her eyes, clearly attempting to tell me she thought I was a dumbass.

"Baby, you are done with work. Let's go home, eat, and you can play and clear your mind."

"Cooper—"

"Kira, you need to decompress. You're prepared for tomorrow. You'll present what you have, the team will listen, then all of us *together* will start brainstorming. That's how this works. No one person is responsible for gathering, evaluating, and deciphering the data. We do that as a team. You have everything we need to get started. You're going to burn yourself out and get tunnel vision if you don't let the rest of us do our jobs."

It took a moment, a lot of them actually, for Kira to finally agree.

"Okay. Your place tonight or mine?"

Her apartment was seriously kickass. She lived in the building Zane used to live in before he married Ivy and started having kids. Kira didn't live in the penthouse, but her view didn't suck, and the building had top-notch security. But I still liked my house better. No, I liked having Kira in my house. I liked her in my bed. I liked her sitting on my couch, cross-legged with her laptop propped up on a pillow. I liked her next to me in my living room while she played her game and I watched TV. This didn't happen every night, it didn't even happen three nights a week, but it happened enough that I knew I liked watching her and listening to her joke with her squad while they played. I also liked it when she gave me a running commentary of what was happening as she played. I liked knowing she was comfortable in my home while I was out in the garage working on a car.

So my choice was easy.

"Mine."

As I waited for Kira to pack up her laptop something dawned on me—I'd said, let's go home, and her response was to ask *which* home. She didn't ask *if* I was staying with her or *if* she was coming to mine.

And as stupid as it was, I couldn't help wondering what it would feel like if she didn't have to ask. If the home I was talking about was the one we shared. If what was mine was hers and there was no going back and forth.

Yep, I was in so deep there'd be no digging myself out. When she left me, I'd still be stuck in my hole. And it was going to be dark as fuck and lonely as hell in there.

5

NORMALCY WAS something I hadn't had for so long that I was still trying to wrap my mind around how regular my life was now.

So, when I asked Cooper what he wanted for dinner I wasn't paying attention to my surroundings. I was too busy thinking about how easy my new life was. How good it felt to live without the weight of five men's lives resting on my shoulders. How natural it was to walk out of work with Cooper holding my hand, so I wasn't paying attention to what was going on.

Thus, I missed it—totally—until his grip became painful. It was only then I looked over at him and found his eyes squinted, his gaze laser-focused on something across the street, and when my eyes followed his, I saw a car parked.

"What's—"

"I want you to slowly walk backward," Cooper interrupted me. "Don't run. Just get back inside the building."

Cooper let go of my hand, and while I had questions, about a hundred of them, the first being why he wasn't coming with me, I held my tongue and took a step back. Then another until there were a few feet separating us.

I saw Cooper's right hand go to his hip and I knew what that meant. It was too dark, even with the moon and street-lights, to make out the person inside the car. And after the year Z Corps had with Theo's brother, Bronson The Dumb-ass, terrorizing the guys, I understood Cooper's vigilance. But I thought unholstering his weapon might be a little over the top.

How wrong I was.

So very wrong that it would change my life. Years later, I would look back and still not understand how it happened.

One second I was slowly backing up toward the build-ing. The next, gunshots rang out.

Three to be exact.

Three very loud bangs.

"Go!" Cooper shouted and took off across the street.

I didn't go. I stood frozen with my heart thundering in my chest.

I saw the first bullet hit Cooper.

His body jerked, but the crazy idiot continued running toward the car. That was when my heart stopped thun-dering and started pounding so hard my chest hurt.

Physically ached.

The next bullet sent me into action. It was so close, I actually heard it whiz by me. I was too far from the door, and besides, due to Zane Lewis's insane security protocols, it would've taken forever to dig my keys out of my bag, scan my fingerprint and my badge, and use my key to unlock the door and get inside. So, I did what I'd seen in the movies; I threw myself on the ground. This was not smart. It wasn't even logical. Now I was a motionless target.

Cooper was sprinting across the street as the car was

pulling away from the curb—not slowly, not watching for other cars or pedestrians; it was taking off like a bat out of hell. I couldn't lie on the sidewalk and watch Coop get hit by a car. I couldn't lie there and make myself an easy target. I couldn't lie there like some sort of spineless twit.

I had to do something.

Anything.

I got my knees under me and was standing when the car sped off.

All of this happened in a matter of seconds.

It happened so fast, I wasn't sure it actually happened. But when Cooper craned his head over his shoulder, I saw it.

Pain.

That was, until pain turned into extreme anger.

"Get the fuck in the building."

It was on the tip of my tongue to argue, to tell him he was insane if he thought I was going to leave him on the street all alone. But I didn't get a chance to argue. The next thing I knew Cooper was running full speed in my direction. He didn't stop or even slow down when he made it to me. His hand tagged mine and I had no choice but to run with him. We got to the door and instead of using his key card he flipped open a metal cover and punched in a code. I heard the lock disengage and he yanked open the door. Cooper shoved me in, pulled the door closed, and since it was after hours the lock automatically engaged.

What the hell was that?

"I didn't know you could do that."

Cooper didn't respond to my asinine statement as he continued to pull me farther into the reception area.

Call it nerves or hysteria or my inability to process what had just happened, but I blathered on.

"What else don't I know?"

Again, there was no response as he pressed his hand on the palm reader next to the door that would lead to a bank of elevators. Belatedly I saw the blood staining his shirt.

"You're bleeding. Shouldn't we go to the hospital?"

Cooper opened the door, gave me a shove, and when I was two steps into the hall, I found myself pinned against the wall.

"When I tell you to get inside," he growled, "you get the fuck inside."

It took me a moment to understand the change in my circumstances and the huge shift in Cooper. And when I did, I needed another moment to stop my head from exploding.

"Step back."

"No, Kira. Not until you confirm you get me."

Was he freaking serious?

"Oh, I get you're an asshole," I spat, then added, "and a jerk."

"I'm an asshole?" he asked and leaned closer.

"And a jerk," I confirmed. "And a fool if you think for one second I was going to leave you out there alone."

I watched up close and with morbid fascination, Cooper's face go soft.

Oh, no.

Hell, no.

"Baby—"

"Step back."

"KK, you scared the fuck out of me."

I scared *him?*

How did I scare him? I wasn't the one running toward the danger, he was.

"You're bleeding, Cooper." My eyes dropped to his left

shoulder, then traveled down to the sleeve of his shirt that was soaked through. "Someone shot you and *I* scared you?"

His right hand lifted and wrapped around the side of my neck.

"Look at me."

I didn't look at him. I was too focused on the blood.

"I'm not Layla," I announced.

"I know—"

"She would've known what to do," I interrupted him. "She would've been able to help."

Layla was a badass, former CIA officer who'd spent years in war zones. I was the one who sat behind a desk. I didn't get shot at. My brother had taught me how to shoot, he'd taught me self-defense, and he'd even gone so far as to teach me how to properly use a knife. But when the time came for me to put all that knowledge into practical use I froze like an idiot. I dropped to my belly and my mind failed me.

"Okay, KK, let's start again. This time I won't be an asshole."

"Maybe we should get you to the hospital first."

Cooper's fingertips dug into the back of my neck and his forehead dropped forward until it was resting on mine.

"Are you okay?" he whispered.

Hell, no, I was not okay.

I wasn't close to okay.

I was so far from okay I was the definition of *not* freaking okay. Now that my heart rate was back under control I felt dizzy. My stomach was in knots. And I was unexplainably angry. Not mad at Cooper for snapping at me and acting like a jerk. Not at myself for freezing like one of the bimbos in a horror movie. I was seriously outraged at the universe.

"You're bleeding!" I shouted. "Someone shot at you, Cooper. Who the hell would do that?"

"I'm not shot. At most, it grazed me."

That did it.

I was done.

"There's *fucking* blood on your shirt," I seethed. "Blood, Cooper. And a lot of it."

Our conversation was cut off when Cooper's phone started to ring. I felt his body sag and his forehead put pressure on mine before he straightened.

"So much for dinner and getting you to relax," he mumbled and answered the call, "Yeah?"

I watched a slew of expressions mar his face—his lips flattened, his brows pinched together, and his jaw tightened. And then it hit me; Cooper was completely unfazed—about all of it. He was unbothered that shots were fired outside our work and that he was bleeding. His concern had not been for his safety; it was for mine. He was upset I hadn't gone into the building like he'd told me to do. But mostly he sounded disgruntled that I wasn't going to be home relaxing on the couch.

The man had blood oozing from his body.

And he was thinking about me.

I wasn't sure how I felt about that. No, that wasn't right, I knew how I felt—safe and protected and loved. But the flip side to that was devastation. It was then I truly realized how dangerous his job was. And for a woman like me who lost everyone who meant anything to her, that was terrifying.

More than terrifying—paralyzing.

I couldn't lose someone else I loved.

I wouldn't live through it this time.

When my parents were killed, I mourned their loss. When my brother was murdered, I grieved so deeply, I thought I'd never recover. If something happened to Cooper, the man I wanted to marry and spend the rest of my life with, it would end me.

This changed everything.

6

THE RECEPTION AREA was packed full—police, Zane, my brother, Layla, Owen, Gabe, Myles, Kevin, Garrett, and two EMTs. I saw the agitation on the first responders' faces. I knew they were pissed I'd refused medical attention. I'd listened to them for about thirty seconds before my attention had gone to Kira and the two detectives who were interviewing her. Shortly thereafter the EMTs had given up trying to take me to the hospital over what amounted to a nick and bandaged my bicep.

My brother looked worried—which was understandable; if he'd been the one who'd been grazed with a bullet I would've been, too. Zane wasn't hiding his irritation, though he never did. Layla was talking to Garrett, and Kira had joined them once the police had concluded their questions. Now the three of them were standing close and all three had matching scowls. My guess was they were jonesing for the police to leave so they could go upstairs and get to work. Which meant it was going to suck for them when I grabbed Kira and took her home.

My team was in a huddle, their conversation was a crapshoot. Best guess was they were dishing out assignments and since Kira and I would be the assets I was not a part of that conversation.

I'd been a cop, I knew the drill. I knew what the detectives were up against, and I knew time was not their friend, but I was fresh out of professional courtesy. It had been hours. And every minute that passed I felt Kira pulling away. The physical distance she'd put between us was obvious. The emotional distance gutted me. And the longer it took for me to get her alone the further she'd slip away until she completely closed herself off and I lost her. I could feel it happening from across the room. I saw it in the side-eye glances. I saw in the way her gaze settled on the bloodied sleeve of my shirt before Jax had gone upstairs and got me a fresh tee. I saw it in the way she was now studiously avoiding looking at the dressing wrapped around my bicep.

That shit was not happening.

The smart thing to do would've been to let it happen, let her walk away now. But I wasn't ready. I'd never be ready to watch Kira Winters walk out of my life, but tonight was definitely not going to be the night I wised up.

I was so intent on watching Zane talk to Detective Garcia, a woman in her sixties who looked fed up with whatever line of bullshit Zane was feeding her, I missed Jaxon's approach.

"You good?" he asked.

"Not even close."

"Want something for the pain?"

"No."

"Cooper?"

"What?"

I was being a dick, I just didn't have it in me to care.

"Brother, look at me."

I slowly turned my head, pausing on Kira long enough for her to catch me. Her eyes slid away immediately. That pissed me off more.

As soon as I made eye contact with Jax he asked, "Are you in pain?"

Fuck, yeah, I was in pain. My heart felt like it was being torn out of my chest.

"I'm good."

"You're not good, told me yourself not two seconds ago," he reminded me. "If you need something for the pain, then take something. I'll drive you back to your place."

Jax meant well, but there wasn't a pill that would alleviate the burning in my chest.

"You saw it. It's nothing more than a graze."

A graze that bled like a motherfucker. A graze that if it had been a few inches to the right would've been a chest wound.

Jaxon stepped closer to me as Zane and the detectives moved our way. When they stopped, it was Garcia who spoke.

"Thank you for your time, Mr. Cain." I dipped my chin and she continued, "Mr. Lewis has my card. If you think of anything else, please call me."

The younger detective said nothing, but his body language said it all. He was unhappy, he had questions, and he wanted to push, but his partner, or more likely Zane, had shut him down. The guy didn't care I was a former police officer, he didn't give a shit it was almost midnight and I'd given a detailed statement, so had Kira, and Garrett had given them security feed from outside the building. He was impatient. If I had to guess, I'd say he only recently passed his detective's exam, and he was itching to make a name for himself. He wanted to close cases quickly.

Stupid.

"I will," I confirmed.

I didn't extend the same invitation for her to call me if she had further questions. I knew she'd call me bright and early tomorrow and ask a dozen more as well as go over the ones she'd already asked.

"One last thing before we go," Garcia went on. "What drew your attention to the car?"

"My gut," I answered.

Detective Garcia gave me a swift nod, understanding without me having to further explain.

The new guy didn't get it, which confirmed my suspicions. He wasn't happy that he didn't have a chance to question me. Garcia had done all the talking and when Detective Thompson opened his mouth to speak, I understood why.

"Your gut?" Thompson asked. "What does that mean?"

I took a moment in an attempt to gather a measure of patience. However, I didn't have it in me. I was exhausted. I was also pissed as fuck Kira had been in the line of fire. I wanted this over with so I could take her home and figure out what was going on.

So I didn't moderate my words when I told him, "Seeing as you're standing in front of me with a badge clipped to your belt it's baffling I gotta explain to you situational awareness. I came out of the building, quickly surveyed the street, saw the car, noted someone was in it, and I got a bad feeling. I was a cop long enough to know I don't dismiss bad feelings. Something felt off. I looked closer and saw the person was pointing something in my direction. At first, I thought it was a camera. Now, taking pictures isn't illegal but like I said, I had a feeling. I walked over to investigate, obviously it wasn't a camera but a gun. Now you get me?"

"You unholstered your weapon *before* you took on fire," Thompson noted. "That can be, and just so you *get me*, I do take that as an offensive measure. Maryland wear and carry permit or not, your weapon can only be used if you feel your life is in grave danger. You just stated you thought the subject was holding a camera."

"I've got a flesh wound that states plainly I was in grave danger. And I didn't use my weapon, I unholstered it and I did so because at that juncture I was in fear for my life."

"How's that?" Thompson shot back. "You were advancing on a parked car."

I was done. To communicate this I looked at Garcia and said, "Call me if you have any questions."

I sidestepped Jaxon and was clearing the group when Detective Thompson called out, "We're not done, you and me."

"You're done," Zane told the rookie detective. "Unless you're going to charge him, I'd like you to leave."

"You're impeding an investigation," the detective unwisely accused.

"I am in no way impeding an investigation. You've asked your questions, I saved you the time and aggravation of getting a warrant and provided you with security footage from my outside cameras. You have everything you need and if after three hours you don't have what you need, too fucking bad."

"Mr. Lewis—"

"Garcia," Zane rumbled clearly as fed up as I was.

I didn't slow my pace to hear the end of the conversation. I was focused on my target. Kira was focused on Layla, and Layla was just as focused on Kira, but Garrett caught sight of me as I approached. His frown deepened and I wondered what they were talking about.

I heard the tail-end of what Kira was saying. "I'm thinking it was too dark, but I'd like to try."

"Try what?" I asked.

Kira's posture snapped straight, her shoulders stiffened, and fear washed over her face.

What the fuck?

Layla didn't miss Kira's response, therefore when it became clear Kira wasn't going to answer, Layla did.

"She wants to run the footage through Patheon."

Patheon was the facial recognition software Kira had developed. The program used two hundred forty reference points, local feature analysis, and surface texture, but the part of the program that made Patheon stand above anything else on the market was the advancement of vein matching. So even if someone was wearing a disguise they couldn't slip past detection.

"Has the program ever been tested in low light conditions?" I inquired.

"Low light, yes," Layla answered. "But inside the car was dark."

"Worth a shot," I noted then looked from Layla to Kira. "Have you checked your laptop's not broken?"

Someone had brought her purse and bag into the lobby. I didn't see what happened, or how her bags had ended up on the sidewalk, just that they'd somehow ended up there.

Kira stiffened further at my question.

I'd been wrong—something hadn't changed, everything had. Everything about Kira was different. She didn't stiffen. She didn't clam up. She always had something to say and had no issue saying whatever was on her mind.

"It's fine." Her retort came out cold and distant. Something else I'd never felt from her.

My Kira was warm and affectionate with everyone.

Garrett picked up on the tone. So did Layla, but it was Garrett who said, "Go home. We'll run the searches in the morning."

I thought that was a great idea until Kira asked, "Do you and Kevin mind dropping me off at home?"

That was obviously directed at Layla.

And if I was pissed before I was now furious.

"I...um...let me...sure," Layla sputtered.

"That won't be necessary," I contradicted. "I got her."

Kira's eyes cut to mine and narrowed.

"Actually, Cooper, it is necessary. I'd like a ride home."

"You wanna do this now?"

"I'm tired and I want to go home, so no, I don't want to do anything right now."

"I'm taking you home."

"My home."

I could feel my blood pressure rising.

"Funny you felt that need to make that distinction."

"What?"

"How long have you been in—"

"Brother," Jaxon rumbled from behind me. "Easy."

"I haven't had to do this since the beginning with my brother and Jasmin," Zane's voice boomed in the room. "Normally, I don't have to deal with employees doing the chitty chitty bang bang then having a domestic in the office. Typically my men think with their little heads and bonk the clients. I see new additions have to be made to the handbook."

I clenched my jaw and held Kira's gaze.

I was not in the mood for Zane's antics. Unfortunately for me, my boss was in the mood to be himself.

"Now, I've got a notarized promise from Cooper and a contract signed in pink ink which I've been assured is still binding even though it was endorsed with a glitter pen, that neither of you would engage in activities that would cause me mental anguish. This..." he motioned between me and Kira. "...right here is causing me mental anguish. Go home, work it out, glove up, make up. It doesn't have to be in that order, but you've got eight hours—which is probably seven hours and forty-five minutes more than Cooper needs—but it's yours nonetheless to work this shit out."

Zane paused then ordered, "The rest of you stay out of it. That includes you, Jax. Your brother's a big boy. And you, too, Layla. As you once told me, Kira can handle herself. Now I got a wife, a kid, and a newborn to get home to. Someone lock up when y'all leave."

"I don't need—"

"I get you," Zane interrupted Kira. "What you don't get is that right now you're making a mistake."

"Zane," I warned.

"You know I'm right, Cooper. All of us in this room see it. But, brother, I know you feel it. You let this happen, you let her carry this out, for you it won't be a mistake—it'll be a regret."

My eyes shot to Garrett; he was staring at Zane, but his eyes slowly drifted until they locked with mine. Years' worth of pain shone back. A mountain of regret. I didn't know the whole story, but I didn't need to know Garrett lived with regret. The part of the story I did know was he was in love with a woman who he'd lost. I didn't know why, or what the circumstances were, but the pain told the tale. Regret.

"I'm going home," Kira hissed. "My home. Alone."

Warring emotions collided.

I wanted to give her what she wanted. I was not a man who forced a woman to spend time with me. I was not a man who needed to beg a woman for attention. Nor was I a man who was prone to making rash decisions. Though I'd never been in love, I was finding that to give Kira what she needed I was going to have to ignore what she wanted.

"I don't much care whose house we go to, but straight up, KK, you're not going there alone."

"I'm going alone."

Stubborn.

Christ.

"You want this to end, then it ends," I told her and my stomach roiled as the words came out of my mouth. "Me taking you home isn't about that. It's me taking care of you whether you think you need it or not. And I'm not leaving you alone. Again, that's about me making sure you're okay when the adrenaline wanes and your mind starts to replay what happened. Now, you want your house or mine?"

I watched the fire ignite, the fury build, and that stubborn take hold.

I felt a hand on my shoulder. I turned my head and found Jax leaning close.

"Go easy," he said, mostly reiterating his earlier advice.

I wasn't going easy.

And besides, I couldn't be anyone but myself. I could and would give Kira anything, but if she wanted to get shot of me, I wasn't going to let her go without a fight.

"We can do this all night, baby, and you know I'm gonna win."

She knew damn good and well I was right. She might've been good at the stare-down, but she lacked patience and restraint.

"Yours," she ungraciously spat.

"Perfect. Let's go."

Her eyes sliced through our teammates and landed on

Layla. Her former team leader gave her an encouraging nod. I knew Layla didn't mean it. She wanted to take Kira home with her. Under any other circumstances, I would've appreciated the bond they had and respected their friendship. But right then, too much was on the line.

If I let Kira go now, I'd never get her back.

And that was not happening.

7

THE DRIVE to Cooper's house was a blur.

An uncomfortable blur.

I must've replayed what could only have been at most sixty seconds from start to finish a hundred times. And each time I got angrier and angrier with myself. One minute had ruined everything. One damn minute put everything into perspective.

I'd been silent on the drive, but so had Cooper. We continued our silence when we walked into the house. Cooper went straight to the kitchen and I went to his bedroom. It was gross but I didn't bother washing my face or brushing my teeth. Okay, so the not brushing the teeth thing was super gross but brushing them would've meant standing in front of the mirror and I couldn't bear to see my reflection. I also didn't bother to undress or pull back the covers.

Cooper joined me in the bedroom a few minutes later. I heard something clatter then the lamp on his nightstand went on.

"Eat, baby."

God, he was killing me.

Killing. Me.

"I'm not hungry," I mumbled.

The bed dipped and my heart clenched.

Everything about this was wrong. He should've let me go.

"You skipped dinner," he reminded me. "I made you a peanut butter and honey."

My favorite.

Something my mom used to make for me all the time. Sometimes, she'd switch it up and slather peanut butter and honey on crackers and smash them up over a bowl full of cut-up bananas. If she was feeling it, she'd drizzle chocolate over the concoction and call it dessert.

Finn hated peanut butter, my dad did, too. So, Mom made it special just for me. She did stuff like that a lot.

I missed my mom.

I missed my dad.

I seriously missed my big brother.

Some days it hurt so damn bad it felt like the pain would tear me apart. But what hurt worse were the days when I shoved the memories away so I wouldn't break.

"Kira?"

I couldn't do this.

I couldn't take another minute of Cooper's kindness. I stayed lying on my side, my back to him, my eyes closed because I was too much of a coward to look at him.

"This needs to stop," I told him.

Those words came right out of my mouth and when they did, I felt the cold creep in.

No more normal.

No more Cooper.

I had to let him go now before he left me. I had to stop

loving him before something happened to him, too. He had a family. A brother and sister-in-law and a nephew and parents that loved him. He had everything. Everything I didn't have. Everything that was taken from me.

The people I loved died.

And tonight proved I wasn't meant to love. I was better off alone. No one would get hurt. No one would get murdered. No one would get shot walking out of work.

I had to protect Cooper and leave.

"Why?"

He didn't sound angry, just curious. And he would be curious—four hours ago we were happily going home and having dinner, same as we did pretty much every night.

"I think we should go back to being what we were before the wedding."

Lies.

"Okay. But I need you to tell me why."

Cooper's quick concession felt like a knife to the heart. I closed my eyes tighter and absorbed the devastation. I should've been happy he wasn't arguing with me, that he was happy to let me go. All he wanted was an explanation and he'd let me walk out of his life.

Why did that hurt so freaking bad?

Because he didn't care.

Damn.

"Because..." I trailed off, unable to think of a lie.

"Look at me," he gently demanded.

Hell to the no. I wasn't going to look at him. If I was being forced to stay at his place, I was sleeping fully clothed, above the covers, with my back to him. He had a king-size bed; if I stayed on my side, I was practically in a different zip code.

My side.

God, that hurt, too.

I could've fought harder to go home. I could've put Layla on the spot. She'd looked torn. I knew I could've guilted her into taking me and it wouldn't have taken much. But I'd made the decision to get involved with Cooper, and when I did I promised myself no matter what, even if it went bad, I wouldn't involve our team. I'd keep it professional. So I did the right thing and let my friend off the hook. I could've called a Lyft but that would've caused more of a scene. So I made the choice to go home with Cooper. Now I had to woman up and face the consequences of the last few months.

I had to untangle myself from Cooper.

"It's for the best," I told him. "We shouldn't've let it get this far."

"How far have we let it go?"

How was he so calm?

Why couldn't he be pissed? It would've been so much easier if he was acting like a jerk. I could deal with that Cooper. Or at least I thought I could. I'd only ever seen that side of him once in the hallway when he was mad, and I hadn't run away.

No, he was mad because I hadn't run to safety.

"Too far," I answered him.

"Right," he mumbled. "So, if you want things to go back to the way they were before we hooked up at the wedding explain to me why you're not looking at me. Way I see it, the only thing that changed is we added orgasms and sleepovers."

Ouch.

Though he wasn't wrong since I was already in love with Cooper before Gabe and Evette's wedding. It was just that night in the parking lot outside the reception we'd finally given in to the attraction. Or more to the point, Cooper had. I'd been ready for weeks—dropping hints, flirting, doing everything short of throwing myself at him. We'd added fantastic sex and orgasms to our friendship, but nothing had changed. We still did all the other stuff, too.

Cooper Cain was my best friend, and I was going to lose that, too.

"I'm tired."

"If you're gonna lie to me the least you can do is put some effort into it. You forget, I know you. You're the only woman I know who can put in a twelve-hour day at the office, go out after and drink me under the table, come home and fuck me all night, get a two-hour power nap and be ready to go bright and early the next morning and look like you've had a full night's sleep and a spa treatment. So don't bullshit me, Kira. You're not tired, you're scared. You don't want to look at me because you know I'll see how full of shit you are."

I felt the vibe in the room change; the calm had slipped out and anger was inching in. That feeling wasn't coming from me, it was all Cooper. I opened my eyes and glared at the wall. I kept staring, hoping beyond all hope Cooper's anger would take over and he'd leave me both physically and emotionally.

He'd leave and I'd go back to being alone.

"You don't know—"

"Don't bullshit me," he cut me off. "I know you so well I know you're lying there right now scared as fuck. I have no idea what tweaked you, but I know the woman who rolled out of my bed this morning was smiling and happy. I know the woman who's determined to suck all the good out of life she can. And I most certainly know the woman who I've fallen in love with, so this shit I know is shit. Turn around and tell me to my face you want this end. Look me in the eye and tell me. But know this, baby—I won't believe you. We haven't discussed it, we haven't put any labels on what we have, but honest to God, what we have is good and you fucking know it. So if you're gonna tear me apart the least you can do is buck up and look at me when you carry out this bullshit."

Oh, yeah, he was mad.

Seriously *pissed*.

But I was stuck on the part where he told me he'd fallen in love with me. For months and months, I wanted those words. I ached to hear them. I yearned to tell him the same. Now all I felt was a hole where my heart used to be.

"You can't love me." The words sounded tortured to my own ears. Hollow and laden with unending grief.

"I can't?" Cooper rasped. "Or is it that you can't love me?"

God, if he only knew.

I felt my body stiffen—my shoulders all the way to my toes. My muscles contracted until I felt like my bones were going to break. My lungs were going to stop working. My heart might as well stop now because once Cooper was gone it might still beat but it would be empty.

"You can't love me, Cooper. You can't. You have to stop."

Hours, days, weeks, months ago I would've begged him to never stop, to love me until the end of days. But now I remembered loving me would mean those days would be numbered. It would only be a matter of time before he was taken from me, from his family, from his team. We'd all lose him in a different way—the permanent kind. That was what happened to the people who loved me.

"Baby, look at me."

Baby.

I wished I'd have that for a lifetime.

"No," I denied. He was right, I couldn't look at him while my heart was breaking. "Just promise me you'll stop."

"Warning, Kira," he growled. "I've given you all the time I'm gonna give to this hiding bullshit."

After Cooper delivered that, he didn't give me time to process his threat. His hand went to my hip, and he rolled me to my back. My choices were to keep my head turned away like a sullen child in the throes of a temper tantrum or turn and look at him. I was ashamed to admit I contemplated keeping my eyes trained on the wall or alternately squeezing them closed. That was how desperately I wanted to escape. It was immature and stubborn but that was where I was at—emotional rock bottom.

I turned to look at Cooper and I saw pain so stark it stole through me before I had a chance to prepare. Pain and confusion. Both were my fault and as much as I felt the same emotions battling inside of me, I had to do it.

It was better this way.

He'd likely hate me by morning, but he'd be safe. I'd be safe. I wouldn't have to feel the loss, the guilt, the monumental sorrow.

"You should've let me go home," I whispered from my back.

Cooper shifted and leaned in partially over me until his fist landed on the bed near my hip. My gaze went to the bandage wrapped around his bicep. The t-shirt he was wearing was not his, the blood had been cleaned away, but I could see it.

I would never forget. Just like Finn's murder was forever seared in my memory—my brother on his knees, the hood over his head, the blade—

"Kira!" Cooper's harsh call snapped me back to the room.

A room I didn't want to be in. No, a room I could no longer be in.

I scrambled to sit but before I could get my bearings Cooper moved. Lightning-quick, he had me pinned to the bed, his face close to mine, his wounded eyes roaming my face.

"Let me up," I demanded.

"Tell me what has you tweaked."

"Let me up," I repeated.

"Not until you explain to me what's going on."

Fury hit hard and fast. A lifetime of heartache, hatred at the world, loneliness, bitterness, and resentment, so much of it my vision went hazy. I was no longer in Cooper's room, in a bed I'd spent many nights in with the man I'd fallen in love with. I was not in Maryland. I wasn't even in my right mind.

I was so overcome with extreme, soul-stealing anger, I attacked.

I planted my feet on the bed, bucked my hips, and bared my nails. I vaguely heard Cooper's grunt when I scored the flesh at his throat as we rolled. I felt him grab my wrists and roll us again, his heavy weight over me, and I went out of my mind. All I could see were the carjackers who murdered my parents. My uncle showing up at the house to tell me they were gone. The terrorists who slit my brother's throat. The blood. The carnage. The horrific aftermath. My brother. My Finn, gone. I slapped, I kicked, I bit, I struggled. Cooper groaned, growled, and grumbled.

All of this was in vain.

All of this was exhausting.

"Stop!" he fumed.

I didn't stop. I couldn't. The need to fight the memories was too strong—Finn's body hitting the dirt. Meeting my parents' caskets at the airport. The smell of the funeral home. The taste of my tears as we buried my parents. The numbness when I buried Finn. All alone.

They fucking left me all alone.

I had no one.

"Baby, please stop," he begged.

"I hate them!" I screamed. "I hate them. *I hate them.* I hate them."

"Who do you hate?"

"I can't do this anymore," I wheezed.

My mouth was dry, my throat was raw, and my muscles burned. I needed to leave. I needed away from the pain, from this bed, from the house, from the goddamn memories that wouldn't go away.

"What can't you do?"

I closed my eyes and saw my parents' wedding rings and the anniversary band my dad had given my mom before they left for their vacation. Not on their fingers where they belonged, but on the kitchen table. One wide gold band, a smaller one in diameter and width, a diamond solitaire, and an eternity band. They didn't have an eternity. They'd had twenty-five years then they were gone.

"I have to go."

"Baby, you're scaring the fuck out of me."

The rings morphed into my brother's flag-draped coffin.

"You're gonna die!" I screamed. "If you love me, I'll kill you."

"What?"

"You have to let me leave before you die."

"Kira, I'm not gonna die."

"You were shot," I reminded him. "It was a warning. I'm gonna kill you."

"Baby, how are you gonna kill me?"

How could he not understand?

"Everyone I love dies. They're all dead. If you love me, I'll kill you."

"Kira, look at me."

I was looking at him—straight into his beautiful blue eyes.

"I am."

"No, Kira, look at me. Come back to the room, to me, and *look at me*. I'm right here. Me loving you didn't get me shot, baby."

God, why couldn't he understand?

"Let me go."

"No fucking way."

"Cooper, I want to leave."

"I know you do but you're not going to."

"I have to leave you before you die. I have to, Cooper. I can't watch you die. I can't do it. I have nothing left. I'm so empty that if you were taken from me, I wouldn't survive it. I'm not lying, I wouldn't survive the loss of you."

Cooper let go of my wrists and his right hand curled around my neck. His fingers pushed into my hair until he was cupping the back of my head. Then he rolled to his right until he was on his back and held me to his chest. When he had me where he wanted me, his other hand slid down my forearm until he found my hand, tugged it up, and placed it over his heart.

"Cooper—"

"Shh, baby, just feel."

All I felt was paralyzing fear. He wasn't letting me go.

"Coop—"

"Feel it, Kira. Feel my heart beating. Feel me breathing."

I did my best to fight it. I did everything I could not to feel anything at all. But as the silence stretched and Cooper's body relaxed under mine, I couldn't stop it. I felt the steady rhythm, the strong thump of his heart, the slow, even inhales and exhales, the warmth that surrounded me. So much warmth that over the months it had pushed out the chill. So warm that I'd forgotten to be afraid. So much warmth I knew if I had Cooper's arms around me, I'd never be cold again.

Those were my thoughts as I was lulled to sleep with the steady tempo of his heart under my palm.

In his arms I was safe.

He was not safe in mine.

8

I WAS in the final circle of hell. The first six had played out over the hours Kira had been asleep. Every twitch, every jolt, every garbled word, had been pure fucking hell. Between her nightmares and the shit she'd spouted before she fell asleep, I hadn't bothered to close my eyes. I knew I wouldn't find sleep.

Everyone I love dies.

They're all dead.

If you love me, I'll kill you.

Three statements that would haunt me for the rest of my life.

Kira curled into me and moaned, then she burrowed closer, and I felt her jerk before her body went solid.

Christ.

When the first nightmare hit, I was worried she had them often and I'd slept through them. When the second one hit, I realized there was no chance I'd sleep through her trembling and shaking so violently I had to hold on to her to calm her down. No fucking way I'd sleep through the groaning and whimpering.

"I know you're awake."

Kira didn't respond verbally but she didn't have to. I absorbed the tremor and the waves of apprehension rolling off her. Both of which served as an unnecessary reminder we had shit to talk about before we left for work.

"We need to talk about last night."

"Please don't," she whispered.

"Kira—"

"*Please*, Cooper. I'm begging you, not now. Please give me this. Give me today."

Jesus fuck.

Kira's apprehension had morphed into desperation. And as much as I wanted to push, I found I didn't have it in me. Not when the tone of her voice was flimsy and hollow. Not after she'd had nightmare after nightmare. Not after she'd held on to me all night while she shuddered.

"We've gotta talk about..." I gave her a squeeze when she started to interrupt me again. "Baby, we gotta talk about it but I get you needing today."

Her body sagged in relief, and what I had to say next sucked because I knew as soon as I did she'd tense up. But it had to be said—more, she needed to hear it.

"Today we got a lot going on. The cops are gonna be back around to question us, you, Garrett, and Layla will be going over footage from the shooting, after that we still gotta go over the Langford case, and I need to talk to Zane about what he knows about Detective Thompson. At some point, I also have to look at the footage."

After I was done laying out our schedule but before I got to what I really needed to tell her she asked, "You haven't watched the recordings?"

It was a simple question but there was something in the

way her voice shook when she asked that put me on alert. She sounded almost ashamed.

"Nope."

Now there was something new coming from Kira. It went beyond the way she was holding her body tight. Beyond her futile attempt to roll away, which I stopped by locking my arm around her.

"Kira?"

She did the opposite of what I'd hoped she'd do and dipped her chin toward her chest, making certain I couldn't see her face.

"Baby, what's wrong?"

Two short, jerky shakes of her head against my chest were accompanied with, "I messed up."

"When'd you mess up?"

"Last night."

Fuck.

That was something else I needed to scratch onto my list of shit I had to do today. Last night I acted like a dick, and in the middle of trying to apologize Garrett had called. Then all hell broke loose when Zane and the rest of my team arrived at the same time the street filled with flashing red lights. It went downhill from there when Garrett, Layla, my brother, and sister-in-law showed up and circumstances what they were I didn't get to finish.

"I shouldn't have acted like an asshole. I got no excuse except to say my head was fucked up." I paused, looking for the right words to explain I'd been terrified. Which wasn't an emotion I was used to. Not only had I never been in love before, but the woman I was in love with had never been in danger of catching a bullet. No doubt I reacted poorly, and I didn't know how to convey that without explaining why—and the why would set her off.

I'd spent the majority of the night thinking about what she'd said, dissecting her fear, and as irrational as it was it made sense—at least to her, it did. The way she was, her personality, and the way she smiled, joked, and laughed it was easy to forget. But thinking on it, the way she lived, the carefree, grab-life-by-the-balls, up for anything attitude was a front. I wouldn't go as far as calling it desperate, but it was borderline careless. And if anyone understood how short life was it was Kira. I didn't know her before her parents and brother were killed, but I'd guess she smiled, joked, and laughed a lot. I'd bet she was outgoing, fun, and up for anything. But having all night to reflect, I'd missed it. I'd been so caught up in all that was her, thinking she was the way she was because she'd been stuck behind a computer in near isolation for ten years, I hadn't gone beyond that. I'd been so selfish thinking about myself and the pain she would inflict when she left me, that I didn't recognize the pain she lived with daily.

If you love me, I'll kill you.

She believed that. It didn't matter that she was unequivocally wrong. Her love didn't kill her family. Her family loving her didn't get them murdered. But in her irrational mind, it made sense.

She was trapped in a make-believe world that was as real as it was fake. Her reality was death and love went hand-in-hand. A person didn't lose their entire family and come out unscathed.

I missed it and fucked up.

"That's not what I messed up," she murmured. "I froze."

I wasn't tracking so I asked, "You froze?"

Another swift nod on my chest before she rushed out, "I blanked and messed up. I forgot everything Finn taught me about what to do in an active shooter situation. I just stood there and watched you get hit, then I stood there longer until...until...I heard a bullet whistle by me then I just got on the ground. It was like I couldn't think, I was totally frozen. Frozen and blank."

Until I heard a bullet whistle by me.

Fucking hell.

Fucking motherfucker.

My cop brain kicked in, running over the specifics of the night. The car parked on the street—not late at night, but late. The window rolling down as soon as I stepped into the street. And finally, both of us taking fire. The shooter would have to adjust his aim to target Kira. That was not a missed shot at me that she heard whistle by her.

One shooter, two targets.

Something to think about, but right then not the most important topic to address.

"I've known cops with years of training who have frozen. There is no shame in that. You can run drills all day long, be an ace marksman, a master at tactics, but until real bullets are flying in your direction no one can say with certainty how they'll respond. And that goes from situation to situation as well. We'd all like to think we'd react appropriately but when danger is present and the heart is pumping, and outside variables creep in, shit happens. That's the God's honest truth. You didn't mess up. And I was out of line last night. I shouldn't have lost my temper. All I can say is, I've never felt fear like that in the field. Which goes to my point—last night you were the variable. My need to protect you overweighed my training. I was careless and because of that, I left you on the sidewalk with no regard to how you'd react. That left you vulnerable, and when I turned and saw you still there, I was pissed at myself and took that out on you. It wasn't cool, it makes me a dick, but that's the truth."

"You were afraid?"

"No, baby, I was fucking *terrified*. I had you at my side, no cover, no backup, and everything to lose. I didn't know if the guy in the car was alone or if there was someone else in there or on the street. I wanted you in the building safe and had no thoughts about how you were going to get there. My fault. My fuck-up. Not yours."

Kira pressed closer and her arm which was draped over my stomach tightened. I took that as her acquiescence and continued.

"Now, about what you said to me last night when we got home, we'll table that discussion until tonight. But, Kira, we are talking about it."

"Coop—"

I didn't let her finish. I knew she was going to argue, pull away, and shut down. In other words, piss me off. So I shut her down.

"That part's not up for discussion, Kira. We're talking about it, period. I get it, all of it, why you said it, why you feel it, and why you don't want to talk about it. But that shit's not right and if the only thing that comes out of you and me being together is you understanding that you are meant to be loved and there's not one fucking thing wrong about that, then I can I live with that. If I can't have you, I'll settle for knowing that you're heathy and happy and loved."

"Why?"

Her barely-there question hit me square in the chest. I knew love—my parents had demonstrated it my whole life. They showed me by loving each other and loving me and Jaxon. I didn't watch my brother fall in love but that didn't mean I didn't witness it all the same. I met a bruised and battered Violet right after a horrific trauma, and when I did, I met a side of my brother I'd never known existed. I saw a man deeply in love, a man who would protect his woman at all costs. A man who knew the woman he'd found was his better half, a woman who would challenge him to be more, a woman who would give him everything, and in return he could give her the same.

I knew love.

I knew Kira.

I knew that I loved her more than was reasonable.

"Because I love you, Kira. And if I can't have you, I love you enough to want you to have it however that comes about."

That was a goddamn lie. Not me loving her. Not me wanting her to be happy however that came about, and not me loving her enough. But I wouldn't settle, not in the sense I'd settle on another woman. Not in the sense I'd get over her and fall in love with someone else. Like my brother, I knew I'd found the one I wanted to build a life with. The woman who would challenge me in the best of ways. The woman who would give me everything I needed to be happy for the rest of my days. The woman I wanted to give that back to.

Lying there in my bed with the clothes I wore yesterday still on, with Kira's head on my chest, curled into me after a night where her dreams had terrorized her, I was still content in a way I knew I'd never find with anyone else. Not pleased she'd had nightmares. Not happy we'd been shot at. Not relaxed by any stretch. Yet I was completely at ease with her in my arms.

And the longer we laid there in silence the more I wondered if I actually told the truth at all, if I was lying to myself thinking I could let her go. Maybe loving her enough meant fighting to keep her. Maybe it meant protecting her from herself.

It was at that moment, with those realizations, I rolled Kira onto her back and climbed partially on top of her. Her startled eyes lifted and locked with mine. I brushed her hair off her face and tucked a hank behind her ear. I ignored the surprise I saw and concentrated on what needed to be said so we could get on with our day.

"Brace, baby."

"Huh?"

"I need you to dig deep and find that strength I know you have. I *know* it's in there, I've seen it, I've felt it. I cannot promise you easy, but I can promise you I'm gonna do everything in my power to cushion this as much as I can. I've been holding myself back thinking you weren't ready. I see now that was a mistake. Instead of spending my time waiting for you to get your fill then leave me I should've been using every minute making you realize even if you could, you wouldn't want to live without me. I should've been paying more attention."

I dipped my head until my vision was filled with nothing but beauty, which had the added benefit of me being the center of her focus. "Now, you need to brace, baby, I'm paying attention—a godly amount—that means I won't be missing a damn thing. You retreat, I'm coming for you. You think you're gonna hide—physically or emotionally—you need to think again because I'm not letting that happen either. I'm gonna fight you. Fight to keep you. Fight to love you. Fight to have you love me back. Fight until you understand love and death are not one and the same. But just to say, I'll state it plain right now, that I will love you until my dying day."

I felt her swift inhale, let the wetness in her eyes settle over me, then I continued.

"Now, we got a full day that's likely to be total shit. I don't want you having to deal with what's ahead and stressing about the conversation we're having tonight so I'm gonna add, when that conversation takes place, you can trust I'll go easy, I'll handle you with care, and I'm giving you everything you need to get through it."

I did not like seeing the tears in her eyes. I wished there was something I could do to make them stop but that would take time. So I did the only thing I could do and kissed the corner of each eye. I tasted her tears, committed them to memory, and silently vowed to best any obstacle she put in my way.

This was a battle I was going to win, and I'd fight as dirty as I had to, to prove to her I loved her more than enough to be the man she needed.

"Cooper?"

"Yeah, KK?"

"I don't know if I'll be able to find that strength."

"Told you once, and I'll tell you again, I believe in you, so I know you'll find it."

"What if I can't?"

The sadness in her voice tore me apart. The disbelief and uncertainty gutted me. It also strengthened my resolve.

"How about we take this one step at a time and not worry about things that might not be a problem?"

She looked like she wanted to argue, the doubt and indecision were clear, but she did exactly what I knew she was capable of doing—she found her strength and tamped it down.

"I'm gonna hurt you."

"I know you are."

"I won't mean to."

Fuck, she was killing me.

"Know that, too, baby."

"Promise me, no matter what, you won't hate me. You'll find it in yourself to forgive me."

That was easy. The hurt she was going to cause me was the kind that didn't need forgiveness. It would require grace and understanding. Both of which I had.

"I promise."

"One more thing," she whispered. "I need until the weekend to talk about this."

Fuck.

"Kira—"

"Hear me out," she pleaded, and I shut my mouth. "I was up all night, my nightmares were so bad I barely slept. That happens when I think about what happened to them. When I let the grief take over. When we talk, I need it to be on a day when I don't work the next day."

I did not let on I knew she'd been ravaged by nightmares. That would mean I'd have to admit I was up all night with her and she'd feel guilty about that. So I let that lay.

"We'll talk this weekend," I gave in. "But I want you in my bed between now and then."

She nodded but didn't add a verbal confirmation.

"Good. You get the shower first," I unnecessarily told her since she got the shower first every morning. This was multipurpose—a time-saving measure since she took twice as long to get ready as I did and it also meant I got to bring her her first cup of coffee when she got out.

"I'm sorry."

Oh, yeah, my insides were hemorrhaging.

"You have nothing to be sorry for. Not today and not in the future. We have a lot to work through but not to work out. I know what I want and I hope I've made it clear that's you and it's not going to change."

I watched her eyes slowly glide closed; it looked painful and raw.

I let that score through me and bent to kiss her.

I didn't linger nor did I push for more. I'd had weeks of sex-filled morning kisses, precursors to my mouth traveling other places, her naked body wrapped around mine taking my cock, her moans filling the room, my grunts accompanying her cries of pleasure. This was not the time for that. It was time I started taking care of my girl the way she needed.

I pulled away, rolled off the bed, and when I was standing at the side I turned to glance at her still lying on the bed. It was for no other reason than I liked seeing her there. I wasn't taking time to memorize the look of her lazing in bed. I didn't need to. I knew I'd see it again and again and again.

9

THE DRIVE into work was only a shade less uncomfortable than the drive the night before. But unlike last night, this morning's drive I was paying attention—to everything. I was acutely aware Cooper was in the car with me. I was hyper-aware of every breath, analyzing every exhale, looking for any sign he'd changed his mind in the last forty-five minutes since he'd told me he was going to fight for me.

No, he didn't say that.

He said so, *so* much more.

And I would remember his words for as long as I walked this earth. I'd never forget them. I'd never let them out of my heart.

I'm gonna fight you.

Fight to keep you.

Fight to love you.

Fight to have you love me back.

Fight until you understand love and death are not one and the same.

Not only would I never forget them, but they scared the

holy hell out of me. They terrified me so badly I forced myself to stop replaying them. The minimal sleep I got last night did not clear my head. The light of day didn't bring lucidity. I was more messed up this morning than I was after getting shot at last night.

I did not want Cooper to let me go.

I desperately wanted him to love me as much as I loved him.

But with the same desperation, I wanted him to stop. I wanted him to be safe.

My mind and heart were at war; they were in a battle and there would be no winner. The outcome would crush them both. Crush *me*.

Cooper turned down a side street three blocks before where he normally turned, and I knew why. He was avoiding taking me back to the scene of the crime. He was going to drive in the back way so I wouldn't be confronted with the memory of the shooting. Another example of his kindness. One more way he put me first. Not that navigating the small back street was all that difficult but it would add some time onto the drive; one-way streets meant he'd have to go out of his way. But he'd do that—for me.

I pushed those thoughts aside, too, and remembered something I forgot to ask him earlier.

"Why do you need to ask Zane about Sam Thompson?"

Cooper's concentration was on the road when he answered, "The guy's an ass."

"He's actually not that bad. He just has a shit attitude."

Cooper's attention came to me for a moment before it went back to the road.

"You know him?"

"I wouldn't say I know him. We're not friends. But I met him when I first moved down here."

Once again, Cooper's gaze sliced to me, and I saw the question brimming in his eyes.

"You were still in Turkey," I answered his unasked question.

"Where'd you meet him?"

"The Iron Rooster."

I was hoping Cooper didn't ask how that meeting came to be. Not that I had anything to hide. I hadn't even met Cooper in person the night Sam Thompson asked me out, but I still didn't want to discuss it.

"The restaurant?"

"Yeah."

Cooper pulled into the parking garage attached to the building and I knew this was something else he was doing for my benefit. Cooper hated parking garages. He developed that hatred at an early age growing up in Southern California and having experienced earthquakes. The man avoided them at all costs. Or, as it would turn out, he avoided them unless he was trying to protect me from being out on the sidewalk in front of the building.

He pulled into a spot next to two motorcycles and I smiled. I knew one of those bikes was Jasmin's. I'd been begging her to take me out on the back of her bike. Unfortunately with all the work I had to get done, today wouldn't be the day.

"Not tracking, KK. If you were new in the area how'd you meet Thompson at a restaurant?"

My hopes were dashed.

"Well, I was sitting at the bar eating my first ever Maryland crabcake, which in case you were wondering was divine, but I could've done without the chipotle hollandaise. Not because it wasn't good but as you know, I'm not a fan of chipotle seasoning—"

"Baby, jump to the part about how you met Sam Thompson."

Right, I was blathering to avoid telling him.

"He sat next to me and asked me out," I rushed out.

Cooper's left hand paused on its way to turn off the ignition.

Yes, his left hand lifted to turn his car off—perhaps I should note we were in his super-cool, bad-ass 1964 Pontiac GTO. Backing up further from that, Cooper had fully restored the Starlight Black muscle car. He even did his own upholstery work on the doors but had sent out the seats to get those done. I couldn't say it was the most comfortable car to drive in but it was by and far the coolest car I'd ever been in.

The GTO's engine shut off, meaning the car stopped vibrating and Cooper turned to me when he asked, "Come again?"

"I obviously turned him down. I was nice about it. But I said no. Then I've seen him a few times in the grocery store. We've exchanged a few words but nothing that would constitute him being a friend or me knowing him. I just know him in passing. And that's to say, loosely in passing. But I've seen him around enough to know his attitude kinda sucks. He scowls a lot, but the times I've talked to him, he wasn't an ass just...maybe...gruff."

"You turned him down? But you were nice about it?" I didn't miss Cooper's incredulous tone, I just didn't under-stand it.

"Obviously."

"Let me get this straight. You were sitting in a bar eating and a man walked up that you've never seen or spoken to and asked you out?"

"Well, no, he sat next to me and started talking to me.

Five minutes later, he asked me out. Five minutes after that he was finished with his beer, and he got up and left."

"Why'd you turn him down?"

Was Cooper jealous? That was not the response I was expecting.

"Because he told me he was a cop, and I don't date cops."

That wasn't the truth. I didn't give a rat's rear end Sam was a cop. The truth was I'd already had a crush on Cooper. But I wasn't about to tell him that.

"I'm a cop," he noted.

"You're a *former* cop. And why do you care why I said no? Bottom line is, I turned him down."

"I care because I'm trying to figure out if the guy's creepy or just the dick I think he is. I can understand him seeing you in a bar and making a play. You seeing him a few times in the grocery store is a little weird. Annapolis isn't exactly small. I can only think of a handful of times when I've seen the same person at a store more than once. A few times, that's weird. Last night he came at me pretty hard. Could be he was having a bad night. Could be he saw you, remembered he was denied, and was embarrassed. Or, could be something more."

"Honestly, I think that's just him. The times I've seen him, he looked like he was in a bad mood. I didn't turn him down because he gave me a bad vibe or he was a jerk, I just wasn't interested."

"Good enough."

"Good enough?"

"If he didn't give you any signs he was a creep, and your opinion is he's just one of those people who walks through life being assholes then that's what it is. I trust your instincts on this and won't worry about looking into him."

I wanted to lean over and kiss Cooper so badly it was a miracle I didn't jump on his lap and attack him. Car sex in the GTO was awesome. As a matter of fact, it had been so hot, I'd scratched it onto my Try A Second Time list just to verify it was as good as I remembered it being. Unfortunately, we hadn't had an opportunity to do it again, and in the parking garage with cameras all around, it wasn't going to happen then either.

But I wanted to.

Instead, I settled on gratitude.

"Thank you."

I watched Cooper's blue eyes dance, something I'd witnessed a lot over the last few months. They always got a little squinty and wrinkled at the corners when he thought I was amusing. Normally this was when he kissed me, especially after we'd added sex to our relationship. Before that he'd just mumble and shake his head.

And right then he was shaking his head, smiling at me. What he didn't do was kiss me.

"Ready?"

I wasn't ready to present a case and face the team but I was ready to get this day over with so I answered in the affirmative.

"Ready."

———

FORGET MY PALMS BEING SWEATY, I could feel the boob sweat collecting in my bra. Kevin, Owen, Myles, Gabe, and Cooper were fanned around the conference table. Zane was at his normal seat at the head of the table and Garrett was opposite him at the other...well, head or foot or whatever the hell it was called. Right then with seven men staring at me expectantly I could barely keep a straight thought. I was blaming this on lack of sleep, a phone call from Detective Garcia, and nerves.

The nerves started yesterday when Garrett told me I'd be presenting, and they'd gotten progressively worse since then. I was being ridiculous; I might not have been used to facing down seven men, but I was in my element.

Intel was my jam.

The collection and compiling of data was what I did. I was good at it.

My gaze skidded to Cooper, but his head was down as he scrolled on his tablet. I looked at Garrett and he was doing the same. No help from either of them. My eyes caught on Zane and the air whooshed out of my lungs. One could say my new boss was just shy of demonic. I'd sat in on the debriefing after the rescue mission in Turkey. It was a safe assertation that Zane Lewis did not take kindly to being drugged, taken, and beaten. But more, he didn't like his men to be drugged, taken, and beaten. So by the time the team got there the rescue mission was more of a clean-up operation. I only had part of the story. Layla knew a little more than I did since she was there. And I knew without a doubt no one but Zane knew what really happened in that house before his team arrived. That was Zane—he carried the weight so his team wouldn't have to.

And right then he was grinning at me with his features gentled and dimples depressed.

So, yes, the oxygen left my lungs. There was no denying the Dimple King was a good-looking man—smokin' hot was more like it. But at that moment it wasn't his looks or the dimples or his blue eyes that were a shade darker than Cooper's. It wasn't even the grin. It was so much more. He'd deny it happened but all I could see was kindness. Belief. Confidence.

Garrett might've been testing my skills, but Zane Lewis believed in me—one hundred percent. I could see it, I could feel it radiating off him; it was so obvious I could smell it.

"That was a good catch," Cooper started, and my eyes skidded to him. "How long ago did Caroline Langford report her laptop stolen?"

"Five months ago. She didn't report it to the police, but I found an internal memo to her boss notifying him of the breach."

Cooper's index finger slid down the surface of his tablet.

"And he advised her not to report it to the police or to GM's upper management, correct?"

"Correct."

Cooper's head lifted and he turned to look at Garrett.

"Missed that, too, G," Cooper noted.

I noted Cooper's lips were twitching.

"In my defense, it's not my case. I ran a cursory search, then gave it to Kira. Though, she found that faster than I would've. My first thought would've been Langford paid someone to hack into his ex-wife's computer. That rabbit hole would've taken me a few days to exhaust."

I was staring at Garrett, so when he tilted his head to look over at me, I didn't miss his smirk.

"What're your thoughts?" he asked me.

Oh, shit.

I felt a bead of sweat form and I wondered why the hell I was standing while everyone else was sitting. I reached for the back of the chair but before I could pull it out Zane stopped me.

"Nope. Presenter stands."

"Why?"

"Listen up, Kid Genius, I totally respect a healthy disregard for authority, actually, I encourage it. Just not when I'm the authority issuing orders. Then you question nothing and obey blindly."

There was the Zane Lewis I'd grown accustomed to.

I pulled the chair out and sat.

The laughter started as chuckles but soon grew to roaring, obnoxious titters. I sat back and crossed my arms and dared Zane to tell me to stand.

He didn't. To my shock, he winked and went back to scrolling on his tablet.

"You're all fired."

"Kira?" Garrett called out, ignoring Zane's idle threat. "Your thoughts."

Right.

My thoughts.

"I think James Whitmore is exactly who he seems—a political thriller author. I went over every search that was flagged and cross-referenced it with his published work. And I may've gotten on to his machine and checked his latest manuscript as well. I skimmed it. Plot has some holes, but he's incorporating the information Kingston Langford is feeding him. Langford has me stumped," I admitted. "I looked into his background, crawled through his machines, his cloud accounts, and I'm not finding a motive. I think he stole his ex-wife's work laptop. Whether he broke in or for some reason she invited him to her house and he snagged it without her seeing him, I don't know. But he has the plans for the Presidential limo on his computer and he doesn't have the means to pay someone to get them and he doesn't have the skill to get them himself. And now James Whitmore has them, too—or he did until I deleted them. But he could've backed it up to an external device, and unless that was plugged in while I was on his machine, I'd have no way of knowing."

When I stopped speaking the room went silent.

"What if I told you Kingston Langford was plotting to assassinate the president?" Zane asked.

"I'd laugh at you and tell you, you were wrong."

"Are you sure enough to put President Grant's life in potential danger?" he pushed.

That gave me pause.

Garrett had been semi-right; for ten years I'd analyzed intel as it came in. I shifted through it until the bigger picture was formed. I had five men's lives depending on my ability to present the information to Layla so she could make decisions.

"Yes, I'm sure. If you'd asked what I thought about Kingston Langford stealing the plans to get his wife fired, I might agree. If you told me Kingston was a lonely man with no friends so he built the fake persona I'd totally agree. That man is bored. He's a liar. He pretends to be a former spy online to make friends and feel important. The six months he's spent chatting with Whitmore is the most interaction he's had in years. So, yes, I'm willing to risk the President's life on my intel. The only thing Langford's capable of is performing Google research for an author who could've found all the information himself if he would've spent more time looking. The guy's not an assassin, he's a virtual assistant to a successful writer."

"Agreed." Zane dropped his tablet on the table. "I'll send the report to..." He paused and smiled. "I'll send the report and alert the Secret Service The Beast has been compromised. Does anyone have anything else to add?"

There was a round of "nos" so Zane pushed his chair back and stood.

"Wait, that's it?"

Zane looked down at me and smiled, "What? You didn't think every case that comes in is a high-speed, door-kicking, fun time, did you?"

"Well, yeah, kinda. Or at least I kinda hoped that was the case."

Zane flashed a smile that if I was not madly in love with Cooper might've given me a tingle.

"I know everyone seems to think money magically appears in my bank account, but we actually have to work to finance the Prophylactic Fund. Something that seems to dwindle faster than the money's deposited."

"Don't blame me. I buy my own condoms," I returned.

"I knew you were my favorite."

And with that, he strolled out of the conference room.

What the hell just happened?

I'd been nervous as all hell for nothing.

I had boob sweat for nothing.

"I think we should look into Langford more. Maybe search his house," I suggested.

"Hate to break the news, Kid Genius, but our job is mostly boring," Garrett told me. "Which I tried to tell you, but you had your undies in a wad and wouldn't listen. And for what it's worth, I agree with you and your intel backed up your evaluation."

"I'm grabbing some lunch," Kevin said and stood. "Anyone want anything?"

Garrett, Gabe, Owen, and Myles followed suit, leaving Cooper and me the only two still sitting. One look at Cooper told me he was holding in a laugh.

"What's funny?"

"Nothing, baby."

"Something's funny, you're pinching your lips together."

"You look totally dejected," Kevin told me.

"I was worried for nothing. My boobs are sweating!"

"T.M.I.," Myles groaned, and Cooper grunted.

Garrett was grinning at me with the soft brotherly look he was sporting yesterday.

"Told you," he muttered.

"Huh?"

"You've got it. What can't be taught. You either have it or you don't, and, Kira, you have it. Trust it, build on it, use it."

Conflicting emotions swirled. I wanted to feel the full impact of his praise. I really did, but I was so confused about everything else I couldn't.

"Thanks."

"Gabe's buying," Myles announced.

"I'm not buying," Gabe rapped out.

"Well, I'm not buying either," Owen announced. "I'm taking Nat to Vegas next week."

"Let me check what Layla's doing," Kevin joined. "You two coming?"

Kevin was looking at me, but Cooper answered. "Yeah, we'll meet you downstairs in a minute."

"Jasmin has her bike today. I was going to ask her to give me a ride," I denied. "You all go without me."

Now, see, I had no idea how most men would respond. I had zero experience with relationships and practically none with men. But Cooper shaking his head and giving me his familiar, easy smile while doing it was not what I'd expected.

I was still staring at him when he said, "I'll bring you back a BLT."

My eyes were still glued to him when he stood and added, "Helmet, baby."

As if I wouldn't wear a brain bucket.

I was gathering my things as the men left the room, but Garrett paused in the doorway and turned back.

"Meet me in my office after lunch. We'll go over the traffic cam footage and see if there's anything useable."

"Got it."

Running the facial rec on the guy in the car was a bust so Garrett had spent his morning pulling the recordings off traffic cameras in the area while I prepared for the meeting.

With all the guys gone I finished packing up my stuff thinking I needed to find Layla before I hit Jasmin up for a ride. This morning when she'd stopped by my office she looked worried, but I'd been too nervous about presenting the case to talk to her. I needed to find her and put her mind at ease. I also needed advice and Layla was the perfect person to give it.

I had until the weekend to figure out what I was going to do with Cooper.

Or I could take the coward's way out and just quit and move on.

I glanced around the empty conference room and my belly flip-flopped at the thought.

What was worse, leaving the men, women, and kids that I'd grown to love or facing my past and the pain that came along with it?

10

I WAS NEARING the elevator when my phone vibrated in my pocket. I pulled it out and barely contained my groan. After reading Zane's summons I shot off a quick text to Kevin bagging on lunch but asked him to bring Kira back her BLT and gave him my order.

By the time I made it up the stairs to Zane's office, Kevin had confirmed, which was good seeing as Zane wasn't alone and it wasn't only the infant he had strapped into a contraption on his chest who was waiting for me in the office.

Layla was sitting on the couch, ass to the edge of the cushion, back straight, hands in her lap. There was no missing the look of apprehension and worry.

Theo Jackson was standing with his back to the wall of windows, eyes trained on the doorway waiting for my arrival. He didn't look worried or apprehensive—he looked furious. I also hadn't seen him in weeks. Easton, Smith, Jonas, Cash, and Theo were all taking an extended, much-needed vacation before they started work at Z Corps. Theo was back and forth between Maryland and Canada reconnecting with his mom, stepfather, and brother while trying to set up a new life back in the States after not having a home for a decade. But the last I'd heard; he wasn't due back for a month, at which time all the guys would start work.

"What's going on?" I asked.

"How's Kira?" Layla shot back and bolted to her feet.

Instead of answering, my attention slid to Zane. It was hard to take a man seriously when he had bright pink fabric with flowers wrapped over his shoulders bundling a baby to his chest, but if there was a man who could get away with it, it would be Zane.

"What's going on?" I repeated.

"How's Kira?"

That was not Layla repeating her question in response to mine, that was Theo.

I felt the muscles in my neck tighten and irritation slid in.

The ambush was unappreciated, and I was having a hard time remembering that Layla and Theo cared about Kira. They'd known her a long time. And I suspected Theo carried some of the same unwarranted guilt surrounding Finn Winters's murder that Garrett dragged along with him. But guilt, friendship, concern, or anything else besides didn't mean I was happy I'd been summoned to my boss's office to talk about her.

"I hope you take this as sincere when I tell you, I get where you're coming from," I started and held Theo's stare. "I also hope you'll take no offense when I tell you to ask Kira directly how she's doing."

I watched Theo's cheek jump then I watched him cross his arms across his chest and seriously hoped this wasn't going to turn into a brawl. I had a few inches on Theo, matched him in body weight, but the dude had spent a decade in the field. He wouldn't think twice about fighting dirty.

"What's with the evasion?" Theo pushed.

From the little time I'd spent with Theo and his team, I liked them all. Garrett had nothing but good things to say about them. And I knew he respected them all.

But right then, I wasn't feeling the love. I was pissed. Which sucked because in a few weeks I'd be working with Theo.

"I'm not evading shit. I'm telling you to ask Kira and hoping you'll take that as a read that I'm not talking to you or *anyone* about Kira. Especially while Kira's not present." I looked back at Zane and continued, "Was there another reason you called me up here?"

It was a good thing Zane was Zane, meaning he employed over a dozen Type A personalities, thus he was used to the abundance of attitude aimed his way. Which was good seeing as he'd recruited five new men who obviously carried the same traits. Though, truth be told it was typically us having to deal with his brash and opinionated views.

"Kira's not here—"

"Cooper's made himself clear," Zane cut in. "Which I warned you both would be his answer. Kira went out with Jasmin, you can talk to her when she gets back."

Theo looked about as pleased to be interrupted as I did for being called up and interrogated about my girlfriend.

"I'm worried," Layla murmured. "I've been worried for years. She talks about her parents and about Finn. She's not hiding from the deaths, but I don't think she's ever properly mourned them. Straight away she went after the organization that murdered Finn. And after I recruited her, I kept her as busy as I could hoping if she was doing something good for the world, continuing her brother's mission, she'd find peace in that. But I never...I didn't know...I let her down."

Layla was right to worry. She was also right that Kira hadn't properly mourned. But that was where the accuracy of her statement ended.

"You didn't let her down," I told Layla. "And you did give her something to help her through losing her brother. There are lots of ways for someone to mourn, lots of ways for them to twist death and internalize things that are not right. You saw her last night. You saw how tweaked she was. Not because she was shot at—because *I* was. I'm not going to go into details, that's not mine to give. Not to you or Theo or anyone. She has to be the one to decide who she shares with. Last night she trusted me with something she's struggling with, and I will take that to my grave. It's mine. And I'm sorry, Layla, I will not betray her to put your mind at ease. You're gonna have to ask her yourself. But I will tell you that I've got her back. Not only with this but with everything. I shared with her last night, and I don't think I've made it a secret or tried to hide it so it shouldn't be a shock that I'm in love with her. I've also made it clear the shit she pulled last night wasn't going to fly."

Theo didn't delay asking, "What shit did she pull?"

Before I could answer Layla did.

"As Cooper said she was tweaked and tried to push him away. She asked me to take her home—home being her house and not Cooper's where she'd been staying with him most nights."

Theo's narrowed eyes landed on me when he half-growled, half-grunted, "You forced her to go home with you?"

"No one forced Kira to do anything, Two," Layla

corrected, using Theo's callsign. "It was a shit night and she put me on the spot in front of Cooper, One, and Zane but if we'd been alone, I would've told her she needed to go with Cooper. You haven't been around, but she loves him."

Fuck, that felt good.

It also made Theo relax—or at least that was what I thought. But what came next proved the man cared about Kira. He thought of her as family and he, too, had her back.

"I want all the footage from last night and everything else One pulled. I called the team and prepped them."

Shit. Theo had also switched to using callsigns, Garrett being Drifter One or One for short.

"Two, you're in the—"

"Exactly," he seethed. "We're in-country and Kira takes fire walking out of work. Who's next? You? Me? Cash, Smith, Jonas, Easton?"

I looked back and forth between Layla and Theo as a chill slithered up my spine. Through clenched teeth, I asked, "You think this has something to do with Patheon and your op?"

"Other than my brother," Theo started and rolled his eyes, "has anyone ever taken a shot outside of the office?"

Theo's brother Bronson didn't shoot at anyone. He'd set off a pipe bomb in the parking garage and threw rocks. Thankfully no one had been injured during Bronson's misguided reign of nuisance.

"There's nothing that suggests this has anything to do with Patheon," Layla asserted.

But now that the seed had been planted, I couldn't let it go.

"What happened at your last briefing?" I asked Zane.

"Confidential."

Fury burned deep.

"Confidential?" I spat. "Someone shot at me last night. Me and Kira. Theo brought up a good theory that we should explore."

"Theo is wrong."

Oh, no, *now* I was furious.

"You willing to risk Kira's life? My life? Maybe Layla's?"

"Yes. Every damn time I send one of you out in the field I'm risking your lives. Yet, I do it time and time again. And every damn one of you trusts me to mitigate and calculate the risks. But with this, Theo is wrong. I am a hundred percent sure of it. And you know the terms of the agreement were and still are confidential. That means, I break those terms, Layla, Theo, Cash, Easton, Smith, and Jonas are facing jail time in a faraway jungle. It would be highly unpleasant for them, but if I thought any of their lives or Kira's or yours was in danger I'd break the contract and expect one of you assholes to formulate one hell of a good prison break because my ass would be right along with them."

Fuck. I knew he was right.

But I wasn't ready to give it up yet.

"How can you be so sure?"

"Because I made goddamn sure all of you were safe," Zane snarled as he shifted from side to side and patted little Rose's behind through the carrier. "Kira isn't good at her job, she's exceptional. Patheon went above and beyond what's imaginable, and what they had made it so Kira's exceptional intel made a lot of people uncomfortable. So uncomfortable, I had the upper hand and used it. No one connected to that operation would dare breathe in your direction let alone shoot at you and that's a motherfucking promise."

Zane didn't ever make a promise he couldn't keep. His word was gospel.

"Not that you need my two cents, and I wasn't in on the final meeting, but Zane's right. That case is closed and locked up tight." Layla paused and her attention went to Theo. "Stand down."

"Layla—"

"That's an order, Two. We're playing on US soil."

Theo's right eye twitched, and his forearms folded over his chest bunched.

He was pissed and attempting to leash his ire.

"I think Kira should go to a safehouse until this is over."

Jesus.

Did Theo have a death wish? Kira would go ballistic at the mere mention of going underground. Hell, if I thought for a second I could've gotten away with it I would've taken her to her apartment with the excellent building security and asked her to work from home. However, I liked my balls attached to my body, so I refrained. And not for nothing, but the woman had spent many years hiding away, I hated that for her, and she had me at her side so it made a safehouse unnecessary.

But before I could relay this information Zane had his phone to his ear and was answering a call.

"Please tell me you didn't lay down that crotch rocket and you're calling me to break it to your..."

Zane abruptly stopped and just as tersely went solid.

What the fuck?

Kira was on the back of Jasmin's motorcycle.

"Hold on." Zane tossed his phone on the desk and in a move that could only be described as magic had a sleeping Rose out of the contraption and was handing her off to Layla. "Ivy's in her office sleeping. I don't want her woken up. I need you to take Rose down and hand her off to anyone but my brother or Garrett."

Layla nodded, gingerly cradled Rose against her chest, and quickly made her way out of Zane's office.

He picked the phone back up and put it on speaker while ordering, "Text Garrett and tell him to get his ass up here." I pulled out my phone and Zane went back to the call. "What's your location?"

"450 East," Jasmin's muffled voice filled the room. "I just crossed the bridge."

"Are you sure you're being followed?"

Hot and cold clashed inside of me until I felt like I'd been hit with a bolt of lightning.

"Yes," she snapped. "Black Sentra has been on me since the Capitol and if you ask me if I've tried to lose him I'm gonna stab you."

I finished texting Garrett and glanced at Theo. I gave him a lift of my chin letting him know it was the same color and model from last night.

"Tag number?"

"No front plate. Just passed the World War Two Memorial."

Garrett came into the office and I took off for the door.

"I'm headed that way, patch me in."

"Wait," Theo called out. "I'm coming with."

I didn't give a fuck who was coming with me, but I was leaving.

"What's going on?" I heard Garrett ask but I was taking the stairs two at a time, so I missed Zane's answer.

A babyless Layla rushed past me on her way up with Lincoln on her heels.

We were in my GTO and pulling out of the parking garage when Theo's phone rang.

"One," he told me, or maybe that was his greeting to Garrett.

Either way worked for me when I heard Garrett's voice come over the speaker.

"Jas is headed to 50 East. Traffic's light. With Kira on the back, she's keeping the speed as low as she can. I'm pulling traffic cams now. And Linc's out the door on his bike so expect him."

"Copy," Theo returned.

"If I haven't got a read on the tag Jas is gonna go over the Bay Bridge and I'll catch it at the toll. Hopefully, I'll have it and she'll take exit 28 and get off the highway."

My jaw clenched as I navigated the narrow side street. I wasn't a fan of motorcycles, I preferred classic muscle cars, but if there was ever a time I wished I owned one it was now. With cars parked at the curb, and the two-lane street barely passable, I was forced to go the thirty-mile-an-hour speed limit.

Fucking shit.

"I'll call you back with updates. But Jas says they're safe and Kira has no idea what's going on."

Only Jasmin would think they were safe while being followed by the person who shot at me and Kira.

Jesus.

I didn't waste time trying to modulate my breathing or regulate my heart rate. The effort would've been in vain. I didn't bother restraining my rage—that, too, would've been futile.

As soon as I hit Baltimore Boulevard, I hooked a right and I pressed down on the accelerator. I gave zero fucks when cars honked at me as I passed them using the turn lane. Absolutely no shits were given when I crossed the double yellow lines as I sped over the Naval Academy

Bridge to get by slower drivers. I did this uncaring I was acting like a maniac and hoping like fuck Jasmin had the situation under control.

The woman was badass. I had no reason to doubt her ability, yet with the woman I loved on the back of her bike, I had my doubts.

Fear crawled deep and I drove faster.

11

HOLY SHIT! I had no freaking idea riding on the back of a motorcycle would be so damn terrifying and awesome at the same time.

The world zipped by at a frightening speed, my thighs burned from holding on, and the helmet was a tad cumbersome and a little heavy. But I was having the time of my life.

The only thing that would've made my first experience riding better was if Cooper were the one driving.

I was pressed pretty close to Jasmin's back, my arms were wrapped around her, but there was still a little space between us. If I had Cooper in front of me I would've scooted closer.

I felt Jasmin tap my forearm and I knew what that meant.

It was go-time.

Yay!

Before we got on the motorcycle, she'd given me a rundown and explained how I was to hold onto her. She also told me that while we were riding if she tapped my arm that meant she wanted me to slowly lean closer into her back and hold on tighter. And when she tapped my knee, I could loosen and ease up.

I took a deep, excited breath, slowly leaned forward with Jasmin, and wrapped my arms tighter around her.

The bike shot forward and suddenly everything was a blur of excitement.

Freeing and refreshing yet scary.

Oh, yeah, this was awesome.

This was exactly what I needed to get my mind off last night. A moment to just be and feel something other than anxiety and fear. I couldn't dwell on the dangers of Cooper's job while my heart was pounding with exhilaration. With the wind whipping past me I couldn't think about my nightmares, or how good it felt to have Cooper holding me through them. I couldn't contemplate quitting my job and moving so I wouldn't have to face the consequences of my loose tongue. Cooper was giving me a reprieve, but my reckoning loomed.

All too soon Jasmin exited off the highway. The exit curved to the right—she leaned into the turn and I leaned with her, but not too much. She'd explained that as well— my body needed to be an extension of hers. She slowed at the bottom of the ramp but didn't stop completely before she turned left, then she made a quick right and that was when I heard it—the revving of another motorcycle. I turned my head and saw Lincoln beside us.

He was using his hand to gesture to Jasmin. She nodded then sped up.

I thought nothing of Linc joining us on our ride; I was too busy taking in the beauty of the tree-lined street and how different everything looked being on a motorcycle. That was until Cooper's GTO shot past us. I did my best to look over Jasmin's shoulder while holding on the way she'd told me, and not leaning to the side. Cooper was stopped at the stop sign where the road dead-ended.

Jasmin slowed the bike, tapped my knee, and at the same time, Linc pulled back up beside us as Cooper exited his car.

What in the world is happening?

I didn't get an answer—what I got was Cooper jogging to the bike and plucking me off the back. My feet never touched the ground as he ran back to the GTO and shoved me through the driver's side door. A new set of hands yanked me to the passenger side and Cooper followed me in. I heard the engine whine and I felt the powerful car accelerate. My body pitched to the side, then someone was taking my helmet off.

I still didn't have my bearings when Theo's angry face came into focus.

"Back seat, KK, and buckle up."

Again, what in the world was happening?

I was too stunned to move, so I didn't.

I was too freaked out to respond, so I didn't.

"Seven!" Theo snapped, using my callsign.

"What are you doing here?"

"Get in the back and buckle up," he told me instead of answering.

I didn't listen to him. Partly because I had no idea how I was going to climb into the back seat. I was sitting on Theo's lap with my legs bent awkwardly, my knees up to my chest, my back leaning against the door, one hand on the dash for balance and the other clinging to the top of the seat.

Cooper tapped my shin and said, "I can't shift with your legs in the way."

I balled up but didn't move.

"What's happening?"

"Get in the back and I'll tell you."

"Cooper—"

"Back, Kira. I need you in a seat belt. Now."

Alrighty then.

Cooper was seriously pissed, too.

How long had Jasmin and I been gone? When we left, the team was going out to lunch, and everyone was happy and smiling. Okay, they weren't happy and smiling, they were concerned about the shooting, but none of them looked like they were ready to go ballistic.

"How?" I asked.

"How what?" Theo's voice rumbled in my ear.

"How am I supposed to get back there?"

"Like this."

Next thing I knew Theo heaved me head-first over the seat. Then Theo gave my ass a shove, I felt my foot connect with something, heard a grunt, and tried to right myself.

"You could've warned me, asshole," I grumbled and very awkwardly got myself into the seat.

"No time, Kira."

"Really? There weren't three seconds for you to tell me you were going to throw me over a seat? What's the rush?" As soon as I asked a knot formed in my stomach.

Did the shooter from last night come back and hurt someone else I cared about?

With a rush, a mix of emotions bubbled up.

Emotions that felt ugly and cruel.

My gaze locked on Theo's profile, I took him in, and the realization hit—for ten years I'd been surrounded by dangerous men. Five men who every day put themselves in extreme danger. When Patheon was created, they were nothing but numbers. I knew their names and their backgrounds. I'd been given limited information on their service then I'd done a full-scale dive and found everything those initial reports didn't tell me. Over the years they became something more to me. I grew to care about them, but it was easy to stay detached. There had always been an ocean between us. Thousands of miles separated us. So it had been easy to care about them in a distant kind of way.

But now I couldn't.

It was in my face.

I couldn't deny how deeply I loved Theo, Easton, Cash, Smith, and Jonas.

I hadn't tried to stop myself from getting close to Owen, Myles, Gabe, and Kevin. I didn't stop myself from falling in love with Jasmin, Robbie, Asher, and little Eric. I'd grown to care about Zane and Linc and Garrett and the rest of the men and women.

Then there was Cooper. Even if I'd wanted to, or tried, or put up a fight I wouldn't have been able to stop the pull. It was too strong, magnetic, overwhelming.

Now I was living my worst nightmare.

Everyone I cared about lived dangerously.

I could lose any one of them or all of them.

How in the hell had I let this happen?

A cell phone ringing pulled me from my thoughts. Then seconds later my world was rocked.

"Anything new?" Theo asked after he answered the call.

"Tag belongs to a 1987 Jeep Wrangler," Garrett weirdly announced. "Jas and Linc are attempting to locate. I need Kira back at the office."

Attempting to locate?

What the hell?

"She's not coming back to the office," Cooper declared. "I'm taking her to Kent Island."

"What's going on?" I asked.

"Can't use that one. Z's got Bridget there," Garrett returned.

Bridget Keller was a witness in a federal case. Zane had been asked to hide and protect her until the trial. Leo Gillonardo, Colin Doyle, Lincoln, and Cooper's brother Jaxon had been rotating shifts as her bodyguard.

"Why would I go to a safehouse?"

My question was ignored.

"What's open?" Cooper continued.

"The Cape, Providence, Charlette."

"Why would I go to a safehouse?" I shouted.

The inside of the car filled with tension. It reeked of anger. And it was coming from both men.

"You didn't tell her?" Garrett broke the silence.

"Tell me what?"

"You and Jasmin were being followed."

"Followed?"

"Same make and model from last night," Garrett went on. "I ran the plate, and it was switched. I'm running the owner of the Jeep now, but I'm coming up empty."

"What do you mean empty?" I asked.

"Owner's a twenty-year-old college student. No priors. Totally clean. I'm expanding to family now."

"Did you get a hit on facial rec?"

"You will not believe this but the guy's wearing a baseball hat, mirrored sunglasses, and a Santa beard complete with mustache. I'm going through frame by frame to see if I have a shot of his neck."

Yes, if there was a clear image of his neck Patheon would be able to pick up surface texture and vein patterns. But that would only help if the subject was already in Patheon's database.

"Okay, we'll be back in..." I paused to take in my surroundings.

We were back on the highway but I still wasn't a hundred percent familiar with the area this side of the Severn River.

"You're not going back to the office," Cooper barked.

The hell I'm not.

"I'm going in to help my team," I contradicted.

"You don't need to be in the office to do that," Cooper rightly pointed out.

"Well, I'm sure as fuck not going to a safehouse," I argued.

"You are, Kira. Twice in two days, you've been targeted."

Normally the growl I heard in Cooper's tone would send a shiver over me. But the last thing I was feeling was a tingle—at least not the good kind. I *was* feeling something—it wasn't fear, and it wasn't anger—it was extreme disappointment that Cooper would suggest I hide.

I'd spent ten freaking years semi-hiding. I wasn't locked in a safehouse; I could and did go out, I'd even been on a few dates, but every interaction I'd had outside of Layla and the team had been a lie. I'd introduced myself to people using a fake name and a fake life. One that included my parents and my brother still being alive and well and living in different states and that was why I wasn't close to them. I'd spent the majority of the time I wasn't working online playing video games like a teenager because I was so damn lonely, I needed something to connect to. Human interaction in any form I could get it.

That was part of the reason why I understood Kingston Langford. He was so lonely he'd made up an online persona. A spy, something other people would find exciting, something others would gravitate to. I hadn't gone that far but I had created online friendships. I couldn't say those friendships were built on lies but they certainly weren't built on the truth. For ten years I'd played End of World with five men who didn't know my real name or where I lived. They were fake friends, but real. They were nameless, faceless character skins yet these men were my closest friends outside of Layla and the team.

Wasn't my team nameless and faceless, too? Hadn't I kept them at arm's length so they would remain numbers? Hadn't I pretended that the very real operation I was a part of was nothing more than a simulation? I'd moved the players around the board, sent them where I needed them to go like they were avatars instead of real-life, breathing men.

Now Cooper wanted to take away my freedom and lock me in a safehouse.

That was not happening.

"Is Jasmin being sent to a safehouse?" I snapped. "Are you? Is the rest of the team?"

Cooper didn't respond, Theo did.

"No one's cutting you out of the—"

I didn't wait for him to finish before I spoke again, "No, Two, I won't be cut out of the investigation because my skills are valuable. But you know what's not valuable? My opinions and thoughts. I'm telling you I'm not going to a safehouse. If you try to take me to one, I'll leave. If you drag me back, I'll find another way out. What I will not do and will never do again is hide. This isn't up for discussion or debate. I am more than my skills behind a keyboard. I'm a fucking person and I get a choice. No, actually, I get more than a choice. I get the final decision on what I will and will not do. I want to go back to the office."

"We'll be at the office in fifteen minutes," Cooper told Garrett.

There was something devastatingly broken in Cooper's voice. It sounded hollowed out and flat. No anger or worry. No inflection, no pitch, just flat and uncaring.

"Copy that."

An uncomfortable silence fell. Part of me felt bad, I knew Cooper was trying to protect me. But the manner in which he was attempting to provide it was not cool and he knew it. However, the bigger part, the part that made me who I was, felt no remorse for shutting down the plan to hide me away.

I ignored the vibe in the car, I ignored the irritation I felt coming from Theo, I ignored the weirdness coming from Cooper and I sat back and stared out the windshield.

Now that I'd experienced the thrill of a motorcycle, the view sucked.

"I need to stop at my apartment and pick up an external drive if you don't mind," I mumbled.

Cooper changed lanes.

He didn't speak.

Nor did he say a damn word until he exploded.

And when he did, I realized he carried more baggage than I'd ever imagined.

12

IT WAS COMING.

I could feel it bubbling up and getting ready to boil over. It was so close to the surface that when the doorman at Kira's building said he had some envelopes for her that didn't fit in her mailbox, I had to bite the inside of my cheek to prevent myself from telling the innocent man to hurry the fuck up.

However, when we entered her apartment and she opened the first envelope and out slid a stack of eight-by-ten images, I saw who they were of and I lost hold of my temper.

I couldn't give two fucks that I was staring at photos of my face with red ink scribbled over it. But I went from already pissed to goddamn furious when I saw the pictures of Kira.

Kira on the street in front of work. She and I walking into a restaurant. Kira getting into her car. She and I coming out of the rock-climbing center. Kira smiling huge after we'd gone skydiving. More pictures of us together, her alone, and one with she and Garrett sitting across from each other, empty plates in front of them, both smiling.

Garrett's face was not scribbled on, just mine.

Hearts and happy faces drawn around Kira.

Creepy shit.

Sick shit.

Obsessive, stalker shit.

"Cooper," Theo rumbled.

It was a warning to lock down my anger.

I ignored him, snatched the rest of the envelopes out of Kira's hand, and flipped them so I could see the postmark.

All local.

I was arranging them in chronological order when Kira spoke.

"Has anyone else received pictures in the mail?"

They had not. If someone had it would be all hands on deck.

I didn't answer. Instead, I ordered, "Go grab your drive."

"Cooper—"

"Go get the *fucking* drive, Kira."

Her hands went to her hips, her head tilted to the side, and she scowled.

"This isn't my fault, so I don't know why you're pissed at me."

"No, you're right, none of this is your fault. But you being stubborn about a safehouse is."

"Stubborn?"

"Kira, go grab the drive. Give me a second with Cooper," Theo interjected.

"No. I wanna know how me not wanting to hide equals me being stubborn."

The gruesome aftermath of a man's psychotic break

dotted my vision. A whole family murdered due to an obsession he couldn't control. They'd done all the right things.
They'd followed the directives of law enforcement to the
letter.

Five dead bodies.

Five lives gone in the most horrific of ways.

A sixteen-year-old took her last breath while I was less
than twenty feet away outside of her home waiting for a
command that came minutes too late. Three children barri-
caded in a home with their dead parents.

She had a stalker, too.

A sick fuck fixated on her.

Now she was dead.

"Coop?" Theo called.

I allowed the memories and the guilt to invade my
mind. I allowed them to wrap around me and seep into my
skin. I reveled in the reminder of my failure. I forced myself
to visualize the crime scene, the blood, the gore, the heinous
smell.

Then I detonated.

"You have no fucking idea what happens to women
like you," I seethed. "It's not stubbornness, it's selfishness.
You don't *want* to be hidden in a safehouse, fine. Live
your life out in the open and wait for more of these to
show up." I shook the envelopes and somewhere in the far
recesses of my mind, I knew what I was saying was
wrong. I knew I needed to shut my mouth and back off,
but I was too far gone. "Since you don't know, let me
educate you. It gets worse from here. The obsession
grows. The need for a response turns into a perverse
hunger until that interaction is no longer good enough.
The compulsion requires direct contact. Direct contact in
the form of assault. Then after he's got his fill and he's

done playing with you, he'll end your life. That's how this shit goes, Kira."

I was so deep in my thoughts I missed the color draining from Kira's face. I missed the way Theo was frowning.

"Brother, you need to take a breath and think about what you're saying."

"*You know*," I seethed. "You know how this shit goes. I'd bet you've seen it worse than me. So, tell me, Theo, am I wrong?"

"Nothing's gonna happen to Kira."

"Right," I huffed. "Bet the Petersons thought the same thing. Bet they thought moving would protect their daughter. Bet they thought leaving the state would keep her safe. I got five dead bodies ranging from fifty-two to ten that say they were *dead* wrong. I got communication that started with instant messages, progressed to calls, went to pictures being sent to the house, and visits to the girl's school. But the one thing that sticks in my head, that tears me apart, that makes me fucking sick to my stomach is knowing we were too fucking late. That sweet little girl took her last breath in the arms of the man who had terrorized her and her family. The man who had murdered her family right in front of her. And that sick motherfucker cradled her as she died. So, don't bullshit me, Theo. You know how fast shit goes sideways, and when it does, we'll all be fucked."

I heard Kira's inhale as it whistled by her teeth. I saw the swing of her ponytail as she turned to flee. I didn't bother watching her go. I looked down at the thick envelopes and braced.

"That might've been overkill," Theo noted.

"Yeah, was it?"

"Her family was murdered," he unnecessarily reminded me.

"I know, Theo. And trust me when I tell you she feels that loss every day. She feels it and she entombs it so deep sometimes I wonder what's gonna happen when the force of it comes out. Last night, I got a taste of what she's going through. Just a taste, and it was so foul I choked on it."

"Yet, you still treated her like that?"

"Yep. *Fuck, yeah.* I'd rather her be pissed at me and breathing than oblivious to the truth and dead."

"Got it," Kira announced.

I noted the tinge of apprehension in her tone, and her slow, sluggish gait as she came back into the room.

Knowing her tone and unsure steps were my fault burned my chest.

I didn't feel a little remorse—I felt a lot of it. But the fact remained, she was in danger. She was the target of last night's shooting. She'd been followed today, and she was blowing it off like it was no big thing when it was anything but.

"Let's hit the road," I suggested.

"Why haven't you ever talked to me about being a cop?" she asked.

I could ask her the same—I'd known her for months; she'd been in my bed for the last four weeks and she'd never told me the fears she'd kept bottled up. She'd never told me about her insecurities. And she knew damn good and well I couldn't turn the tables and point out she was just as guilty as I was for harboring secrets without giving hers away.

Kira had perpetrated the ultimate sneak attack and tied my hands tighter than they already were.

"I have talked to you about being a cop. I also told you why I quit," I reminded her.

"You told me you quit because of the red tape."

"That's the reason I quit," I confirmed.

"It sounds like you left the department for deeper reasons."

Fuck, yeah, my reasons for leaving were deeper. So deep, it took a great deal of effort not to ring my captain's neck for delaying the call to enter. He'd been so worried about protecting his ass that he'd held my team out on the lawn. That delay had killed a sixteen-year-old girl. That delay meant when we entered, we were treated to the most horrific crime scene any of us had ever seen. The smell of body decomp alone was enough to make the most veteran officer on my team gag. The parents had been dead a while. The two younger siblings for at least a few days. The beautiful teenage girl—minutes.

Minutes.

Every man on my team had shed tears. A man didn't have to be a father to mourn what those children saw. He didn't have to be a husband to imagine what that father felt knowing his family was going to die—or at the very least, he was—and his wife and children would watch. Alternately, he watched his wife take her last breath and died in fear of his children following her into the afterlife.

Pain and sorrow were human conditions. They didn't discriminate, didn't care if you were a husband or a wife a father or a mother, a cop or an accountant.

But that day, as a man, my insides rotted. As a cop, I knew I'd failed.

So, yeah, much deeper than red fucking tape.

"How about this?" I started. "This weekend after we finish talking about what you laid out last night, I'll give you mine."

It was a dickhead thing to say and when Kira's eyes flashed fire I learned I'd underestimated the woman's core strength.

"You mean after we're done talking about my nightmares? The ones I know you were awake for. Or do you mean after we talk about what I told you? Which is now truer than ever."

I saw Theo's head swiveling back and forth between me and Kira. I ignored his confusion and focused on the infuriating woman I was contemplating tying up and kidnapping for her own safety.

That might be a deal-breaker for her. Layla would likely think it was a tad over the top. And Theo might try and stop me or maybe he'd help.

"That's not cool, baby, and you know it."

"Oh, so now I'm *baby* again?" she sarcastically drawled.

I glanced at Theo before I moved to Kira. My arm went around her waist, my hand rested on her back, and I pulled her to me.

"Never doubt for one second what you mean to me. You know damn well I love you and you know I'll go to any length to protect you. You wanna be pissed at me for telling you the truth, be my guest. But it changes nothing. I spent thirty minutes scared as fuck I was gonna find your mangled body on the side of the highway. You were on the back of a motorcycle with an experienced rider, but it was *your* first time. An accident can happen at any time. But when a new rider is on the back of a bike it severely limits the driver's options. Jasmin could've outrun a car no problem, but she knew better than to take chances with you on the back. It took me twenty-seven minutes from when Jasmin called in your tail until I got you in my GTO. Twenty-seven fucking minutes of me out of my mind with worry."

I leaned in closer. Kira's eyes skidded to the floor and I waited.

My patience paid off when moments later she looked back up and understanding flared.

"I love you, Kira. Down to my soul, I fucking love you and it took me twenty-seven minutes to get to you. If Jasmin was anyone else, today's outcome could've been different. I get why you don't want to go to a safehouse. But, baby, I also know you're smart. And I know this is gonna set you off, but before, *I* just wanted you to go. When these envelopes get back to the office, you need to brace because Zane will have you behind lock and key so quick your head's gonna spin. That is, if Garrett doesn't get to you first. No one, and I mean *no one* is going to let these pictures slide. They go beyond creepy straight to deranged."

"I'm still pissed at you," she whispered.

"You can be that and I'll take it with joy in my heart and a smile on my face."

"I don't like sarcasm," she bit out.

I wasn't being sarcastic; I was being honest. Her pissed meant she was safe.

"Says the most sarcastic woman I know."

She rolled her eyes to the ceiling and left them for a moment longer than needed for a traditional eye roll, which led me to wonder if she was plotting. And if so, if I should do the smart thing and cup my balls before she kneed them.

Kira's eyes dropped down and I saw nothing but despair.

Fuck.

"I need you to trust me," I murmured. "Trust that I know the woman you are. I know what you want, what you need, and how to give it to you. But, Kira, none of us can do our jobs unless you cooperate. And before you argue, remember—I got a stack of envelopes that don't say you're in danger, they scream it."

When it came to Kira, I was not above manipulation. There was no distance I wasn't willing to go to get her safe.

"Less than twenty-four hours ago you watched a bullet graze my arm. At the time, all you saw was blood and you had no idea how injured I was. With that in mind, tell me, if I was the one in danger what would you want me to do?"

"That's not fair."

She was right, it wasn't.

"No, baby, what it is, is real. With these pictures, we got a starting point. You can do your job from anywhere, and back in the GTO you were correct, your skills are needed. But the jab you took saying your opinions and thoughts weren't valuable was bullshit and I hope you said that because you were pissed off and not because you believe that."

I saw the contrition.

"Good," I whispered in response to her regret. "You ready to get back to the office?"

"No."

"No?"

"No," she affirmed. "I'm not ready because I know you're right and I'm not happy about it. But you were also right when you said I was smart. Contrary to what you think, I'm not naïve. I've seen enough Discovery ID shows to know what happens to women who don't take threats seriously. And I'm not making light of your service and what you've seen. My point is I'm not planning on starring in *I Know What You Did Last Summer* part thirty-two. I do have a brain and if it's proven I'm the target and in danger, I won't put myself or the rest of the team in harm's way."

I didn't know whether to laugh at her joke and fall to my knees in relief.

She was going to the safehouse without too much of a

fight. But more—she wasn't going to try to escape once she was there.

Thank fuck.

"Thank you."

"Don't thank me, Cooper, I'm seriously angry with you."

"Then it's a good thing we'll be locked in a safehouse together and you'll have plenty of time to explain to me all the reasons why you're mad."

Kira's eyes narrowed. Then they sliced to Theo.

I gave her a squeeze and pulled her tighter against me.

"Nope. Don't bother asking Theo."

"I don't like you being bossy when I'm mad at you."

"That's all right since you're rarely mad at me, which means ninety-nine-point-eight percent of the time, you like it."

"You must've been taught that common core math," she snarked.

It was wholly inappropriate, and I didn't give a shit when I tipped my head down and kissed her. It was either that or laugh. And since I hadn't felt her lips on mine in too fucking long, I opted for the kiss. I also opted for tongue and made it deep. It didn't take long for me to coax a sexy mewl from her, and since we had company and the sounds she made when she was turned on were strictly for my ears, I broke the kiss.

"I love you, KK."

She didn't say it back, but her face softened, and her beautiful green eyes danced.

13

I WATCHED a bottle of TUMS slide across the table followed by, "Take three before the acid in your gut eats a hole through it."

The whole room waited for Zane's comeback to his brother's remark, but it never came. Instead, Zane's gaze skidded around the table, his lips turned down, his jaw covered in a few days' stubble, his shoulders slightly hunched forward.

He looked tired, as any dad of a newborn would, but worse.

Battle worn and weary.

I'd known of Zane Lewis long before I'd met him. I'd heard fabled stories of his bravery. I'd heard not-so-nice things about him. I'd heard downright scary tales recounting his legendary missions. I'd never once heard anyone call him weary, but that was exactly how he looked. Worn-out and tired. And when his eyes hit mine, I saw sorrow.

"You're going to a safehouse," he commanded.

Any other day, I would've bristled, maybe argued just to push his buttons because one thing I learned about Zane after meeting him—he was easy to rile up. Something else I learned was that he was a marshmallow—a big, tall, broad, sardonic marshmallow, especially with the women in his life.

His wife walked around with a smile that broadcasted how well-loved she was. His sister-in-law, the guys' wives and girlfriends, and even me and Layla being the newcomers, were all shown—no, we were *given* the utmost respect, care, and concern. Of course, we were also on the receiving end of his signature asshole remarks. Man or woman, he pulled no punches. But everything Zane did for those around him was shrouded in love. He might never admit it, but it was true.

So, knowing all of that and seeing his fatigue, I decided to give him a pass and relent on going.

"Okay."

"Cooper's going with you. Garrett will rotate with Theo."

"Okay."

Zane turned to Garrett and asked, "Any luck with the footage you went over?"

"No. I'm sending it with Kira for her to look at."

Zane nodded, then turned to Theo.

"I assume you're good staying."

"Yes."

"Good, then I'm putting you on rotation with Bridget. I need to pull Linc off her detail and put him on something else. I'll have him take you over there tonight to make the introductions. Your living situation sorted?"

"No, not yet."

"You can stay with me and Ivy."

"Respect and I appreciate that offer, but, brother, you look tired as fuckall. If that's what living with a newborn does to you, I'm never having kids. I think I'll stay at a hotel."

Not even a twitch of a smile from Zane, even though Kevin, Owen, Gabe, Myles, and Linc were all chuckling.

Zane gathered up the pictures that were laid out on the table in front of him and stacked them into a pile. In all, there were twenty-seven pictures, and it wasn't lost on me that was how many minutes it had taken Cooper to get to me. Twenty-seven supremely unnerving pictures that I would never admit to Cooper scared the crap out of me. I'd glanced over them briefly, but I knew that the next step would be looking at them closely to see if I could date them. Some of them were obvious, like the lunch I had with Garrett and the shots of me and Cooper rock climbing and skydiving, and one of us at the movies. But the rest I'd have to look at closely—something I wasn't looking forward to doing. However, before I did that, Kevin was taking them to get printed.

So, I had a small reprieve. Just a small one, seeing as in a few hours I'd be living in a safehouse with Cooper, and for some reason that felt different than me staying at his house or him spending the night at mine. I also knew he'd want to hash out the last two arguments we had. That was Cooper; he didn't let a thing go unfinished or unsolved, and he didn't do uncomfortable. Which was why him giving in that morning and not pushing a conversation I wasn't ready to have had shocked me. But I had a feeling once we got to the safehouse and got settled, he'd want to clear the air—immediately.

"I need a word with Kira. Everyone out," Zane barked.

There was the grumpy boss we all knew and loved.

Zane waited for everyone to file out of the room,

Cooper being the last. But before he left, he turned and glared at Zane.

"She's had a rough day," Cooper said.

"And? I've had a rough life," Zane shot back.

Cooper's jaw clenched and he growled his one-word warning, "Zane."

Zane dipped his chin and sat back in his chair. Satisfied with Zane's acquiesce, Cooper left.

Something was seriously wrong with Zane. No reminders of the handbook, no jokes about our contracts, no cocky smirk.

What in the actual hell was wrong?

As soon as the door clicked closed behind Cooper, Zane's gaze swung to me.

"I need a favor," he started.

Zane Lewis needed a favor from me?

"Anything," I quickly replied.

"You might rescind that offer when you hear my favor."

"What's wrong? You're not yourself."

Zane took his time before he answered—long moments to gather his thoughts, his eyes never leaving mine, his posture stiff.

This was not the Zane I knew.

"Cooper didn't want you in a safehouse," he told me. "Before the call came in from Jasmin, he and Theo were arguing about it."

"Theo *wanted* me to go to a safehouse and Cooper argued with him about it?" I asked to clarify.

"Yup. Theo cares about you. He worries, and he was pissed you weren't already under protection. Cooper made it clear he was not going to force you to go. He knew you'd hate it, and he didn't want that for you. Of course, that was before someone followed you and Jas."

Holy shit.

I knew Theo thought of me as a little sister, and he didn't hide how much he cared about me. That wasn't what blew my mind. It was Cooper going to bat for me. Maybe it shouldn't have been such a surprise—he knew me. I guess I just never thought about how *well* he knew me. Going back to a life in hiding—even for a short time, was not something I wanted to do. And Cooper understood that; maybe better than I did.

"Why is Theo here?"

Zane's features became guarded when he said, "I called him."

"You're worried."

"No, I'm not worried. Never thought the day would come when these words would leave my mouth but I'm goddamn exhausted. We've been at this a long time. I've asked a lot of my men and they've never complained. I've sent them out on ships, I've sent them to hellish countries, I've put their lives at risk and in danger. And they've always done what I've asked. A situation pops up, we best it, and another one hits. They just keep on keeping on. Now they all got women and families and I'm still putting them out there. But now I'm not just risking them, I'm endangering their families."

Holy freaking shit.

Who was this man?

"They don't follow you blindly, boss. They follow you because they trust you. They're loyal to you because you've given them the same, tenfold. And you have to know that the women they chose, they did so for a reason. They're strong women, they fully understood what they signed up for."

"Do you?"

"Do I what?"

"Do you understand what you've signed up for?"

"Yes."

"You're sure about that?"

The tone of his question made me think maybe I didn't know what I'd signed up for. I mean, I'd read the job description Layla had typed up. I'd read the employee handbook that Ivy had made, including the handwritten notes that looked like chicken scratch that Zane had added. Garrett had been clear in what he needed from me. I didn't receive any formal training when I'd started Z Corps but then I didn't really need any training.

"Positive."

"And you trust me? You're loyal to me and to your teammates and not just Theo, Cash, Easton, Smith, Layla, and Jonas but *all* your teammates?"

What the hell?

That was out of line and quite frankly offensive.

"Have I ever given you a reason to doubt me?"

Again, Zane sat quietly and took me in. When the silence went on too long and started to grate on my nerves, I asked, "What's going on?"

"Has Cooper told you about why he quit the LAPD?"

If Zane had asked me that yesterday I would've confidently said yes. Cooper had told me he left the force and his SWAT team because of the bureaucracy. He explained that some of the new procedures that were put in place made the police ineffective. But after his outburst in my living room, I knew there was way more to the story he'd never shared. And thinking back to his eruption, it was like he wasn't in my living room. He looked like he was far away in an unpleasant place, like he was reliving something horrible.

"We've talked about it, yes. But today I found out I don't

know the real reason, or I didn't until he..." I trailed off, not knowing the right way to explain Cooper's reaction without it coming across like I was bad-mouthing him.

"Had a flashback," Zane supplied.

"I guess you could call it that."

"He told you about Linsey and her family?"

"Is that the sixteen-year-old's name who was killed?"

"Yes. By her *stalker*."

I felt the beginnings of a shiver, but it turned into a full-on quake.

It would seem someone had fixated on me, as well. And as much as I didn't want to use the term stalker, the sheer number of photos that someone had taken of me suggested that was exactly what I had. But what worried me was in all the pictures of me and Cooper, it was Cooper's face that had been graffitied over.

"Does he have flashbacks often?" I asked, hoping I hadn't missed any signs.

Cooper was easygoing and fun. He was full of life and energy and always happy. He'd never snapped at me, never scowled at me, or acted in any way other than as a gentleman. And in the beginning, he was far too chivalrous and was exceedingly cautious not to get too close or touch me in a way that could be offensive.

It was only after I was in danger that a switch flipped inside of him and my laidback Cooper was gone and the bossy, protective Cooper was now in his place.

"No. And I'm asking you to give him some leeway. These pictures." Zane leaned forward and tapped the stack. "Are sure to set him off. Linsey Peterson's stalker followed her. The family reported it to the police. When nothing was done, they moved. The guy found her, they reported it again, and they moved *again*."

Holy hell.

"Maybe you should let Cooper tell me the rest."

"Cooper didn't tell Layla and Theo."

Zane's statement was so bizarre I jolted.

"He didn't tell them what?"

"Layla looked like she was near tears and worried out of her skull. He had Theo bearing down on him ready to engage, and Cooper would not budge."

I was lost and confused.

"Budge on what?"

"He kept your secret. Whatever you had going on last night that had you shutting down and pulling away from him after you finally landed him after months of the most ridiculous, boring game of playing hard-to-get. That was him being ridiculous. You were the boring one. We have an armory packed full of tasers, handcuffs, zip ties, ropes, you name it we got it. I was thoroughly disappointed you didn't take advantage of the tools you had at your disposal and didn't just tase his ass, cuff him, and tie his big, dumbass to your bed. I would've helped a sister out, but you never called."

There he was.

Zane was slipping out of whatever funk he was in.

He'd given me something important, telling me that Cooper hadn't told Layla and Theo about our private conversation, but in true Zane fashion, he cloaked his worry in wit and smartass.

"So what's your favor? You wanna help me get in tune with my inner Domme and teach me how to use a bullwhip?"

Zane made a gagging sound and shook his head.

"I provide condoms and wisdom, not in-person instruction."

And he was getting even closer to being back to himself.

"Then what do you need from me?"

"I need you to put Theo's mind at ease."

"And how do you want me to do that?" I asked even though I knew how.

I swallowed down the icky feeling that was crawling up my throat and waited for him to confirm what I knew.

"Talk to him. Tell him what's going on with you."

"Why?" I choked out.

"Something I've learned. That stupid saying *it takes a village* pertains to more than raising children. You're young but I reckon you got more life experience than someone twice your age. You've lived through more tragedy than most people will ever feel. You lived through it, Kira, but you haven't overcome it. To do that, you'll need your village, your tribe, your people, whatever you want to call it. But bottom line, you need to trust those who care about you to help guide you. When you came here, when you signed on, you didn't get a job, sweetheart, you got a family. None of us can or want to replace the family you had. Your brother was an exceptional man—a warrior. His death was felt by an entire nation, but you bear the worst of that. But those of us who served, who by the grace of God came home, we've got a responsibility, one that every man in this company takes great pride in shouldering. You've found yourself a slew of big brothers, of mentors, of protectors. Use them wisely. And you've got sisters, a lot of them. They're nosy as shit and they'll get in your business and probably give you bad advice that will include how to wear your man down until you get your way, and you'll fill his house with cats and toss pillows and shit-filled diapers."

I couldn't breathe, my heart was so full of the most

beautiful, exquisite pain I'd felt outside of when Cooper told me he loved me.

"I hate cats," I noted.

"And that's why you're my favorite."

"And I've never owned a toss pillow, but I might want one in the future."

Zane shook his head and informed me, "No, Kira, toss *pillows*, plural. For some reason unknown to me mainly because I don't have a vagina, they come in pairs. You can't just have one, you have fifteen to throw on the floor every night and put them right back on the bed in the morning even though no one but you will see them. And since Cooper doesn't have a vagina either, don't expect him to arrange them the way you want them. Accept that if you want the damn pillows to look a certain way, you'll have to do it yourself. And don't get pissed at him when he tells you he doesn't care if they're on or off the bed."

That sounded like sage advice, so I nodded.

"I'm scared."

"No shit."

Well, all right, I guess I hadn't fooled Zane.

"I'm afraid for Cooper. What if it's me?"

I didn't need to explain further; Zane got me.

"Life's a gamble, sweetheart. It's all about risk versus reward. You make your bet and roll the dice. Some hands you win, some you lose. You take your winnings and celebrate your success. Or you take your losses and move on. I can't predict the future, but I do know Cooper's worth taking a roll of the dice. I know he feels that way about you. And I know without pause, without doubt, without hesitation what happened to your family had nothing to do with you. Not one thing, Kira. They loved you. You loved them. And what happened was so far beyond a tragedy, beyond horrific, there are no words to explain how heinous."

Zane leaned forward and rested his palms on the table before he continued, "Finn died by the sword he faithfully and wholeheartedly believed in. As his sister, you will not understand this, and honestly, you're not meant to. To you, Finn was your big, loving big brother. To those he served with he was someone else. To us, he's *our* brother. A man who knew the risk, made his bet, and rolled his dice. He celebrated his wins. And when he rolled his last hand and knew he lost, he stayed the warrior he was. He died a hero's death. The families of our fallen bury their sons, daughters, brothers, and sisters. They mourn the loss, they bear the sacrifice. You, Kira, bear the weight and you will for the rest of your life. But men like me, men like your brother, men who truly down in their guts are willing and ready to sacrifice their lives knowing their families will feel that loss, we see it differently."

At some point during Zane's speech, tears had formed in my eyes. My chest hurt so bad I wanted to rub away the pain.

But I still asked, "How do you see it?"

Without hesitation, he told me, "Noble."

That word tore through me and sliced me to shreds.

Noble.

Finn was certainly that.

He was also kind, considerate, and loving.

"What if it's me?" I whispered. "What if Cooper loving me means something bad happens?"

To his credit, Zane didn't look at me like I had a screw loose—which I was fairly certain I did. My logical mind told me my fears were irrational. But that part of me that was frenzied and scared didn't care about what was rational.

Once the fear took root, all logic was shoved aside. The anxiety and dread that filled my heart invaded my every thought.

"What if it's not? What if you succeed in pushing Cooper away? What if one day you wake up and it dawns on you that you are surrounded by people who love you and people who you love, and nothing has happened to them? But the one person who you loved the most wasn't there because you were too afraid to take a chance."

Damn.

That made sense.

"I want a family. I want kids."

"Then have them."

I couldn't stop my lips from twitching when I reminded him, "My contract states I may not reproduce until I have written approval from leadership."

Zane smirked, one of his dimples depressed, and he shook his head.

"Your contract does not say that, though that must've been an oversight. I'll have Ivy add that in."

"In bold, capital letters in the first paragraph, it states, *failure to properly use prophylactics is cause for termination.*"

Zane waved his hand and gave me a full-on, wide smile.

"That's for the dummies who think the condoms I stick in the go-bags are for making balloon animals. And, yes, a certain dumbass makes wiener dogs out of them."

I seriously wanted to know who knew how to make balloon animals out of condoms because I kind of wanted them to teach me how to do it. But thoughts of wieners and condoms flew out of my mind when Zane's smile faded.

"You gonna do me that favor?"

I didn't want to talk to Theo. Not because I didn't care

about him or I wanted him to worry, but because I was emotionally drained on top of facing a long talk with Cooper. A conversation in which I needed to face my fears and admit I was struggling to come to terms with my parents and Finn being gone. There was only so much I could handle in one day and Cooper had to take priority.

"I'll talk to him," I agreed. "But I have to talk to Cooper first."

"I'll accept that."

Pure Zane.

"Glad to see your funk's worn off."

"I've got a baby girl at home who is on a mission to see the sun rise every morning. I have a boy who is dedicated to the task of destroying my house every minute his eyes are open. I have a wife who has devoted her life to giving her children whatever they want so she is no help in my attempts to control the toddler, and since she loves holding and staring at her daughter, she makes no effort to make her sleep in a crib."

Zane did his best to make his explanation sound like complaints but it was far from a grievance. He was just as guilty, if not more so, of spoiling his children.

"Then I come into work," he continued, "and after years of lying to myself I have finally come to terms and given up on the notion that I have the slightest bit of control over what you people do. I thought I was done with lectures no one pays attention to. Cooper was the last one, and he swore, went as far as having his promissory note notarized, that he'd never fall in love. Then you came along, he saw you over the computer, and *bam* he's down. Then I take on five new guys and I know I got more years of strays being dumped on my doorstep, wisdom not being listened to, and the mayhem that comes with all of that. I'm too fucking old to be babysitting grown men with high sex drives and who get bored if they're in the mix of a good battle."

Gross. I didn't want to think about the men on my team's sex drive.

Ick.

"You forgot about Garrett," I reminded him.

"Garrett does what Garrett does but he will never replace her."

"Her? Who is she?"

Zane shook his head and frowned.

"As far as Garrett's concerned, she's a ghost."

"Is she dead?" I whispered.

"For him she is, but she's very much alive. Out of reach but alive."

"Why—"

"Respect, Kira, but don't go there. Not with Garrett, not with the guys, not with the women."

Zane's tone left no room for argument, but I really wanted to argue.

"Maybe—"

"No! Garrett had his reasons for leaving her and he has his reasons for not going after her now. Those are his. Trust me—do not go there with him."

Damn.

"Fine."

"Good girl."

My eyes narrowed and Zane smiled huge.

"That was condescending."

"Was it? I thought that was all the rage. Did I not say it right? Should I have deepened my voice?"

"Gross."

Zane pushed his chair back and stood.

"Be smart and stay safe."

"Copy that."

I stood and followed Zane to the door.

"Oh, one last thing," he drawled and I braced. "Don't be a dummy...wait, that doesn't work. Cover your Peter...damn, that one doesn't either. Before you tap it...you know what? Never mind."

"Seriously? You got nothing for me?"

"Nope. I got nothing. Never had The Talk with a woman before."

"I feel so cheated. What about, sex is cleaner with a packaged wiener? Or even, if you're eager, protect your beaver?"

Those dimples popped out and Zane roared with laughter.

Perfect.

14

"YOU'RE ALL SET," Gabe said as he dropped my backpack on the floor.

"Appreciate you swinging by my house before you came by."

"Don't mention it."

There was a glint in his eyes and humor in his tone that I couldn't quite read. Though admittedly, I was more focused on Kira and the shift in her demeanor. She came out of the conference room after talking with Zane laughing. But before that, she hadn't argued about being holed up in a safehouse. She hadn't asked how long she'd be stuck here, she hadn't asked about being followed, she'd hadn't asked about anything except Jasmin. But once she ascertained that Jasmin and Lincoln were fine and still driving around looking for the car, she asked nothing else.

I wasn't sure if I was grateful or worried about the change.

Gabe turned to look at Kira setting up her laptop at the kitchen table and asked, "Layla get you everything you need?"

"I haven't looked," she returned. "But whatever she packed will be fine."

Kira went back to plugging in her external drive and Gabe's attention came back to me.

"The perimeter alarms are set," he told me something I knew. "Owen's still patrolling the area and I'll do one more drive through the neighborhood before I head back."

I nodded but had nothing to add so I didn't.

"Strange, isn't it? Being on the receiving end?" he asked and looked around.

The man would know. He and his woman had spent some time in one of Z Corps safehouses. Only that time, it had been me playing bodyguard while Gabe was busy falling in love with Evette.

"It's good she didn't pitch a fit," he went on quietly as I followed him to the front door.

"She did," I started. "I lost my shit when I got her in my car and told her she was going into a safehouse, she disagreed. We got to her house, she opened one of the envelopes, I saw the pictures and went ballistic. Said a bunch of shit I shouldn't've or I should've at least cush-ioned. She relented but only because I was a dick."

"What'd you say to her?"

I winced at the memory.

"That bad?" he inquired.

"Yep. I told her she was stubborn and selfish, then I explained to her what happens when a stalker fixates on his prey."

Gabe ignored the insults I'd hurled at Kira and focused on the bigger issue.

"He's not gonna get to her."

"You're right, he won't."

I'd die before some lunatic got close to Kira.

"How's your arm?" He changed the subject.

Other than a dull throb and a small chunk of flesh missing, it was fine.

"Nothing to worry about."

Gabe nodded; having seen the graze he knew I wasn't blowing sunshine.

"You need anything before I go?"

The fridge was fully stocked and there were more toiletries than in a five-star hotel. We could be locked in the house for a month without needing any additional provisions.

"Nope. We're good."

"Not what I asked. Do *you* need anything before I go? I know you play it close to the vest, you don't talk much about what happened in LA before you came here, but we all know *something* happened. I hope you know when you're ready to talk about that, we're all here to listen."

Within weeks of me joining the team, Gabe and the rest of the guys made an effort to welcome me into an established, close-knit group. They'd made it easy for me to let my irrational insecurities go. All of them had made it clear they wanted to get to know me as Cooper, not Jaxon's little brother. But even knowing they had my back, I'd never opened up to them. It wasn't because I didn't trust them or felt the need to keep my past a secret, but from the day I'd started Z Corps, there'd been one trauma after another. Evette needed protection after she'd investigated the wrong people and found information powerful men wanted to stay buried. Myles had been on a mission to find an intel specialist who'd been kidnapped and taken into Mexico. Next was Layla needing our help rescuing Theo. Then there was Zane and Kevin being taken hostage. Back-to-back operations with little downtime wasn't conducive to deep conversations about shit I'd rather not talk about.

"I know you are, and I appreciate it. But I'm good with that, too."

Gabe shook his head disbelievingly and stepped closer.

"You can pretend it's not there. Some days you might even be able to forget, but, brother, that doesn't mean it's still not there. I know you're close with your mom and dad, closer with Jaxon. You got blood who will listen but sometimes it's easier to unload with someone who wasn't around while you were running around in diapers. You need us, we're here. But don't try to bullshit me and tell me you're good. If you were good you wouldn't have lost your shit on Kira. Not that I'm judging you; I would've done the same thing to get Evette safe. I would've said whatever I had to and dealt with the fallout later. But that's not you. Out of all of us, you're the most levelheaded."

I didn't feel levelheaded. I felt out of control and out of my element.

"We'll talk when this is over and Kira's safe."

Gabe dipped his chin and thankfully let it go.

"Stay sharp."

And with that, he was out the door, leaving me and Kira alone.

I locked the door, set the alarm, and peeked out the curtains to the mostly empty street. I cataloged the cars parked on the street and in the driveways knowing it was unnecessary since Owen and Gabe had done the same. One or both would be back every few hours to drive the neighborhood.

Kira was safe.

On an exhale I turned and found Kira standing in the

middle of the living room. The look on her face could only be described as timid.

What the fuck?

"Everything all right?"

"No."

Right. That was a dumb question; of course, everything wasn't all right. Once again, I'd been a dick. That was three times in the last twenty-four hours I'd stepped over the line and said shit I shouldn't have. Three times too many. Not to mention, Kira was somewhere she didn't want to be. She'd made it abundantly clear she was against going to a safe-house and only relented after I'd pressured her into it.

I wasn't a dick. I was a motherfucking asshole.

"I know you don't want to be here."

Before I could continue, Kira shook her head in short fast shakes.

"I don't. But it's where I need to be."

I should've felt relief. I should've been pleased as fuck she'd seen the light and was going to cooperate. Instead, I felt loathing. Kira was being forced to do something she didn't want to do, and I'd help make that happen. My response to her being followed was a knee-jerk reaction to *my* fear.

"What I said earlier—"

More shaking of her head as she said, "You said exactly what I needed to hear to wake me up. I was hellbent on *not* coming here and I was prepared to be stubborn about it. Which would've been selfish. It would've put myself and the rest of you in more danger. You were right to point that out. Though, I will ask that if something like this occurs in the future, you don't tell me where I'm going or what I'm going to do. You talk to me about it, and we discuss what needs to happen."

Okay, what the fuck?

"We'll discuss it," I easily conceded.

I was unsure what to say next, therefore I remained quiet, hoping Kira would guide the conversation where she needed it to go.

Apparently, she didn't feel words were necessary. Instead, she walked across the room, placed her hands on my chest, leaned in close, and kissed the underside of my jaw.

My hands went to her hips while her lips traveled over my neck, skimmed the line of my jaw, and stopped at my ear. Then those lips whispered, "I love you, Cooper."

I love you, Cooper.

Good Christ.

My eyes drifted closed, my chest burned, and fire shot through my veins.

"I love you, Kira."

Her lips were back to moving, this time across my cheek to my mouth. I held still letting her do her thing. She brushed her lips over mine, then on the second pass she used her tongue to trace my bottom lip, and that was all the invitation I needed. My tongue slid in, hers found mine, and she didn't hesitate to kiss me back. Not only that, but it was Kira who deepened it and moved one hand up my chest, over my shoulder, and curled it around my neck to pull me closer.

I'd kissed Kira hundreds of times but none of them had felt quite like this. The perfect mix of lust and love. Frenzied hunger with slow glides. When she arched into me, pressing her tits into my chest, I knew it was time to end this before it went too far. But before I could pull back she groaned, the sound so fucking hot I forgot why I wanted to stop.

I felt Kira yank my shirt up, then her knuckles were grazing my stomach on her way to the button of my pants.

Right.

Too far.

I broke the kiss but didn't go far when I muttered, "We need to talk."

"No more talking."

Her hand was intent on unbuttoning my jeans and I couldn't believe I was going to stop her but I had to.

"Baby, we should really talk before—"

"We talk too much," she said right before her mouth hit mine.

With the button undone, she went for my zipper while at the same time sliding her fingers into my hair. Kira engaged her nails and scraped them over my scalp. Getting her intended reaction, I growled at the feel and she broke the kiss, hooked her finger in my belt loop, and tugged.

"Bedroom," she rasped. "Now."

Kira pulled and I silently followed as she led us through the living room, down the short hall, and into the bedroom. Once there she let me go and tore her shirt over her head. Next to go were her jeans and panties then finally her bra.

There she stood naked and so fucking gorgeous I needed a moment to take her in. From the first time to every time after her beauty never failed to steal my thoughts and leave me stunned. From her full breasts, to her rosy nipples, to the flare of her hips, the woman had curves. There was nothing pointy or hard about her. She was toned but managed to stay on the right side of soft.

"Cooper?"

"Yeah, baby?"

When she didn't say more my gaze lifted from the juncture of her thighs to her face. Her lips were parted, her eyes hooded, and she was lifting her hands to cover herself.

"Arms at your sides," I ordered, and her arms dropped. "You love me?"

"Yes."

No hesitation.

"Tell me."

"I love you."

Christ. Beautiful.

"You gonna run from me?"

"No."

"You ready for me? For us?"

"Yes."

Relief, fast and sure, washed over me.

"No more playing. For real. You and me building a future."

"Yes."

Those pale eyes held mine, nothing but the truth shining from them.

Thank fuck.

"I want a family, Kira."

She pinched her lips but nodded.

"Kids, KK, I want kids," I clarified.

"I do, too," she whispered.

Fuck, but she was amazing. Standing in front of me, shoulders back, body bared, hiding nothing.

Finally.

I pulled my shirt off and tossed it aside. Toed my shoes off and yanked my already undone jeans down my legs and kicked them off. As I bent to remove my socks, I started issuing orders.

"Bed, baby. On your back, knees bent and wide."

Kira whirled, giving me a view of her heart-shaped ass.

Her knee went to the bed and I watched as she scrabbled to do my bidding.

"In a hurry?" I asked and stepped closer to the bed.

She stayed on her knees, craned her neck, and glanced back over her shoulder. I caught her sexy smirk before my attention went to between her legs and my dick started to throb.

Fucking hot.

My hands went to her hips to halt her progress.

"Change of plans," I muttered.

I bent forward, one hand going to cup her breast, the other going between her legs.

"Cooper."

My name came out as two breathy syllables.

As hot as it was when she breathed my name it was better when she moaned it. So, I set about getting that moan.

Two fingers circled her clit and I heard her breath hitch. My thumb grazed her nipple and her back arched.

I knew from experience I had approximately two minutes before Kira lost patience and started begging. I liked that almost as much as when she moaned my name. I liked it so much I barely teased her wet opening, a featherlight brush just enough to gather her excitement and drew it back up to her clit, and slowly circled again.

"Coop."

I bent deeper, put my mouth to her neck, and gave her a hint of my teeth.

"Coop," she repeated on a whine.

"Yeah, baby?"

I went back to tasting her neck, pausing long enough to take in the smell of grapefruit and mint before I worked my way to her shoulder, gliding my tongue over her smooth skin.

"Cooper."

I lifted my head, rolled her nipple between my fingers, and said, "Baby, you keep saying my name but nothing more."

"Please."

"Please what?"

"More."

Not quite begging but almost.

I dragged my fingers between her legs, slowly pushed two inside, but stopped at the knuckle and pulled out. Her hips chased my hand and she groaned her frustration.

"Do you want my fingers or my mouth, baby?"

"Your cock."

"Patience, KK."

I slipped my fingers back in and she moaned, "Fuck patience."

My cock twitched, wholeheartedly agreeing with her.

To punctuate her statement, she lifted a hand off the bed and reached back, curled her hand around my thigh, and dug her nails in.

"Come closer," she demanded.

Closer would mean my rock-hard cock would be pressed up against her ass, which was way too close to where he wanted to be.

I stopped toying with her pussy long enough to reach for her hand and yank it between her legs. Then with her hand under mine, I guided her fingers to her clit and started rubbing.

"You want my cock, KK? Don't stop playing until you come."

Kira took over rubbing harder and faster than what I'd been teasing her with.

"Want your mouth when you come," I told her and plunged two fingers deep.

"Yes," she hissed and rocked her hips.

With one last tug of her nipple, I released it and leaned back. As I did, I watched my hand trace the line of her spine. I took in the arch of her back, the way her ponytail fell over her shoulder. All of that was beautiful, but when my gaze hit the dimples above her ass my cock jerked at the sight. I slid my palm over the swell of her ass until I had a handful and squeezed.

My mind went to the drawer full of butt plugs Kevin had anonymously sent to my house. Then I began wondering why in the hell they were still in the packaging unopened and unused.

"When we get home, I'm gonna plug your ass."

"Cooper."

There it was, the sexy-as-all-fuck moan.

"Just like this. You on your knees playing with yourself while I fuck you."

I felt her hand work faster on her clit.

I didn't need to ask, I could feel her pussy clutching at my fingers, but since I liked hearing the rasp in her voice when she was turned on, I asked anyway.

"You close, KK?"

"Yes."

I pulled my fingers free and ordered, "Don't take yourself there."

"Too close."

I pulled my boxers down far enough to pull my cock free, lined the tip up, and slammed home. Kira's neck arched, and she cried out. I curled over her and took her mouth while her pussy pulsed around my cock.

Fuck.

Beautiful.

She took my punishing drives and groaned the rest of her orgasm down my throat. When I felt her tension wane, I broke the kiss and straightened. My hands went to her hips, and I pulled her back while I drove forward.

"Ohmigod."

"Tip your ass, KK, I want more."

Her back arched deep, her ass tipped up, and my gaze dropped to our connection.

"Oh, yeah," I started, and moved one hand off her hip to graze the crack of her ass with my thumb. "I'm gonna fuck you with a plug while you're taking my cock."

I felt her pussy contract and quickened my pace.

"Yes," she groaned and rocked back to meet my thrusts.

That was my Kira—up for anything. In bed, out of bed, it didn't matter.

My hand slid up her back and I put pressure between her shoulder blades.

Kira read my cue and lowered herself to the bed.

"Slide your knees wider."

She did that, too, and we both groaned at the new angle as I drove down harder.

My hand on her ass reached around and I went after her clit. Her hips bucked and her pussy clamped tight.

Fucking heaven.

Best I ever had.

"Oh, God, Cooper."

She sounded just as close as I was.

"Tell me," I grunted.

"I'm close."

"No, baby, tell me you love me."

Kira lifted her head, bent her neck, and caught my eyes. Jesus.

Hot and openly hungry for more—a look I was familiar with. One she gave me freely and frequently when I was inside of her. A look I fucking loved. But this time, it was suffused in adoration, which softened the hunger into an emotion that was so striking I held my breath.

"I love you, Cooper."

Jesus fuck.

I couldn't hold back.

"Love you, KK," I snarled and pounded harder.

Kira's eyes drifted closed, her head dropped back to the bed, and she moaned her pleasure. With a deep thrust, I stayed rooted and followed her over the edge. All thoughts of safehouses, stalkers, shootings, and car chases were erased. The pleasure of my orgasm was second to the knowledge that Kira loved me. Not only that, but she'd also said the words.

After a few gentle glides, I pulled out and immediately rolled Kira to her back. I fell to my side and rolled her again so we were face-to-face. Her cheeks still flushed, her ponytail now a tangled mess, strands of hair pulled out and stuck to her forehead, and she'd never looked prettier.

"Hey," she whispered and brought her hand to my face.

I waited while her fingertips skimmed over my lips before I replied.

"You okay?"

"Never better."

It sucked I had to ask but the about-face shift in Kira made me concerned. And as much as I wanted to enjoy it, I couldn't. Last night she'd been adamant she didn't want me to love her, she'd pleaded with me to leave her. And now, she not only told me she loved me, but she was ready to move forward.

"Hate to ask this, baby, but I have to. What changed?"

"Zane and I had a talk."

Zane Lewis, the man who cornered the market of brash, inappropriate comebacks, and cold-hearted comments—*that* Zane and Kira had a talk?

"You talked to Zane?"

"Yes," she confirmed. "He told me that life was a gamble. And you were worth the risk. He also told me that I'd lived through but hadn't overcome what happened to my family. He was right about both. He also asked me what would happen if one day I woke up and realized that I was surrounded by people who loved me and nothing bad had happened to them but the one person I loved most in the world wasn't there because I'd succeeded in pushing you away. And that got me thinking. How that would feel. How much I would regret losing you."

Kira paused, took a breath, then continued. "And he told me it took a village. I think he was talking about me needing a village of people around me to help me through losing my parents and brother. I don't think that's some-thing I'll ever overcome, but obviously, I'm not dealing with it in a healthy way."

I was totally fucking speechless.

I'd been on the receiving end of one of Zane's talks, the talk where he imparts wisdom and does it in a way that leaves no doubt the man cares deeply even though he does his best to keep it under wraps. However, he was far gentler with Kira than he was with me.

Kira's hand still resting on the side of my jaw slid over my ear and into my hair.

"Thank you for not leaving me."

This time when my gut tightened the pain was exquisite.

"You never have to thank me for that."

"I know I sounded crazy—"

"You sounded like a woman who has lost enough and is afraid of losing more. That's not crazy, Kira, that's real, that's honest, and it took a helluva lot of courage to share your fears with me." I lifted my hand and covered hers resting on the side of my head and squeezed her fingers. "I promise you, I'll make it worth it."

"You already do."

"I haven't. But I will."

I was leaning in to kiss her when I heard the alarm beeping. Kira's hand dropped, her eyes widened, and I moved off the bed, tossing the comforter at the same time.

I tucked my dick back in my boxers thinking it was a damn good thing we'd already had the birth control talk, and since Kira was on it, we'd stopped using condoms. I found my jeans and was hiking them up when I heard, "*Honey*, I'm home."

Fuck. Theo.

"Be right out," I returned, then glanced back at Kira now up on an elbow covering her chest. "Get dressed, baby."

"I brought dinner," Theo continued. "And an apple pie, though I think you two already had your dessert if you catch my drift."

Kira groaned and threw herself back on the bed, yanking the covers over her face.

"I can never look at him again."

"That's gonna suck for you, Kid Genius. I brought your favorite," Theo returned from the hall.

"Gyros with extra tzatziki sauce?"

"Yep."

"Damn," she muttered then louder, "Be right out."

"Thought so."

"I need to get dressed."

Yeah, she did, and it sucked we were interrupted. But seeing her on the bed with just her forehead and eyes peeking out from under the sheet, and her hair looking the way it did because I'd just fucked her after she told me she loved me made it suck a little less.

15

"WHAT'S ON THE HARD DRIVE?" Theo asked around a bite of apple pie.

"Files," I mumbled back around a heaping scoop of vanilla bean ice cream.

Which meant my answer came out garbled, but Theo still nodded.

"Baby, your laptop screen is flashing," Cooper told me on his way back from the kitchen with his second helping. "Good call on this pie, brother."

"Shit, I forgot I signed off."

I jumped off the couch, taking my bowl of ice cream with mashed-up pie on the top. Both men gave me a ration of shit about how I smashed the pie and then mixed it in with the ice cream like that wasn't what happened once it hit your stomach. Yet neither of them thought it was strange their pies were topped with the ice cream and that each bite they took had both pie and ice cream in it.

I set my bowl on the table and pulled my laptop in front of me. As soon as I did, I smiled.

The chat box on the side of my screen was blowing up from my squad.

I scrolled up to see if I'd missed anything important. After seeing nothing but my friends asking if I was ready to play I scrolled back down and typed a message.

Hey. Sorry I signed on and something came up.

Three messages popped up right away.

HondaRebel: No probs.

WestSide213:We need u.

VDGeek: U live.

Yes, his screen name was VDGeek, and yes, we'd teased him relentlessly about his choice of names.

I checked the box and saw a green dot next to SorryNot-Sorry's name, yet he had not chimed in. That was surprising. SorryNotSorry was normally the first one to give me shit for not playing and he was also the one who gave me shit when I was online for days at a time playing. That happened rarely, me playing for days at a time. I'd only done it when I was waiting for one of the guys to check in. Or when one of them needed me to get them information and I was waiting on a program to break code. I'd used video games as a way to stay awake. But once Patheon was shut down—or I should say once our mission had been completed and I started working for Z Corps—I'd limited my screentime. Then I'd started hanging out with Cooper and while I still enjoyed playing, I now had better things to do. There were places to go and fun to be had. And human interaction, especially when that human was Cooper, was way better than online friends.

Still, they were my friends and I owed them an explanation.

I'm alive. Just RL stuff. Sorry.

WestSide213: RL sucks.

I'd chatted with WestSide213 in a private box. He was extremely forthright and trusting with his personal information and his real life didn't suck. His real name was Bernard and he was a twenty-three-year-old trust fund kid who'd graduated from UCLA. His mother had paid his tuition using the money she'd gotten from his father in the divorce settlement. And from what he'd told me his parents' favorite pastime besides bickering with one another was seeing who could spoil their kid more. So, maybe his real life did suck, just not the way not-rich-trust-fund people's lives could suck.

HondaRebel: U need a vacay.

That was the damn truth. I needed a vacation. Unfortunately, that wouldn't be happening anytime soon.

VDGeek: As long as there's wi-fi I agree. We're getting our mf'ing asses kicked. Help us out, KidGenius!

I glanced back at the list of screen names in the chat box and saw SorryNotSorry was still active but not participating.

Weird.

Hey, SNS, U there?

VDGeek: He's butthurt you've been MIA. We've slipped into 3rd. Unless we make up our score we're out of the champs.

I felt a twinge of guilt. For years I'd looked forward to playing in the End of World championships. There was a time when mindlessly playing EOW felt like the only normalcy I had in my life. I wouldn't go as far as saying the game had saved my sanity—that would be overly dramatic— but chatting with my squad had certainly been the sun in my otherwise dark world. It had served its purpose. I still liked to play and message my friends but I no longer had the time to sit and play for hours and hours.

So sorry, guys! My life is so hectic right now. New job.
SorryNotSorry: FU, VD, I'm not butthurt.
Whoa, Nelly.

Much like any group of friends, as we got to know each other over the years a fair amount of ribbing and ballbusting went on. They could sling insults back and forth; mostly they were directed at VDGeek and his poor choice of screen names. But it had never gotten ugly or out of hand. There'd been plenty of "fuck yous" tossed out but they were always accompanied by some sort of smiley emoji. Sorry-NotSorry's response felt different.

VDGeek: Damn, dude, take a joke or ice ur balls or do whatever u do to chill out.

SorryNotSorry: Fuck off, vaginal discharge. I don't need your stupid shit. And learn how to spell, dumbass.

What the heck was happening?

HondaRebel: Uncool.

WestSide2 1 3: That sucked.

"Why are you frowning?" Theo asked.

I glanced into the living room to find both men staring at me with identical assessing gazes.

"I didn't know I was."

"You were," Theo confirmed. "What's going on?"

"Nothing."

Not wanting to deal with any more drama, I signed off and closed the game.

"Didn't look like nothing to me," Theo pushed.

"Damn, Two. Or should I call you mama bear? Nothing's wrong."

"I prefer Big Papa."

I made a loud, obnoxious vomiting noise that told Theo exactly what I thought about calling him Big Papa. Cooper busted out laughing and my gaze shot to him in time to watch his big body sitting on the couch shake with humor.

Maybe being in a safehouse wasn't so bad as long as I had company. Maybe it wasn't being stuck in my house for days working that was the issue. Maybe it was that I was there alone. Maybe it was the silence. Not literal silence because I worked with music playing, but silence as in, no conversation. No one to talk to or bounce ideas off of. No one to complain to, or bitch when some program crashed, or I couldn't crack a code.

There were only so many discussions a woman could have with herself before she concluded she wasn't a very good conversationalist.

I'd come to that conclusion in year five and spent the next five years talking out loud but telling myself not to answer.

Can you say batshit crazy?

"That's never coming out of my mouth," I told Theo.

"What isn't?"

"Big Papa."

Theo's brow rose and Cooper's died-down laughter ramped back up.

Whatever.

I went back to my bowl of mostly melted ice cream pie, scooped a spoonful, and debated whether I should look over the pictures Garrett had emailed me or go through the traffic camera and Z Corps security footage.

Footage.

I wasn't ready to face the pictures just yet and what they said.

How in the hell had I not known I was being followed? Layla had taught me better than that. I knew how to spot a tail.

"How'd we miss it?" I mumbled and set my bowl down. "Huh?"

I ignored Cooper's question and pulled up my email. I found the one from Garrett I was looking for and opened it.

"Kira, what?"

"How'd we miss a tail?" I asked louder and clicked on the zip file.

I was entering in my password when Theo spoke. "Let us in on where you're going with this."

"I find it hard to believe we missed a tail," I clarified. "Me, Cooper, *and* Garrett. None of us saw someone following us or taking pictures."

"Those images could've been taken from a hundred yards away," Theo noted.

This was true, but a high-power zoom lens that could produce a crisp image from that far away would be expensive—very expensive and it would also require a tripod.

"What are you thinking?" Cooper asked.

I glanced his way and watched him place his empty plate on the coffee table. I watched Theo do the same and I did this thinking how life was not fair to women. Both men had eaten two huge slices of pie with a mound of ice cream on each of those slices and neither of them had an ounce of fat on them.

Bastards.

"Kira?" Theo called.

"I don't know what I'm thinking."

Cooper had come out of his lazy sprawl on the couch and was now sitting on the edge of the cushion, and while Theo was still lounging back, he was alert and staring at me with a look that told me I wasn't going to like what came next.

"I'm not trying to be an ass, but," Theo began, proving I

was correct in my assessment. "It's easy to miss a tail when you're preoccupied. You were out with your man and had no reason to be hyperaware, so you weren't. You were having lunch with a colleague and no reason to think someone would be watching you, so you weren't on the lookout. This isn't the days of Patheon when you had to employ anti-surveillance to move around."

I might've found Theo's accusation that I'd become complacent offensive if it weren't true. He was right; I hadn't been vigilant about checking my surroundings. I hadn't cataloged the people around me. I'd been so caught up in my newfound freedom I'd stopped paying attention.

So it sucked I had to admit someone could've been ten feet from me, taking pictures with their cell phone, and I wouldn't have noticed.

Shit.

"You're right," I grumbled and went back to my laptop.

I placed all the images in a folder on my desktop to look at later and went in search of the security footage—specifically the traffic cameras from today. All I needed was one good angle and then I'd let Patheon—the facial recognition program, not the team—do its thing and we'd have a name.

I was a minute forty-five seconds into the first clip when I felt hands on my shoulders.

"Want something to drink?" Cooper asked.

Damn, but I loved him.

I loved that he didn't tell me that Garrett had already gone over all the footage. I loved that he didn't tell me I'd had a shit day after a shit night and I should rest. I loved that he knew it wouldn't matter how bad of a day I had, how long it had been, how tired I was, or how many people had looked over the videos; I wouldn't be able to settle my mind until I watched them.

"No, thank you."

Cooper gave my shoulders a firm squeeze and started to move away.

"Did you watch last night's—"

"Yep," he cut me off before I could finish. "And seeing it from your angle, I get why you thought I was shot and not grazed. I didn't feel my arm jerk back as hard as it did. And I know you're beating yourself up for getting on the ground, but again, seeing it from where you were standing with bullets flying you did the right thing. And as far as you not going into the building, I know I apologized but it's worth the repeat—I'm sorry I was a dick."

I didn't need him to apologize again. And as embarrassed as I was, I'd dropped to the sidewalk like a moron, I had bigger things to worry about.

"Did you back up the video? Or just watch it from when we exited?"

"I started it a few seconds before we came out."

"I need you to see something," I told him and minimized the video I was watching to pull up last night's footage.

It might've been nothing, but it had been bugging me since I'd watched it this morning.

"He was parked out there over an hour. But he'd circled the block for more than thirty minutes before that."

"Not unusual," Theo rejoined, sounding closer.

I glanced to my right and Theo was right next to me—as in super-close and I hadn't heard him move.

"You need a collar with a cowbell," I grumbled.

"I'm up for a lotta kinky stuff, KK, a collar isn't one of them."

"I don't know what's gotten into you," I groused. "I'd blame it on Zane, but you haven't spent enough time with him for his inappropriateness to rub off on you."

"Fresh air and clean living brings out all sorts of shit in a man," Theo rapped out. "And just to add, Zane will never rub anything on me or off me."

"Now I understand why Layla had her rules and Zane has his handbook. If left unattended with no adult supervision you all would run amuck, and no work would get done."

"It's cute you still think we followed Layla's rules."

"It's cute you think I didn't know."

That was a lie. At the time, I'd thought the guys were following Layla's rules, especially the one about none of them having direct contact with one another. And I'd never in a million years thought they'd break the golden rule, the one that was paramount for operational security, and come back to the United States before the mission was over. But then, I was a little naïve in my thinking. I was a rule follower unless the rule had to do with hacking a system or a database, or a foreign satellite. Basically, I followed the rules until I needed something. So why I thought a group of former Ground Branch operators would follow the rules, when I, an average citizen, bent them to my needs I didn't know. But they'd all broken all the rules that Layla had put in place. However, by the time she'd found out, the operation was over.

I held Theo's stare until he smiled.

He knew I was lying, he just wasn't going to call me on it.

"Pull up the footage, Kid Genius, before I slip into a food coma standing here."

I went back to my keyboard while pointing out, "If you hadn't stuffed your face with gyros and pie you won't be experiencing gut rot."

"Woman, I spent ten years in dozens of counties. Some

of them beautiful, some of them hellholes. But even in the beautiful ones, I was stuck in the shittiest parts with the dregs. If I had a weak stomach before I went over, I promise you I don't anymore."

Theo's tone was teasing, but I knew what he'd done during those ten years. I knew what he saw, I knew who he met with, I knew the horrific things he'd had to do.

Guilt gnawed at my insides.

I hadn't made the decisions, but my intel had led to those decisions being made. I'd never given Theo or any of the guys a direct order to take out the enemy, but I had provided locations when needed.

"Hey." The back of Theo's hand nudged my bicep. "Don't go there."

Jeez, the guy wasn't only stealthy, he was a mind reader, too.

But he was right; I needed to push aside the guilt and concentrate on what I was doing.

I found the footage I needed and played the video. The black Sentra pulled into a parking spot right across from Z Corps. A few moments later a man stepped out—jeans, gray t-shirt with no logo, a green John Deere trucker hat, very obvious fake beard and mustache though this disguise was brown and not the stark white one he wore today. The guy walked to the trunk, popped it open, pulled out a backpack, then walked back and got into the car.

"Rewind that," Cooper said.

I did as he asked and waited to see if he saw the same thing I saw.

"Pause it and zoom in on his forearm."

Oh, yeah, Cooper saw it.

Thanks to Zane's high-quality cameras, even though it was dark and the image was at a ten-times zoom, we could make out numbers inked on the man's forearm. Unfortunately, with the brim of the hat pulled low and the fake beard and mustache we had no clear shot of the guy's face.

"Four dash eleven dash twelve," Cooper read the numbers. "April eleventh two thousand twelve?"

"I'd read that November fourth," Theo said. "In the military day goes before the month."

November fourth? There was a nagging in the back of my brain; I knew that date. It wasn't anyone in my family's birthday, not an anniversary, not the day they died. But I knew that date was important.

"Is that one of the guy's birthdays? Layla's?" I asked Theo.

"Nope. Why?"

"Something important happened on that date. I know it. Was it a mission?"

Theo thought for a second before he shook his head.

"Not one of mine. At least not one that stands out. And Zane was adamant that what's happening isn't retaliation."

I know why Zane thought that. His deal with the government was comprehensive. But that didn't mean shit. I knew from personal experience that bad people meaning to do bad things didn't respect deals. They didn't honor agreements because they had no honor. But the CIA wasn't why I'd backed up my files and lied to Zane. The U.S. government wasn't why I hadn't turned over all of my drives even though I'd signed a mountain of paperwork declaring I had. It wasn't even the foreign governments I was worried about. It was the warlords, the pirates, the terrorists, gun runners, drug dealers, and traffickers I was worried about.

They'd seek retribution and want restitution for all the money Patheon had cost them. They wouldn't care that

Zane Lewis had struck a deal. And since knowledge was power, I'd kept everything.

But this didn't feel like vengeance, at least not from the actors Patheon had dealt with. If one of those people had wanted Cooper dead on the street, they wouldn't have missed. They had the means and connections to pay for the best. Jasmin and I wouldn't have been followed; we would've been taken out.

But I knew that date meant something to me. I just couldn't place it.

"What did Garrett say about it?" Cooper asked.

"We haven't had time to discuss anything. We both have full caseloads on top of the shooting last night and what happened earlier. I'm hoping to connect with him tonight." I paused and frowned. "Hopefully, we're all done with the stupid tests."

"I told you the Langford case wasn't a test," he reminded me. "Neither were the other cases Garrett put in front of you. It's about teamwork and trust—you learning how to use your team and trusting yourself to make decisions without going to Garrett, Zane, or Layla. You know you're good at your job. You know it and you have no issue rubbing it in Garrett's face when you find something before him, but you still don't trust your instincts."

My instincts were screaming that the numbers on the shooter's or stalker's or whatever he was forearm were the key to cracking the case.

I just had to remember, and I wasn't going to do that with two men staring over my shoulder.

"Go. Turn on ESPN or a car show or a movie. I need to concentrate."

Cooper chuckled, kissed the top of my head, and asked, "You sure you don't want me to put you on a pot of coffee?"

Yep. He knew me well.

"Yes, please."

"You got it, baby."

I felt Cooper's hands leave my shoulders. A few beats later Theo leaned closer and whispered, "Whatever was fucking with your head last night, if it comes back, you find me."

Shit. I'd talked to Layla before we'd been escorted to the safehouse, but I still needed to talk to Theo.

I opened my mouth to explain I was too emotionally drained to talk right then but Theo beat me to it and continued. "We'll talk later. But for now, you need to know that man will go to bat for you, he has your back, and when you find yourself a man like that, you hold on to him, sweetheart. You don't push him away, especially in the middle of trouble."

Theo's whole persona had changed. Gone was the teasing friend and he looked nothing like the rogue commando I knew. The softness in his eyes made me wonder if Finn were alive if he would've looked at me the same way.

"I'm not going to push him away."

"Good. Now get to work. Use that big brain of yours and find me a fuckwit to kill."

I felt my eyes get huge and Theo smirked. "Kidding. Sorta. Not really."

I smiled back at him and went back to my computer.

November fourth two thousand twelve.

I knew that date and it was going to drive me crazy until I figured it out.

16

I HEARD Kira's laptop close, the chair scrape on the wood floor, and checked the corner of my tablet for the time. Just after two in the morning. Kira had been at it for hours. Theo had long since gone to bed. I was sitting on the couch waiting for her to be done. And by the sound of it, she was finally ready for bed.

I got my confirmation when her ass hit the cushion next to me and the top half of her toppled into my lap and she declared, "I'm done for the night."

One hand went into her hair, the other on her hip and I asked, "Find anything?"

The thing with Kira, and the habit that Garrett was trying to break with what she called "tests," was that she liked to work alone. Seeing as that was how she'd worked the last ten years it was to be expected, but that was not how Z Corps operated. We shared information even as it was being gathered.

Kira was an island unto herself.

That meant, even though Theo and I had been sitting on the couch she hadn't said a word to either of us. She'd had a brief conversation with Garrett and by brief I mean it lasted long enough for Kira to tell him she'd gotten into the Maryland Department of Transportation's files and had pulled all the footage from all the traffic cameras within a twenty-mile radius of Annapolis, then she hung up and went back to work.

"Do you know how many black Sentras there are in Maryland?" she asked instead of answering.

"No."

"Too many." She blew out a breath. "But I caught him at an intersection in Glen Bernie. There's a camera at a bus stop across from the MVA. Bad news is, I knew it was him because he was wearing the Santa beard. More bad news is he's wearing a hat and sunglasses and a collared shirt with the collar popped up. If I didn't know any better, I'd say he knows how to evade facial rec. I ran some of the images through Patheon and I got nothing. Tomorrow I'm gonna go back into the DOT's files and get more footage now that I know what direction he came from. But I'm too damn tired tonight."

Kira rapped all that out like it wasn't damn impressive that it had only taken her hours to find a very popular car.

"How'd you find it?"

"Garrett had a program. I made a few tweaks. After that, I just had to run the footage while the program ran in the background. When I have time, I'm gonna make a few more adjustments. It's still too slow."

Again, like making tweaks to a program is no big deal.

"English, baby."

"I had the car's tag number, so it was easy once I made a few changes to the program that Garrett wrote. Surveillance and verification tech isn't his thing. He's more into encryption and...sorry, I'm geeking out. Anyway, that's how I found the car."

"Do you have any idea how much of a turn-on it is that you're so smart?"

I felt Kira's body shake until the shaking turned audible and I heard her soft giggle.

It wasn't until right then I realized I hadn't heard her laugh since I found her in the conference room with Lincoln's twins. And it wasn't until right then I realized how much I'd taken it for granted. She laughed all the time, so much so I'd forgotten to appreciate the gift it was.

"You're a strange man, Cooper Cain," she teased.

"Lots of men find intelligent women attractive."

Kira pivoted to her back, stretched her legs over the armrest of the couch, and with her head still in my lap looked up at me and smiled.

"And here I thought men were attracted to boobs and booty."

Oh, yeah, there was a lot I'd not taken the time to fully appreciate. From the first time I heard her voice over a video call, I was taken in by her feisty attitude. And from the time I saw her smiling on the screen I was a goner. And as the months went on, those smiles kept coming along with her energy and wit—all of that consuming me. Yet I'd never fully comprehended the beauty of it until I didn't have it. Sure, she'd smiled in the last twenty-four hours but not like she was doing right then with her head in my lap. Not the kind of smile that lit her face. Not the kind that made her eyes dance.

"Yeah, baby, we like boobs and booty, too."

"What's wrong?"

I shifted my hand in her hair, found the rubber band that was holding her ponytail, and gently pulled it out.

"Nothing's wrong."

Her eyes roamed my face searching for the veracity of my answer. Apparently, she didn't find what she was looking for because she pushed. "Are you sure?"

"Have I ever told you how much I love hearing you laugh?"

"Huh?"

"Or how beautiful your smile is?"

"What—"

"I've never met a woman who makes me laugh as much as you do. I've never had more fun with anyone, man or woman, as I do with you."

"Coop," she whispered.

"Everything about you is captivating. When I'm with you I feel good. More than content, more than happy. It just downright feels *good* to be near you."

Kira's lips turned up but the smile was soft and full of worry, not exactly what I was going for.

"Not that I don't love hearing you telling me that, but, honey, why do you look like..." she trailed off and bent her head back and to the side keeping her eyes locked on mine. "I don't know how you look. Unhappy? Upset?"

"I'm neither," I told her then amended, "Maybe I'm upset with myself for not realizing how much I take you for granted."

Before I could stop her, Kira scrambled out of my lap only to get right back into it, this time sitting astride me. My hands automatically went to her hips. Hers went to my chest and she put pressure there as she leaned into me.

"What are you talking about? You don't take me for granted."

"Yeah, I do," I admitted. "I had no idea, because you're you. You smile, you laugh, you tease, you're always in a good mood. I had no idea what it would feel like not to have that. Then I didn't have it for a day, and I feel like an asshole. I just assumed I'd never go without. I took each smile without thought. I laughed with you never considering what you were giving me. And something else—I took you as you came and held pieces of myself back from you out of fear of you leaving me. I think earlier we agreed we're moving forward, together."

"Yes, that's what we agreed," she confirmed.

"That means I'm not gonna hold back."

Kira frowned and asked, "What have you been holding back?"

"You talk about your parents and Finn," I started and her body jolted. "I love that you talk about them, I love that you smile when you tell me stories about them. But you never talk about *you*, how you feel. And after last night, I agree with Zane. You lived through not one, but two life-changing tragedies. But I'm not sure Zane's right about over-coming that sort of a loss. I don't think that's something you overcome. I think that when you love someone as deeply as you loved your parents and Finn, the loss stays with you. It shapes you, it takes a piece of you. There's beauty in that. There's something special about that kind of pain, the kind that is born from deep abiding love. But to get to a place where you can feel the loss and the pain without the sharp edges ripping you to shreds, we have some work to do. That starts with us talking about how you feel. I didn't think that was my place before, but now it is. And that's what I'm not gonna hold back. I'm gonna push you to open up to me."

Kira leaned back until I had to loosen my grip on her hips. But when she'd put enough space between us, I slid my hands around her and locked her place.

"I miss them."

"I know you do."

"No, Cooper, I *miss* them. Every day. Every hour. I miss them so much that sometimes it steals my breath. Sometimes I think about it and I'm still in shock. I still don't believe it. I can't get over how one day I had loving parents and the next day I didn't. One day I had a big brother who loved me and teased me and was a great son and the next day I didn't. Just like that. Just. Like. That. Poof, it was over. My parents were gone, but I had Finn. We had each other. We missed them together. Then he was gone. And I had no one to miss him with. I was alone. That's how I feel."

Christ.

"Baby."

Kira's chin tipped down, her body went solid, and waves of grief were rolling over her, filling the room. Grief so thick it stuck in my throat. Heartache so potent I realized I was wrong; each smile, each bubble of laughter, every witty comeback, they weren't gifts—they were miraculous. It was astounding she hadn't crumbled under the loss, and not only that, she still had it in her to be sweet, caring, and funny.

And when she went on, I understood why her sorrow was leaching into my pores.

"There's this soul-crushing yearning to have them back. Another day. More time. An hour. Something. I'd literally take anything. Another second. One more phone call with my mom. One more hug from my dad. Another smile from Finn. I just needed more time and I'll never ever have it. They're gone. Time's up. It's over. I had a family, now I don't. It's been over a decade since I lost them and sometimes, I still wonder how it happened. I mean I know how they died, but how did it *happen*? How does life just go on? After Finn and I buried my parents, I stood there and watched the people leaving the cemetery thinking how strange it was that some of them might be going to work that day, some might've been going home, but all of them were going to go and do *something*. Live their lives. But my parents were in the ground. And after I buried Finn, I thought it strange that the next day, and every day I had left, I'd just live my life, but Finn wouldn't. I still think about that. The strangeness of death. How life goes on. How there is nothing I can do to get more time with them. Time doesn't heal the loss. The loss is always there, and the only thing time does is make you wish you had more of it."

There wasn't a damn thing I could say. First, because I'd never experienced the kind of loss she had, and second because she was right. She'd never get the time she yearned for. She'd never see another smile, feel another hug, hear any of their voices—not in this lifetime.

"You're right, Kira, and I'm sorry you can't have that time."

She blinked as if she was startled, then she reared back like I'd slapped her.

What the fuck?

"Baby—"

"I'm right?" she interrupted me in a whisper.

"Kira, if you had them another day, another year, another twenty years it would never be enough time. You could get a thousand more hugs from your dad, and you'd always want another. A million more phone calls from your mom and more smiles from your brother. That's the beauty of loving someone—you never get enough, you always want more, you mourn all the things they gave you when they're gone."

Suddenly she pitched forward, her chest hit mine, and

her face went into my neck. My arms slid around her as the first sob racked through her.

"It would never be enough," she cried.

"No, Kira, it wouldn't be."

I felt her body buck, then I felt wetness on my neck. But more than that I felt her devastation blanket the room and honest to fuck, her anguish was so heavy it winded me. Which made me suck in a breath and when I did, I tasted her pain. It was right there, surrounding her, surrounding us. Raw and ugly. A decade of misery that was as fresh as the day it happened. But it wasn't a day—it wasn't pain from the day they died, or sadness from the day she'd buried them, it was all the days after. It was the absence of them. Each new day a reminder she'd never get the time.

Fuck.

"I want more."

Her words fanned across my neck.

"I know you do."

"That's beautiful, right?"

Good Lord, she was fucking killing me.

Killing.

Me.

I tightened my arms around Kira and I did the only thing I could do while she trembled, I held on. I locked her body to mine and stroked her back while her tears soaked my shirt. I did what I could to push aside my guilt for missing all the signs, though she was damn good at hiding her pain. But thinking back, it had been there, just disguised. I'd been so caught up trying to protect myself against the heartbreak I knew would come when she left me, I mistook her adventurous spirit for making up for lost time, packing in as much fun as she could since she'd spent ten years working nonstop.

I'd been wrong.

So fucking wrong it ate at my insides.

Kira Winters wasn't making up for lost time; she was running from her pain. And I'd fucking missed it.

But now wasn't about me or my guilt.

It was about Kira.

It was about her giving me the ugly and raw so later I could help her find the beauty and peace.

I couldn't give her more time, but I could give her this. I could bear the brunt of her weight, I could hold her close, I could soak in her pain, but I couldn't take it from her.

"Yes, Kira, it's beautiful. So damn beautiful the way you love them. Nothing more beautiful, baby."

She nodded her head, her breath hitched, and she sobbed and sobbed and fucking sobbed rivers of tears. So many tears by the time she'd passed out in my arms my tee was soaked. So many tears, she didn't flinch when I stood and carried her to the bedroom. So many tears, when I laid down beside her and gathered her in my arms she didn't wake up.

And once again I held her close while she slept and didn't bother closing my eyes.

Yes, there was work to do. There was healing to be done to dull the sharp edges. But the longer I laid there with Kira tucked close, having experienced her grief in a way I'd never experienced before, I started to understand why when someone dies, we call it loss. It's more than the loss of their physical presence. It's the loss of time, the loss of what was to come, the loss of all the tomorrows. We don't lose the memories; we lose the future. That's the tragedy, that's the loss.

Time.

It rolls on.

Sometimes painfully so.

———

A NOISE from behind me pulled me from my fatigued haze of another night of no sleep.

"How long you been staring out that window at nothing?" Theo asked as he entered the kitchen.

"I have no fuckin' idea," I admitted.

I reached for my abandoned coffee on the counter next to the sink and took a sip.

Cold.

I dumped the half-full mug into the sink and waited for Theo to finish with the carafe.

Theo leaned his ass against the counter and crossed his ankles but made no other move. Not to take a sip of his freshly poured coffee. Not to slide his calculating gaze away, which had gone from watchful to alert.

I would understand his stare after he didn't delay getting straight to the point.

"I heard."

He'd heard?

"Say again?"

"Last night," he clarified. "I was coming out to grab a bottle of water and I heard Kira. I also heard what you told her."

I locked down my anger at him eavesdropping. Teammate or not, that shit was not on. What was said last night was between me and Kira. And it was not anyone else's business until Kira made it their business—but that choice was hers.

"That wasn't cool."

"You're right, it wasn't. But I did it. And I did it because

I care about her. I get she's yours, I get you love her, and she feels the same about you. But what you don't get and what she sometimes forgets is, before there was you, Zane, and Z Corps, there was Patheon. There was me, Cash, Jonas, Smith, and Easton. There was Garrett. There were six men who went out on a mission to rescue Finn and failed. However that failure came about does not lessen the failure. We all live Finn Winters's death."

I wanted to hold onto my anger on Kira's behalf, but I couldn't. Especially when I understood the guilt that gnawed at a man's insides when he feels responsible for someone else's death.

"She doesn't blame you."

"I know she doesn't. But that knowledge doesn't make me feel a damn bit better about Finn being dead."

Fucking hell, I understood that, too.

"Right," I muttered.

"For what it's worth, what you said was correct. There's no overcoming that sort of tragedy. She's gonna feel that sting for the rest of her life. And that's part of our guilt, knowing what Kira lost and knowing there's no end to her feeling it. But knowing she's got you and you'll give her a place to finally grieve helps."

"She'll have a safe place to grieve," I confirmed. "I understand the guilt, Theo, but she'd hate knowing you and the others feel responsible. She knows who murdered her brother."

"Yeah, I know you understand the guilt. Which begs the question, who hates it for you?"

I felt a chill run up my spine and carefully blanked my expression.

"What are you talking about?"

"This part's gonna piss you off more than me telling you I listened in on your conversation last night."

That was not a good way to start off any statement, but seeing as I was seriously pissed he'd invaded Kira's privacy, I didn't have a good feeling about what was to come.

"What's gonna piss me off?"

"I looked into you. When I got out of the hospital and saw you and Kira together, you not hiding your interest in her and her doing anything and everything she could to get your attention, I needed to make sure you were who you seemed to be. A good guy, loyal friend, and reliable teammate. I know about the Petersons. I know about the stalker. I know you and your SWAT team were standing outside when that girl was murdered. I also read the complaint filed by your captain. I know you beat the shit out of him, I know you stopped before assault turned into premeditated murder. So, I know you've got control. I also know no formal charges were filed because the chief stepped up for you. I also know you're a lot like me; you'd feel that guilt and it doesn't matter that you are not responsible for what happened to that family. They were in two other jurisdictions before they moved into yours. You just happened to be the unlucky team to clean up the aftermath of a madman."

Theo had dug deep, that was for damn sure; that complaint was not on my record. When the chief heard the shit my captain had pulled, he was rightly on the warpath. And the only reason charges weren't filed was because my captain understood one thing, how to save his ass. And me facing charges would mean it would come to light why he got his ass kicked. Since he didn't want to explain how often he'd fucked up and then scrambled to cover his fuck-ups, he dropped the complaint.

But Theo's ability to dig into my past and get my service records wasn't what was on my mind.

"That shit doesn't fucking fly," I told him.

"It does when you love someone."

The stiffness that had crept into my body keeping me rooted to the tile floor turned into a rigidity that could only be described as stone.

"The fuck?" I growled.

Theo pushed off the counter, nabbed his coffee, and fuck me, softened his expression.

"I see you read that wrong. She lost Finn and when she did, she got us. Not a single one of us will ever be to her what her brother was, but that doesn't mean she doesn't have five big brothers looking out for her. I mean no disrespect when I say, you can be as pissed as you want, and I get that, brother, I'd be fucking furious if someone invaded my life the way I did yours. But I got a job to do—protect her. And I feel no remorse doing it."

And with that, Theo took his leave. But before he got too far, he looked over his shoulder.

"Either you'll come to understand and forgive me or you won't, but I'm not gonna insult you by apologizing for something I'm not sorry for."

I clenched my molars in an effort not to say something I'd regret.

With a jerk of his chin, Theo turned and he walked away muttering, "Like I said, a good guy, a loyal friend, a reliable teammate."

I wasn't feeling much like any of that. I was feeling pissed way the fuck off.

"Theo?" I called.

He stopped and craned his neck.

"Next time you want to know something about me, ask.

I get why you did it. I get you care about her, but you want me to trust you, don't ever go behind my back again."

"Copy that."

Jesus.

My hands came up to scrub the sleep from my eyes then I poured myself a cup of coffee and resumed my position at the sink staring out the window into a backyard barely lit by the rising sun.

But I was no longer thinking about Kira. I was thinking about Theo, and as much as I wanted to hold a grudge I was finding it damn near impossible to stay mad at a man who had cared for Kira after she'd lost everything. The alternative meant that no one was at Kira's back and I'd fucking hate that more than I hated someone invading my privacy.

17

I WAS TRYING my best not to turn into a whiny brat. It hadn't even been a full twenty-four hours since I'd been stuck in the safehouse, but I was already having flashbacks from the days when I'd roll out of bed and go to my computer in my pajamas. The days of ordering enough takeout for a family of four so I could graze on it for days and not have to cook or go out. The days of isolation that had become so normal I'd started hating being around people.

But that was no longer my life and I never wanted to go back to being alone and lonely. Not that I was alone; Cooper and Theo were here and I wasn't lonely, but the safehouse was a reminder of how my life had been.

Or maybe I was being dramatic, feeling weird because two nights in a row I'd opened myself up in a way I'd never done before. Actually, I hadn't opened up as much as I'd blown off the doors to the crazy closet and now that I'd torn those bitches off the hinges there was no way to close them. I didn't have baggage surrounding the death of my family—I had a carousel full.

And now Cooper knew it all.

And this morning when I'd woken up, he'd already gotten out of bed.

And I really didn't like waking up alone now that I'd had a taste of waking up next to Cooper.

So now I was back at the kitchen table on my laptop and had been for hours trying to keep my mind occupied with work so it wouldn't drift to last night. Or more accurately—my family.

Cooper was on the couch with his laptop on his lap and he was typing. Theo was sitting in a huge, overstuffed chair that would've swallowed me but fit him perfectly. He was scrolling on his tablet. He was also leaving in a few minutes to go to another safehouse to pull guard duty. I should've been grateful I was not Bridget Keller. That poor woman had been under protection for months and she would be for many more.

But I wasn't grateful. I was grumpy and frustrated.

"Kira, take a break," Theo grunted.

"I don't need a break," I lied.

Actually, I needed a nap and a second computer. Another reason I wished I was at the office—multiple machines to work on.

"Woman, you're over there groaning and growling at your computer."

"I am not," I snapped.

Theo held his tablet up and tapped the screen. A moment later I heard myself growling and groaning and grunting nonsense.

Ass. Hole!

"I can't believe you recorded me."

"You can't?" Theo chuckled.

Okay, I could believe he'd record me.

My attention went to Cooper who had his head turned in my direction. My gaze dropped to his twitching lips, and I asked, "Are you laughing at me?"

"Nope," Cooper fibbed.

"It looks like you're laughing."

I watched his shoulders shake and his lips twitched more until he couldn't stop the wide smile that split his handsome face.

My eyes narrowed and I contemplated the construction of my Yeti. Or more to the point if it would break if I threw it at Cooper.

"Kira." He chuckled. "You've been over there mumbling nonsense at your computer for ten minutes while you pound on the keys."

The downside to no longer working in solitude was coming clearer.

"I'm frustrated," I grumbled.

Cooper closed his laptop and sat up straight.

"If you're frustrated, why haven't you asked for help?"

"Because I don't need help."

Cooper's brow lifted and if I hadn't been in a grumpy, grouchy mood I might've heeded the unspoken notation I was being snappy. But I was tired and irritated, so I ignored the brow raise and held his stare.

"I'm answering emails," he weirdly told me. "Emails that can wait."

"Okay?"

"Use. Your. Team." He punctuated each word, no longer hiding *his* frustration.

"I don't—"

"Did you find where he stayed last night?"

"Yes."

Cooper scowled and when he stopped and opened his mouth, I knew what he was going to ask.

"How long ago?"

Yep. I knew that was what he was going to ask, and I knew my answer would piss him off.

Still not heeding the scowl or his annoyance I answered in a not-so-nice tone, "An hour ago."

"An *hour* ago?"

I didn't answer even though it was clearly a question— one he was going to use to make a point. I'd been sitting on information.

Instead, I informed him, "I pulled the hotel records."

Which was the wrong information to give if I was correctly reading the scathing look Cooper was giving me.

"What else did you find while I was needlessly answering emails and Theo was *reading a book?*"

"I wasn't reading a book," Theo defended. "I was reading an educational article on applied ballistics. Which led me to a great read on weapon employment zone analysis."

"Right because cross wind estimation and ammunition precision are more important than finding the man who's following Kira."

"No, but it'll come in handy when I snipe his ass from five hundred meters instead of having to remove blood stains from my favorite tee."

Oh, boy.

I wasn't sure which had me more worried, Cooper's ire or Theo's comment.

I soon found it was neither.

Theo's chocolate-brown eyes swung my way and I froze

when the intensity hit me. I'd communicated with him for ten years. But during that time, I had never seen him. The first time I'd laid eyes on him he was in a hospital near death. I'd watched him recover, going from crutches to a cane to walking on his own. I'd seen him in pain. I'd seen him pissed when he learned that his half-brother Bronson had been lied to and used as a pawn to fuck with Zane. I saw him angry, embarrassed, and troubled when he learned what Bronson had done. I also saw relief when he learned that despite fucking with Zane and his men Bronson was unharmed. But for the most part, in the last few months, I'd seen Theo happy. What I had never seen was Theo intense and his anger had never been directed my way.

Now it was.

And that intensity held a twinge of disappointment.

"You've got nothing to prove to no one," Theo said.

His calm tone contradicted his irate stare.

"I'm not trying to prove anything."

"You think I was out there alone for ten years, but I wasn't. I had my team. I had you. None of us worked alone."

"Theo—"

"One is none," he rapped.

My heart lurched painfully.

A flood of memories invaded my mind. Finn used to tell me that all the time.

When I had my heart set on which college I wanted to go to and I wasn't going to apply anywhere else.

One is none.

When I was going camping with a group of friends and he called from Alaska in the middle of training to ask me what gear I was taking with me.

One is none.

When he took me outdoor rock climbing for the first time.

One is none.

Two is one. One is none.

Me and Finn.

Now there was only one.

One is none.

How true that was. I'd been living on nothing for ten years.

I looked between Theo and Cooper, then paused on Theo.

I'd been alone, hadn't I?

I lost my parents and my brother and after that I had nothing, right?

"I see you're getting it, sweetheart," Theo softly said.

Oh, yeah, I was getting it. I was coming to understand that I'd lost everything. But when Finn died, I gained something different. I got Layla. I got Theo and Cash and Easton and Jonas and Smith. And years later I got Cooper and Zane and Kevin and Myles and Gabe and Owen and Garrett and Jasmin, Linc, Jaxon, and their kids. I got all of them, too many to mention. I didn't find them, they found me. They pulled me in and gave me a new family. Different than what I had with my brother and parents but no less beautiful.

I was coming to understand all of that but something bigger hit me—I had nothing to prove. Even if I wasn't "Kid Genius" I'd still be welcomed. You didn't have to prove yourself to family. Cooper had tried to tell me. Garrett, too.

Garrett wasn't testing me. He was building my confidence. *He* was proving something to me. He was trying to teach me to trust my team.

Mine.

My team.

My family.

I had my place and I had for a very long time.

"And now," Theo rasped. "I see you got it all."

His face softened and I braced.

"Sweetheart, you had it all along. You've had all of us. We were just waiting on you."

They were waiting on me.

And I'd stuck my head in the sand and buried myself in my work and closed my heart. I knew why I'd kept myself distant.

"I tried not to love you guys," I told Theo but had to stop to control the tears that threatened to form.

"We know."

"I was too afraid to love you guys. I was too scared to love you and lose you."

"We know."

"I tried not to, but I still loved you guys, and every day I was so scared."

"We know."

I glanced over at Cooper and the moment my gaze halted on him I wished it hadn't. Pride and understanding shone from his handsome face and that did it. The tears I'd been able to keep at bay welled over my lids and fell.

Cooper made no move to rush to my side. He didn't come to me and wipe my tears. He sat where he was and gave me everything I needed. The slight nod and the small smile said it all. I had his support and his love, and it was so strong I felt that from across the room. I didn't need his arms around me or him in my space. It was there filling the room.

I looked back at Theo, but before I could say anything he shook his head.

"There's nothing to say, Kira, except to say you have our

love. You've had it from the beginning, and we knew we had yours. We knew you were sitting behind your computer doing everything in your power to keep us safe and you did. You were loyal to us and never wavered. You went days without sleep and now seeing how you work firsthand I know you went days without eating. And you did that because the five of us needed you. You sacrificed for us. That's love, Kira. Doing that for five men you didn't know, that says something else." Theo stopped, drew in a breath, and continued, "Finn would be proud."

That velvet blow knocked the wind clear out of me and I still wasn't recovered when Theo went on.

"Finn would be proud of your intelligence, your intuition, your skills, your kindness, your courage, your loyalty. But he would be so goddamn proud you are what he was—a warrior. Your battles are fought in a different arena but make no mistake, they are no less difficult to win. You've won, Kira, you just haven't admitted victory."

I wasn't sure what I'd won. Most of my life I'd felt like I was losing.

Theo stood, his posture stiff, his eyes unfocused, and pointed at the windows behind me. Then he continued to wreck me.

"Ten years ago, I boarded a plane as a self-righteous asshole who could only see good and bad. I had no concept of the varying shades of evil. I left here knowing I'd never return. I was prepared to die to right the wrongs of others. It is because of you, Kira, that five men made it home safely. It is because you *love* your brother more than yourself and set out to right a wrong that brought you into our lives, and in doing so you saved five men from a suicide mission."

I knew Theo was done when he turned to walk to the front door.

But I had something to say.

"I didn't want to set a wrong right. I wanted vengeance."

Without turning around Theo growled, "And vengeance was had. Trust and believe every last one of them met their end in the most painful way possible."

I heard the door open, the alarm beep, and watched Garrett enter the house. He stepped aside as Theo silently approached, then I watched Theo disappear.

Garrett looked from a departing Theo to Cooper and asked, "What's going on?"

"Closure."

"Closure?" Garrett repeated and shut the door.

Was that what just happened? Was Theo offering me closure or taking it for himself?

Wait.

"Does he feel..." I started to ask Cooper but trailed off when Garrett's gaze skidded to me.

"Does he feel what?" Garrett prompted when I didn't continue.

"Nothing."

The vibe in the room changed. The change wasn't a slow, gradual decline in temperature, it was a sudden and instant chill. And the look on Garrett's face was impossible to miss. If the air around him was chilly his eyes were down-right frosty. And they were pointed in my direction. If I wasn't afraid my legs would give out, I would've gotten to my feet and ran away.

Garrett was *fucking* pissed.

Yes, the f-word was an important emphasis on just how pissed Garrett was. Not only that but he looked like he was angrily shouting seven hundred words at me with just his eyes. His body language screamed more words that were just as angry but also painful.

Okay.

Shit.

This was bad.

Very bad.

And I knew how bad it was when Garrett's rough voice came from across the room. The way it slammed into me, he might as well have been standing right next to me.

"Enough."

That was all he said. One word that said everything.

"Garrett—"

"No, Kira, *enough*," he growled.

Cooper's long frame folded off the couch. He skewered Garrett with a look that couldn't be read as anything other than what it was—a warning. But just to be sure Garrett got the message Cooper didn't delay verbalizing it.

"Careful, brother."

Even though Cooper was on the move, making his way to the dining area where I was still sitting at the table, Garrett's eyes didn't move from mine.

"I've given you months to broach the topic. I've waited for you to bring up what's between us. I've baited you into conversations, but you dance your way out of them."

Garrett had been waiting for me?

I'd been waiting for him.

"I didn't want to bring something up and hurt you," I told him softly.

"Hurt me? Fuck, woman, just looking at you tears at my insides."

I felt the oxygen in my lungs crystalize.

Cooper positioned himself close to my chair and I felt

his hand on my shoulder. His menacing tone reverberated through the house when he said, "Easy, Garrett."

"Nothing easy about this, Coop. Tried careful. Tried waiting patiently. Time's up."

Fuck, woman, just looking at you tears at my insides.

Holy shit. I'd been wrong. So, freaking wrong I'd been on a whole other planet.

"Might be easier if you think about what you're saying before you say it."

"Cooper," I whispered and reached up to cover his hand. "Don't."

"No. Fuck, no, baby. I know when to sit by and keep my mouth shut and let you handle your business. I know you and Garrett got a lot to talk about and that should've happened months ago and I get why neither of you wanted to start that conversation. And, Garrett, brother, I might not know what it is you carry but I know it's heavy. I got a mind to that when I tell you, think before you tell my woman that just looking at her tears you apart. Think real goddamn hard how she's gonna take that. I know what you meant. Kira does not. I suggest you start explaining and do it quick before that seed you just planted grows."

When Cooper was done, I chanced a look at Garrett, ready to commence damage control. The last thing I wanted was for there to be a problem between them. They were friends, and teammates; any issues would carry over into work.

As soon as I shifted my gaze it locked with Garrett's. His expression was no different—hard, angry, glittering eyes still spitting icicles.

"Garrett..." I got no more out.

His hand came up, palm flat in my direction, and since I wasn't a fan of the "hand" I pinched my lips.

"I failed Finn. I failed you. And it tears me apart knowing that it's only a matter of time before you see me for who I am."

"You didn't fail Finn," I contradicted.

"I sure as fuck did."

Cooper's hand dropped from my shoulder as I stood. The moment I cleared the chair he moved to my side—close but not too close. Cooper was there if I needed him, but he wasn't crowding me.

He was there offering me support; he was not there to shield me.

Not that he could protect me from the heaviness that descended on the room.

"You did not fail Finn, Garrett."

"I—"

"No!" I took a fortifying breath, then I let the bitterness I worked so hard to keep at bay move through me until all I felt was the jagged edges of betrayal cut into my flesh. "Leif Robinson killed my brother. Yaser Said sliced his throat, but it was Leif who set it up. It was Leif who sold out Finn's unit. You did not fail him. Zane didn't fail him. Neither did Easton, Smith, Jonas, or Cash. My brother lost his life but all of you lost something, too. You don't think it tears me apart every time I look at *you*? Knowing what you lost. Knowing you left your team. Knowing that your brothers lost you. Jesus Christ, Garrett, we all lost something. That's not on you. It was never about you. It wasn't even about Finn. It was greed that took Finn from me. It was Leif who stole *your* life. But as Theo pointed out retribution was paid. And I wish I was a better person; I wish it didn't make me feel good to know Yaser Said is burning in hell right beside Leif. And I don't care what it says about me but I'm happy Zane did whatever he did to Leif. I'm happy before that piece of shit died, he told you the truth. And, Garrett, I know neither of you will ever tell me what happened and how he died but I hope it was more painful than when Theo took out Yaser. I hope Leif begged for mercy. I hope he pissed his pants. I hope his death was as painful as my brother's."

"We should've—"

"Should've what? Chased bad intel? Gotten yourselves killed? I've read every report, Garrett. I've read them so many times I have them memorized. I loved my brother more than life. Do you understand that? I am still lost without him. I risked everything to find the truth. And when I found it, I gave up ten years of my life to bring down the people responsible. Don't you think if I thought you held even the most minute, the smallest, a fraction of culpability I wouldn't've gone after you? Do you really think if there was the barest hint that Zane had fucked up, I would've done what I did to protect him? Do you think I would've spent years working with Cash, Easton, Jonas, and Smith if I thought for a second, that they'd failed my brother? That's a fuck no, Garrett."

"They didn't fail," Garrett was quick to defend his old team. "I was the TL. I was One. It's on me, Kira. They were following my orders."

"You know what's so messed up about this situation?" I asked but didn't give Garrett a chance to answer. "What is absolutely fucked-up? Theo feels guilt for following orders. He had a job to do, and he did it. And when he found out that his source was a terrorist, he did the right thing and brought it to the CIA's attention. Zane did his job, gathered the intel, and wired it to his CIA handler. You got the intel, trusted the CIA had it right because they're the goddamned CIA, and took your team out on a rescue op. You know who doesn't feel guilt? The CIA. You blame yourself. Theo blames himself. Layla lost her job for backing Theo. You lost your job and with that your brothers, which means they lost you, and, Garrett, they missed you when you were gone. I lost my world. We all fucking lost. But the men who are responsible are dead. When do *we* get our lives back? When do *we* get to move on? When do *you* stop blaming yourself?"

Garrett shook his head.

He wasn't listening.

He was determined not to hear me.

And I was done.

D.O.N.E.

"There's nothing you can say that will convince me my brother died because of you!" I screeched. "Nothing. If you want to wrap yourself in guilt, I can't stop you. It'll hurt me. I'll be sad you feel that. I'll hate you feel that way. But I'm not giving those assholes another minute of my life. I did my job. An eye for an eye. I didn't get to pull the trigger or wield the blade but I sure as shit found that bastard. I found him, and it's because of me, Yaser Said is burning. You and Zane handled Leif. I wish I'd had a part in that, too. But knowing Zane, really knowing the man and not just the rumors about him, I take great pleasure knowing Leif's last few hours were spent with Zane Lewis."

Garrett's expression changed. It was subtle, but it was also scary as hell. He no longer looked guilt-ridden, he looked menacing and ominous. He looked like a man you did not cross without swift punishment.

"It was painful," he ground out.

Leif Robinson's end.

"Good."

"It was not Zane who made that happen."

Translation: Garrett had done the deed.

"Good."

Garrett's eyes narrowed and I felt Cooper's arm brush against mine as he moved closer.

"Why don't you blame me?"

It was as if Cooper knew I'd had enough. I'd been as strong as I could for as long as I could. And hearing Garrett's voice full of agony was the last straw. I swayed into Cooper, his arm swept around my lower back, and his fingers wrapped around my hip to keep me steady.

I didn't remind Garrett I'd just explained all the reasons I didn't blame him. Instead, I asked, "Why would I?"

"Because I should've known."

"Not to be a bitch," I started and paused briefly when Cooper's fingers on my hip squeezed his warning for me to be careful with my words. "But how were you supposed to know? I get all of you think you have superhuman powers, and sometimes even I believe you all do. But bottom line is, you are not omniscient. Trust me, I wish you were. I wish you had some all-knowing power that sent you a vision of where Finn was being held. But you don't and you're not God. So the real question is why do *you* blame *yourself?*"

At that Garrett dropped his head and his hand went up and grabbed the back of his neck.

I didn't know what that meant. I did know that I felt like the bitch I said I didn't want to be. I turned from Garrett to look up at Cooper. He dipped his chin and as soon as his gentle eyes landed on me, I felt the anger that had fueled my tirade and had kept my pain in check slip away.

The pain of hashing out the circumstances that led to my brother's murder. The ache that never went away knowing my brother did not die on the battlefield, he didn't die in the protection of the country he loved, he didn't die defending innocent, good people. Finn was gone because CIA Officer Leif Robinson was a greedy piece of shit who sold my brother and his unit out. Finn was dead because Leif was a traitor.

The anger always simmered just below the surface, lingering under my skin, but it was the constant pang of loss that flowed through my veins. A loss that I would never overcome but I had to find a way to live with. A loss that was so bitter I'd all but forgotten the good my family had given me. I'd only allowed myself a fraction of the happy times we shared—the laughter, the vacations, the goodnight kisses, the hugs. There was so much goodness, but in an effort to protect myself I'd refused to remember it all.

I'd let the darkness of their deaths drown out the love they gave me.

That had to stop.

I needed them now more than ever.

I needed to remember.

I needed to take my life back and let go of the darkness.

I just didn't know how.

That was what I was thinking about when Cooper's hand came up and cupped my cheek.

"You're fucked, brother," Garrett muttered. "She's already channeling Zane. The problem with that is she's smarter than him which means she makes too much sense. Good luck with that."

Cooper's eyes didn't leave mine when in a thick, rough voice he muttered back.

"Think I'll manage."

I was busy getting lost in Cooper—lost in his stare, lost in his support, lost in his love. Yet I still had the wherewithal to hope that Garrett's remark meant he was ready to move on and start living life again. Really live it and let go of a responsibility that was not his.

I wanted that maybe more than I wanted to be happy.

I wanted it because my brother would want it.

I wanted Garrett free because Finn would be pissed a good man had given up so much.

And I wanted to be more like my brother—selfless and noble.

18

I FELT IT, some of the tightness eased from Kira's shoulders. The air in the room was no less uncomfortable but it was no longer coming from the woman in my arms.

Something had changed. The first change happened when Kira was speaking with Theo. I saw it from across the room, the moment the truth hit her. It was as painful as it was beautiful to witness. The realization she hadn't been alone.

There was a second change and arguably the larger of the two, though I was unsure what had settled in her. I just knew it had happened after Garrett had teased her about being like Zane. Her posture was no longer tight, her shoulders no longer stiff, and the intense sadness had lifted.

The foreboding was coming from Garrett, and it was still rolling off him in bitter waves of regret. The fuck of it was I didn't know what he regretted more, Finn dying, Kira feeling that loss so deeply, or Kira *not* blaming him. The man was intent on holding onto guilt that was not his to shoulder. What Garrett hadn't planned on was that Kira was just as determined to make him see the light.

My thoughts were interrupted by Garrett's phone. It was then I saw it. It was not the first time I'd witnessed it, but it was the first time seeing it made my chest burn. All emotion bleached clean off Garrett's face. Everything about the man transformed. He'd slipped back into a place where feelings and guilt couldn't touch him.

I knew Kira saw it, too, when her hand on my ribs flexed and her fingertips dug into my side. Thinking back, I'd seen glimpses of the real Garrett, but mostly I knew the façade. I knew the guy who was quick to hurl quips with Zane. I knew the guy who was always ready to take a teammate's back. I knew the guy who smiled and laughed.

I knew a guy who was a total fraud. A man who hid so much it had changed his DNA, lingering pain that was so immense he rarely acknowledged its existence.

Garrett pulled his phone out of his pocket and he quickly tapped in his code and answered the call.

"Shep," he greeted. "Got you on speaker with Kira and Cooper."

Shepherd Drexel was a hacker Garrett used rarely. The man was a pain in the ass to get a hold of. It didn't matter if he knew you or had worked with you a hundred times, he still made you jump through hoops before he'd pick up the phone. And when you did get him on the line, he only took jobs that challenged him. Then there was the small detail he charged out the ass. The good thing about Shep was he loved working in those gray spaces where illegal and highly illegal mingled. There was nothing Shepherd Drexel couldn't find if given enough time and money.

"I looked into Kira, like you asked," Shep started, and I felt Kira tense right along with me. "I took my time and there's no hit. I checked her aliases, as well. Nothing on the dark web, the deep web, forums, or chat boxes."

I heard Kira draw in a swift breath. She had yet to release it when Shep went on, "Also looked at those pictures you sent. Out of the twenty-seven pictures, twenty of them are still-images pulled from CCTV. The other seven were taken with a Nikon D7500."

"So, the camera's no help," Garrett grumbled. "What about the lens?"

"Standard bundle, eighteen to a hundred and forty millimeter," Shep returned.

"Holy shit," Kira mumbled. "Theo was right; he was close, and I didn't notice him."

"*We* didn't notice," I corrected. "So the new question is, how did he find the CCTV feeds to pull?"

"Facial rec." Kira pushed away from me and once she was facing her laptop she continued in a disbelieving whisper, "I'm being tracked by facial rec."

"Yep," Shep confirmed like it was all the same to him.

My gut roiled at all the things Shep didn't say. Someone had tracked Kira's movements until they either felt comfortable enough or had the means to get close.

"He knows Patheon," Kira said as her fingers flew over her keyboard. "He knows my damn program." After she huffed out an annoyed breath, she switched gears. "I tracked the black Sentra to the hotel he stayed at last night. The hotel has security cameras in the parking lot and in all the common areas. When I went to pull up yesterday's footage it was gone."

"How sophisticated is the hotel's network security?" Garrett inquired.

"Not very," Kira returned. "It took me about ten minutes to get in."

"So someone without your skill?" I rejoined to ask.

"An hour if they knew what they were doing, a couple more if they didn't."

Kira had windows popping up all over her screen. She was obviously falling into a groove, and it was hard to bite my tongue and not remind her to let us in on what she was thinking before she fell down the rabbit hole.

"Let me into your machine," Shep demanded.

Without missing a beat or looking up from her screen, Kira shook her head and denied Shep entry.

"Not a chance."

"You know I'll be in by the end of the day," Shep noted. "Save us all time and let me in."

Suddenly her fingers froze along with the rest of her body.

"He bypassed collection."

"What do you mean collection?" I asked.

Garrett's phone clattered on the kitchen table near Kira's laptop as he slid his backpack off his shoulder and dumped it on a chair.

Before Kira could answer, Garrett did while he unzipped and pulled out his laptop.

"Unlike other facial rec programs, Patheon collects data, stores it, and anyone using the program can access the information. Meaning if the Marshals are looking for a fugitive and uploaded the image into Patheon, the program would within seconds be able to locate the fugitive if they'd passed by a camera that ran Patheon. Kira coded the program as an interface, not an independently run program. Every user has access to all the stored information, not just the searches they've run. It eliminates multi-agency bureaucracy."

"It's also a total invasion of privacy," Shep put in. "It's genius, especially the vein pattern detection. The facial rec is better than any program I've ever used—with a few minor coding adjustments—but I still think it's too far-reaching."

"I'm going to pretend you didn't pirate my program," Kira growled. "I know you didn't purchase a key because I have you blacklisted. I'm also going to pretend you didn't tell me you fucked with the perfection that is Patheon. Though I can imagine—since you stole my work—that you disconnected the program from the interface. Which brings us back around. Whoever is following me knows Patheon and they've used what they know to avoid detection, including the lowlight issues I haven't worked out. And they, too, have recoded the program to disconnect from the data collection portion. There are no images of me, Garrett, or Cooper on the server."

"How many people could recode your program?" I inquired.

"Not many. Shep, obviously," Kira clipped. "Garrett could recode it not to dump into the databank. There's a guy in Pennsylvania, though he would never. Whoever did it is smart, very smart. First, to get a copy of the program without purchasing it he'd have to hack his way through layers of security. Nothing is a hundred percent secure, but Patheon is ninety-nine percent secure."

"How'd *you* get in?" Garrett asked Shep. "I've never tried, though I'm seeing that was a mistake."

"Respect, Garrett, but some things are meant to be a mystery, and this is one of them. If it makes you feel better, it took me over a month to break in. And that was with me devoting all my time and writing multiple programs to get in. Once I was in, I could not access the data, only the program itself. Where are your working files? The lowlight corrections you're in the process of fixing?"

Before Kira could answer, Garrett cut in, "Send me the

hotel information. I want to get started trying to recover the files."

"One second." Kira was back to pounding the keys when she added, "Babe, can I send you the files I have on Toni Rea? She owns the Jeep Wrangler the stolen tags belong to. A cursory background check shows she's clean, but I think we should dig deeper just to be safe. If I remember correctly her major is cyber security."

That was cute—*if* Kira remembered correctly...the woman never forgot anything.

I didn't remind her of this. Instead, I said, "Yeah, send me what you have."

"How'd you get into my machine?" Kira grunted irately.

"Who are you talking to?" Garrett asked. His laptop was open but not powered on. My laptop was still on the coffee table, and I wouldn't have the first clue how to access anyone's machine anyway.

"Shepherd," Kira spat. "What the fuck?"

There was a moment of loaded silence that became thicker as the seconds ticked.

"How do you know someone's on your machine?"
Someone?
Not Shep.

"What do you mean how do I know?" Kira's voice was laden with irritation. "You opened a freaking TextEdit like I wouldn't notice."

"Don't touch anything," Garrett ordered.

"I don't want him in my..." Kira trailed off then her head snapped to look at Garrett. "*He's* in my machine."

She whispered the last sentence like it was physically painful for Kira to utter those words.

"This is good," Garrett returned.

Lightning-quick, Kira reached forward and yanked a

USB cord out of the side of her laptop. I followed the path and saw the external she'd grabbed from her house.

"What's on that drive?" I inquired.

"Files."

"What kind of files?" Garrett pushed.

"Important ones."

I had Kira in profile, her head turned just enough for me to see the color had bleached from her face and her pulse was pounding in her neck.

Garrett didn't miss the flush or the pulse-pounding, and I knew this when his eyes narrowed on her in a menacing way I didn't like much. But as much as I wasn't fond of the look, I understood it. If Kira said the files on her external hard drive were important that could mean anything from pictures of her family to top-secret data to a new program she was coding. So, her 'important' could be *anything* and Garrett knew that, too.

"Kira!" The snap of Garrett's voice rang out and I wasn't fond of that either, but I didn't get a chance to express my dislike before Kira's left hand lifted off her keyboard and she jabbed a finger at Garrett's phone.

Fuck.

Important was *important*. As in, not-for-Shep's-ears important.

This was bad news. Garrett knew that, too. He gave up glaring at her and his gaze went to her screen.

"Backtrack—" Garrett started.

"No," Shep denied. "If you do it, he'll see. Let me in."

Kira was shaking her head in fast, jerky movements.

"Coop, get me your laptop," Kira said without looking up. "Garrett, we need those hotel files recovered. Shep, can you please get into Harbor Hospital's parking lot cameras?"

I had my laptop in hand and was walking back into the kitchen when Shep inquired, "Harbor Hospital?"

"I tracked the car, a black Sentra, to Baltimore," Kira told him. "South Hanover Street and Cherry Hill Road, then it vanishes. That intersection is directly in front of Harbor Hospital which seems the most logical place for overnight parking and an easy swipe of a license plate. I need the old plate number that was used before this one so I can continue to track him."

I handed Kira my laptop and she wasted no time shoving hers to the side and set mine in front of her. Without asking she typed in my password and started opening windows and system preferences.

"What are you doing?"

With her fingers working the keys she answered, "I'm remotely accessing my terminal so I can backtrack the invader's IP address. It'll be masked by a VPN, but it'll give me a starting point. I'm also infecting my computer with malware."

I was positive Kira's explanation was the watered-down, computing-for-dummies version of what she was doing, and I still didn't understand why she'd infect her computer with a virus. I didn't ask for further clarification. First, because time was of the essence, and second because I was uninterested in the answer. I was not a sit-behind-a-computer type of guy. I was a kick-in-the-door type of guy which meant I did the bare minimum when it came to sitting behind a desk. Lucky for me, my boss hated reading reports as much as I hated typing them up. The requirement was all situation reports, after-action reports, and discovery were to only include the pertinent information. If a report included any more than what was absolutely necessary Zane chucked it in the trash.

Another reason I didn't ask was because my phone was vibrating in my back pocket. When I pulled it out and saw Lincoln's name I answered the call.

"Linc?"

"Got a call from Detective Garcia," he launched in. "Our black Sentra is in police impound. It was towed last night."

"Where'd they find it?" I asked as I made my way out of the dining area to the hall.

"No parking zone near the Capitol."

"He wanted the car found," I surmised.

"Yep. Which means we won't find anything, but still, Zane called in a favor. Jax and I are going over there now. Maybe we'll get lucky and he left a print."

Of course Jaxon would be all over this. Not only was he my big brother but I hadn't hidden my feelings for Kira. He knew she meant something to me which meant he had double the incentive to end this quickly and safely. Though he'd do that anyway because he liked Kira.

"Don't forget the trunk and—"

"Not my first go around, kid."

I bit my tongue and tried to remember Linc meant no disrespect, but the quip still pissed me off.

"She hasn't mentioned it, but I know Kira's still thinking about it. Any luck with the tattoo? November fourth seemed to hit with Kira though she can't remember why. But we still need to consider the possibility the date is April eleventh."

"Nothing on that yet. Kevin's looking and Delilah is helping him."

Setting Delilah on the hunt was a good call. Before she'd hooked up with Myles, she worked in IT for a corporation called Abrams. Unfortunately, her boss turned out to be a sick and twisted asshole who tried to kill her when she uncovered information on a brain experiment he wanted to keep hidden. Fortunately, quitting wasn't an option for Myles, and even though it had taken him a long time, he tracked Delilah down and saved her life.

"Right. A few updates on our end..."

I gave Linc a succinct rundown of the current events taking place in the dining room. As I did, my chest started to burn with fear. The motherfucker had tracked her with the very program she'd designed. Then like every sick fuck stalker, when watching her from afar no longer got him off he stepped into the real world to get his fix. Continuing to follow the pattern, he'd made contact by sending her the pictures. He'd made his statement by blotting out my face. His next move would be to gain further access to her, which he'd instigated by accessing her computer.

And I didn't have to be a computer genesis like Kira, Garrett, and Shep to know that if he wanted to remain unseen while he was in her laptop, he would've been just that. But he'd opened a program knowing she'd see his work.

He was setting his trap.

But the real question remained—who did he want?

Me out of the way? Or Kira?

19

I ACTIVATED the kill code and prayed I wasn't too late, and ten years' worth of black ops missions didn't just fall into the hands of an unknown hacker-slash-stalker.

The good news was not only were my files encrypted—which of course could be decrypted. But I'd added another layer of security. To get to the encrypted files he'd have to get into a directory that was hashed. Unlike encryption, there was no unhashing. He'd have one shot to get the password right before the files corrupted themselves.

The bad news was, he was in my terminal. That sent a chill of fear down my spine—more than knowing he'd been close enough to take pictures of me, more than him shooting at me and Cooper, more than him following me and Jasmin.

This guy was smart.

And the evidence was suggesting he was smarter than I was. My security was top-notch. I built the program personally and I tweaked it every few months. There should be no way for someone to get in.

No *freaking* way.

Cooper had disappeared down the hall to take a phone

call, Garrett was next to me trying to recover the hotel's security feeds, and Shep was still on the phone. I could hear him typing so I could only assume he was getting the parking lot footage from the hospital.

I'd opened my search for the Sentra to all of Baltimore, Brooklyn Park, Towson, White Marsh, even Woodlawn going back thirty-six hours. I tracked it to an intersection just before the Hanover Street Bridge, but nothing before that. It was like the car just appeared at an intersection. Logic would point to the hospital. But there was also a boat launching ramp near that intersection and a park, and neither had cameras. I was still betting on the hospital. I was also betting he'd gotten in the hospital's network and deleted the feed. If he didn't, I'd bet he had on his disguise and he left the security footage intact to screw with me.

He knew my program. He wanted me to know he knew it. He wanted me to know he was in my machine, if he didn't, he wouldn't have opened a program. No hacker smart enough to breach my security would make such a rookie mistake. It was on purpose. He was upping the game.

That didn't scare me, that pissed me off. He thought he was better than me. Smarter. Untraceable. That only fueled my desire to best him.

"Got him in the parking lot," Shep announced.

I might not have been scared of the hacker-slash-stalker who was currently poking around in my computer which was a supreme violation of my privacy. But I was scared of Shepherd Drexel. The rumor was, he'd changed the source code of a very popular cell phone and enabled the cellular provider's ability to track through cell towers. He did this not by hacking the company's network but by outsmarting the project manager and the company's security manager into sending him the source code directly. The rumor went he'd actually talked the project manager through how to compress the files and send them using an anonymous file transfer server. To avoid embarrassment and have to publicly admit a potentially huge security breach the company never filed charges. Shep could've hacked the system, but that would've been too easy. In the game of man versus machine, he could win. That stunt was a game of human versus human and Shep had proved with a little research into the company structure, information people divulged in chat rooms and on messages boards, he could get all he needed. Nowadays with social media in the mix, no doubt he could do it again and it would be easier.

Beyond that there wasn't a government institution—foreign or domestic—that could keep him out. Something he'd proven time and time again. Though he was now paid to do so and report back how he got in. The guy was unmarried, had no kids, was filthy rich from the buckets of money he made from his now legitimate, ethical hacking skills and he still charged out the ass to hire him personally. There had been times over the last ten years I'd debated calling him for help. He could do in a few days what would take me a month, but due to the nature of information I was collecting, secrecy being paramount, I'd never used him. That didn't mean I didn't study everything I could find on Shep. And since I studied him and used some of his lines of code in my firewalls, I knew he could break into my computer. Beyond normal security protocol, Shep was one of the reasons I had kill codes written into every program I wrote. If he wanted something, he got it. If he wanted into a terminal, he got in. If he wanted information off a server, he got it.

That meant getting on Shep's bad side, was cyber suicide. He could make your life a living hell if he wanted.

So, knowing all I knew about Shep, it was not a surprise he could get into a hospital's system in under ten minutes.

"Garrett," Shep went on. "I'm sending you the footage."

"Send it to me, too."

"Kira—"

"I want him to know," I cut Shep off. "He's not hiding, he's in my machine. He wants me to know, and I want him to know we're tracking him."

"You're playing into his hand," Garrett argued.

"Yep. It's game on. I need him to make contact with me. I want him to gloat about how he bypassed my firewalls. I want him to think he's got the upper hand. He *thinks* he's smarter than I am and that's gonna make him cocky. I play that up, I let him think he's got the better hand, he'll screw up. But contact is the most important thing. He knows me, and the fastest way to figure out how is to get him talking to me."

"Bold play," Shep told me. "It could backfire."

Shep was right, it could.

And I could be wrong; the guy might be smarter than me. He might be anticipating me goading him. He might already have a counterattack planned for my every move.

"Trust your gut," Garrett said from beside me.

Trust my gut.

Indecision had already crept in. It was strange how I could be so sure of myself, sure of my abilities and skill, yet be apprehensive. I could go from confident to feeling like I was an impostor who had no business being in a room with Garrett in a nanosecond. Add in Shep who was brilliant beyond comprehension, and I felt like a fraud.

What if I was wrong? What if Shep was right and my ploy to instigate contact backfired? What if...

My train of thought was abruptly cut off when I felt

Garrett's hand on my shoulder. I kept my eyes trained on the screen in front of me until Garrett's fingers curled in and he gave me a shake. Slowly, wanting to drag out the moment before I looked at him, I inched my head to the side and prepared for the disappointment I knew I'd see.

I'd failed.

My security failed.

This was undeniable.

Someone had gained access to my machine.

Worse, someone gained access to my Patheon files. Now all the guys were at risk. Theo, Easton, Smith, Jonas, Cash, and Layla. Not that their names or any identifiers weren't scrubbed but their mission briefs were intact. The intel was in those files. Every piece of information I'd collected over ten years and now an unknown bad guy had everything.

Shit.

Zane was going to kill me. He literally might wrap his hands around my throat and choke me to death. I'd put everyone in danger.

Garrett leaned closer and his whispered voice came at me soft and gentle. "You're in your head having a one-sided debate. You're convincing yourself you're wrong. You're talking yourself out of trusting your instincts. Shep was not disagreeing with your initial assessment. I'm beating a very dead and bloody horse with this, Kira, but this is how a team works. A plan is made and it's your team's job to point out the cracks. It's your team's job to deconstruct a mission and find the weak spots. Shep's correct, it's a bold play. But that doesn't mean you're wrong in making it. You have to trust those around you, but more—you have to trust yourself."

The horse was indeed dead and very, very bloody from being dragged around. And every time I thought I was ready to bury the poor thing something else popped up and I fell down the rabbit hole of insecurity.

This had to end.

The cycle had to end.

I had to be a better teammate.

I had to trust myself.

"Shep, code in a redirect script into the video."

I knew I made the right call when Garrett smiled at my suggestion and straightened in his chair.

"A reverse shell?" Shep muttered and if I wasn't mistaken that mutter sounded impressed.

"What's a reverse shell?" Cooper asked from behind me. "And please dumb it down into simple, easy-to-understand lingo."

I couldn't stop my smile from forming at Coop's request. He was a good sport when I got carried away about my work. He could and had many times sat and listened to me go on and on and he did this without his eyes glossing over with boredom. He also didn't stop me even though most of what I was talking about went over his head.

Totally a good sport.

Cooper had zero interest in how to hack a network, but he'd patiently listen to me. He'd sit next to me on the couch and let me talk out a problem until I found where I'd gone wrong.

One of the many reasons I loved him.

"A network is protected by a firewall," I started to explain. "The firewall stops inbound attacks. What it doesn't stop is outbound connections. A reverse shell is an outbound attack. Instead of us attacking his machine, Shep's going to add a line of code into the video he's going to send to me. When the hacker opens the video to watch it on his terminal an outbound connection will be made and a port will be opened. Shep will then be able to open a command line on the hacker's machine."

"What if the hacker doesn't watch the video?" Cooper asked.

"He will. He won't be able to stop himself. He'll want to see what we have."

At least I hoped that was the case.

"And will his anti-virus software or whatever detect the attack?" Coop continued.

"Nope."

"Smart."

"Sometimes simple and stupid is the way to go. He'll be expecting me to come at him. So I'll make him come to me. As soon as he watches that video, we're in."

"Video sent," Shep rejoined.

Yep. Totally scary that he could add the script to the video in a few minutes. Not that it would've taken me much longer, but Shep was definitely better than I was.

"Now we wait and see if he takes the bait."

"As long as we're doing that, Linc called. The Sentra's in police impound," Cooper announced. "Seeing as it was parked in a no-parking zone, he wanted the car towed. Linc and Jax are going to look the car over and dust for prints."

That was bad news.

"Did he tell you where the car was towed from?" Garrett inquired.

"No-parking zone near the Capitol building."

"He switched plates then or Kira would've tracked him there," Garrett noted and pulled up a map of the last location I had on the car. "Jasmin took exit 28, the Sentra stayed on 50 and exited using 29A."

I studied the map Garrett had up on his screen. An auto repair shop, an Exxon, and a Wawa. The gas stations were out. Someone could easily see someone stealing a license plate.

"The auto repair shop."

My declaration was met with Garrett's quick agreement.

"I'll see if they have cameras. If not, I'm sure the Exxon station next door has them."

"I'm in," Shep boomed. "Dude's tidy."

What Shep meant was the guy's directories and files were neatly arranged. Most people save documents, pictures, and downloads all over their computers instead of in the right file folders. It made getting in and getting out undetected easier when you didn't have to poke around someone's computer for twenty minutes trying to find something saved in the wrong place, or the alternate, which was what I normally did, was to transfer all their data and sift through it when I was no longer connected.

"Jesus." Shep's muttered curse had Cooper stepping to my side.

"What?" Garrett snapped, probably feeling as incapacitated as I did.

I was not used to being blind in this type of situation. I was normally the one with the information on my screen. Not being able to see what Shep was seeing had my teeth on edge.

"Two things," Shep started. "He's running Patheon. I'm running the code now against the original version to see what he's changed."

"We already knew he had access to Patheon," I pointed out.

"Confirmation."

"What's the second thing?" Garrett asked.

Shep didn't delay and he didn't sugarcoat his findings;

he just laid them out and when he did I felt a chill come over me. But that cold invading my bones was snuffed out by the tidal wave of fury blasting from Cooper.

"He has two terabytes of files in a directory named Kid Genius. I'm transferring them now. A lot of TXT files, JPGs, file extensions ending in EOW. I don't—"

"EOW?" I choked out.

"I don't know that extension." Shep sounded perplexed.

Which of course he would be.

"Back up," Cooper growled. "Kid Genius? Who else knows that nickname?"

End of World.

EOW.

Fucking shit.

A sickening feeling rolled around in my stomach.

Was it possible?

"My squad," I answered. "Kid Genius is my screen name for End of World."

"The video game you play?" Garrett asked.

"Yes."

My squad.

Holy shit.

No way.

My mind was racing a mile a minute, one thought collided with another as years of gameplay and chatting with my squad sped through my mind. But it was the last interaction I had with the guys that stuck in my head. Something had felt off; the normal fun banter and good-natured jabs seemed sharp and rude.

"What video game?" Shep inquired.

"End of World," I told him. "I started playing it when it was in beta. I was bored and used it as a way to occupy my time while I was waiting on..." Shit, that was top secret.

"Waiting on your team to check in with you," Shep finished for me.

I glanced to the side and saw Garrett shaking his head. I didn't know if that meant he hadn't told Shep about my black op assignment or if no one associated with Z Corps had. I was thinking the latter. I couldn't see Zane divulging that information to anyone—even if he hadn't signed a million ironclad nondisclosures—especially to someone like Shepherd Drexel. It wasn't that I thought poorly of the guy, I actually respected him and admired him. But the truth was, Shep was a collector of information. I didn't think he'd betray Zane and sell out my team. However, if there was a way to exploit Patheon's missions and profit from them, Shep would do it.

"My what?" I croaked out.

I had always sucked at lying and my voice cracking was evidence I hadn't gotten any better at it.

"Truth time. I'll go first," Shep proclaimed. "I've had my eye on you for a long time. You hit my radar when you were in a tech forum discussing the cons of Waymo. It was your opinion that the operating system of the Google X self-driving car could be easily compromised. There was some pompous asshole who argued it would be impossible. Three weeks later you were back in the forum with proof you broke into Google X. You laid out step-by-step how you did it."

Holy shit! That was like twelve years ago. Before Finn was murdered. I was young and cocky and out to prove to myself (and the world) I was good enough. I'd worked on breaking into the Waymo project twenty hours a day for three weeks straight. I'd taught myself back when there was very little information available about programming on the web. That was my first taste of success and Shep had been watching.

Crazy.

"I sent the project manager an email explaining how I got in and suggestions on how to fix their security issues."

"I know you did. When I went to get in, they'd fixed the back door you used. It was impressive work. I knew you'd only get better over time, so I watched you. Two years after Waymo, I was going to approach you to offer you a job. My workload was such I was turning down projects. I figured it was only a matter of time before you became my competition. I wanted to waylay that and get you onboard working with me. I was stalling because your brother had just been murdered and I thought you needed time. I shouldn't have waited; a week after Finn's death you hacked the State Department's network. You were uncharacteristically sloppy and left breadcrumbs. I went in after you and cleaned up what you left behind. A few days later Layla recruited you and I lost my chance but that doesn't mean I didn't continue to watch you."

I heard Garrett rumble something unintelligible next to me. I felt my stomach bottom out and a wave of nausea rolled in.

He knew about my team.

But that was impossible.

"I worked with Layla as an independent contractor for the DOD."

Shep let out an exaggerated sigh that told me he knew I was full of shit.

"I'd go into the details, Seven, but we have bigger issues than you thinking I'm stupid." Shep's retort had my back snapping straight.

It was a sad day when running a five-man black ops

team was less stressful than my current situation. Not only did Shep know my callsign, which presented a metric shitton of problems—including but not limited to Zane birthing a cow—but Theo, Cash, Easton, Smith, Jonas, and Layla were at risk. My boss was not a man you wanted as an enemy; he could burn your world down. However, so could Shep. That on top of being shot at, Cooper being hit, (yes, I was considering a graze as a GSW) me being stalked and followed, the troll breaking into my computer, and learning that it was very possible my stalker was a man I'd been chatting with for years. On top of that, there were the fights with Cooper and the emotionally draining conversations with Theo and Garrett. Not that my arguments with Cooper hadn't been emotional, but he was Cooper. Deep down I'd known he cared about me, as uncomfortable as it was, as scary, as emotionally taxing, I knew he'd take care of me.

So, with all of that, I was done.

I couldn't handle another issue.

Though in reality, everything that had happened was the *same* issue.

Before any of us could ask Shep what the bigger issue was, the troll took control of my terminal.

"What's happening?" Cooper asked as windows started opening and tiling across my screen.

"I didn't play into his hand when he opened the Text-Edit program and make maneuvers to kick him out. Which made him wonder if I saw it. So now he's making sure I know he's in."

The asshole wanted to play, we'd play. But I'd set the rules.

I started closing the programs but left the command prompt open.

"You sure you want to do this?" Garrett grumbled. "He

could have the contents of your hard drive. You know, your *important* files."

I didn't mistake Garrett's inflection for the warning it was. He was a smart man; I had no illusions he didn't know what was on that drive.

"As soon as he attempts to open them, they'll corrupt," I assured Garrett and prayed I was correct.

"I'll be happy when we can stop calling him, "*he*" and start using a name."

I agreed with Cooper for a variety of reasons. Besides the fact calling the jackass "he" was getting annoying as hell, plus once we had a name, we could eliminate the threat.

Which was why I was willing to play with *him*.

I just had to get the upper hand, and the only way to do that was to piss him off and hope his ego kicked in.

"Fucking hell."

At Garrett's curse, I turned from my screen to look at Garrett's.

He had the footage from the hospital parking lot opened and paused on a frame of a man with his back to the camera and I understood what the bigger issue was. It was not the baseball cap the guy was wearing, it wasn't the scarf he had wrapped around his neck to avoid Patheon's vein pattern detection, it was the logo on the back of the guy's shirt. The head of an eagle in profile—just the curved beak, an eye, and the neck, which was encircled by a shield. At the top, a five-point crown broke the outline before it picked up again. Completing the design was a star just above the bottom point of the shield.

Z Corps logo.

And if that wasn't alarming enough, the t-shirt was black, but the logo was printed in silver.

Silver.

A taunt.

"He's been in my machine before," I noted. "He's been through my emails."

That was the only explanation. The only way he'd know I'd been championing our team's color to be silver. Not that the guys or Layla disagreed with my choice, it was the guys from Red, Blue, and Gold who were throwing out suggestions of pink, purple, and the dreaded orange. Zane being Zane had been threatening to name us the Pink Team. Easton had flat out told Zane he'd quit. Surprisingly, Theo had been the only one who'd had a sense of humor and voted with Zane. Since the guys were on leave and taking much-deserved vacations these exchanges happened over emails.

I went back to my computer and opened the standard Notes app. Once it was opened, I added a new folder, named it INTRUDER, and created a note and typed a message.

Find anything exciting?

Cooper read what I'd written, muttered a similar curse under his breath, but clearly articulated his opinion. "I don't like this."

"Which part, brother?" Garrett asked. "The whole thing is a clusterfuck."

"The part where my woman's reaching out to a man who shot at her, followed her, and has been *stalking* her."

I tore my eyes from my screen and wasn't surprised to find Cooper's jaw clenched and his gaze narrowed on my laptop.

For a moment I contemplated continuing down this path. Cooper didn't have to emphasize "stalker" for me to know he was struggling. He was trying to hide it but failing.

He was being strong for me, he was being mindful of my emotional wellbeing. I, however, was not being mindful of his. I wanted to tell him I was not Linsey Peterson. I wasn't a teenage girl being terrorized. But I didn't think that would help. Actually, bringing up the Peterson family at all right now felt like it would be a slap in his face instead of it being what I wanted it to be, which was reassuring.

However, I had to say something to put his mind at ease.

"Coop, we need to know what he knows. I need to egg him on. I need him to slip up and give me something that will help us figure out who he is. I think he's someone I game with. But to confirm, I need to interact with him. While I'm doing that Shep's gonna be in *his* machine. I get you don't want me to engage, and I understand why. But I'm safe here, with you and Garrett."

My explanation did nothing to soften Cooper's expression; if anything, it looked like he was now grinding his teeth.

"And if he's tracking your location the same way Shep's trying to track his?" Cooper ground out.

Yep. Totally grinding his teeth.

"If he tracks my location to this house, you're here. Garrett's here. The team knows where we are. I'm safe here," I reiterated, and Cooper's unhappy gaze cut to mine.

Chaos.

That was the only way to describe the turbulence I saw swimming in his eyes.

Turmoil and sadness mixed in his bluish-gray irises, seeing my Cooper—my funny, charming, protective Cooper awash with despondency made me more determined to end this. Not for me. Not to get me out of the safehouse—which I had to admit wasn't terrible, but I still wasn't happy I'd been taken from my life.

No, *our* life—mine and Cooper's. The life I truly wanted but never thought I'd get. The life I had been too afraid to fully commit to. But I had committed to it and now that everything I wanted was within reach, all I had to do was outsmart some asshole who was threatening to take it away and Cooper would do the rest. He'd eliminate the threat and we could go back to our lives.

Only, when we went back, it would be better.

There would be no more hiding from each other. No more hiding our true feelings. We had what we had, what we'd been growing for months. A solid foundation to build on. We'd established a friendship, a bond, everything we needed was in place.

But until right then, seeing the look in Cooper's eyes I hadn't realized the toll it was taking. I'd seen his worry. I'd felt the impact of his angry outburst. I'd heard the fury in his voice. But I had never seen Cooper Cain sad. Not like he was right then staring down at me. This wasn't the same kind of sadness I saw when he listened to me talk about my parents and Finn—that was empathy. This was something more, something deep-seated. I knew he was worried about me, but the worry was cloaked in memories of a murdered girl he couldn't save and her family.

Murder surrounded both of us.

This had to end for Cooper.

I needed to end this before Cooper got lost in the past. A place I knew from experience was not a good place to be.

Come on, asshole—play.

20

I WATCHED as ten different thoughts raced across Kira's face. Any other time, I would've found it fascinating. I would've been enthralled by her intelligence and the speed at which her brain problem-solved, and in doing so exhibiting her aptitude and resourcefulness in a way that made all my bitching about teamwork and Garrett's attempts to draw her out and use her team seem stupid. This was not the first time I'd witnessed Kira working out a puzzle in her head until all the pieces slid into place. Maybe the rest of us needed to bounce ideas off each other and collectively come together to brainstorm but clearly, Kira did not.

Beyond that, I saw something else, something more important, something meaningful—straight-up trust shone in her eyes as she studied me.

I'm safe here.

Twice she'd said those words and both times I felt them slam into my chest. What I didn't feel was placated. Her trust meant everything to me, but the situation being what it was outweighed her faith in me.

I'd failed before. A failure that led to a family dying and the end of a career I loved. Logically, I understood the circumstances were vastly different. In my mind, I could discern the difference between Linsey Peterson's stalker and Kira's. I could easily separate the difference between working for Zane Lewis and the LAPD.

However, guilt wasn't logical.

Fear wasn't rational and in the last forty-eight hours it had become increasingly harder to rein in the bone-deep fear that one misstep could mean the end of the woman I loved.

Now Kira was making contact and the cop in me was screaming to shut that shit down. Provoking a stalker was never a good idea—actually, it was the worst thing a victim could do.

But Kira's not a victim.

She was however the object of this asshole's fascination. He wanted her attention, and she was giving it to him. She was playing right into his hand.

I sucked in a breath in an effort to swallow my objections.

"Kira," Garrett called out, bringing me back to the room.

Kira blinked, tilted her head ever so slightly, but didn't look away from me when she pleaded, "Please trust me."

The fuck of it was, I did trust her. I spent the better part of six months imploring her to trust her instincts. So had Garrett and the rest of the team.

This was the very definition of a rock and a hard place.

I didn't want her engaging but I had to trust her even though every cell in my body was begging me to demand her to cut the connection and let Shep and Garrett handle the rest.

"I trust you, Kira."

There was a ghost of a smile when she nodded and turned her head back to her laptop. My gaze followed and as soon as my eyes landed on her screen my stomach recoiled.

I find everything about you interesting.

Sick. Fuck.

Kira's fingers flew over her keyboard as she responded to his message.

If you find me so interesting, why are you hiding from me? Afraid I won't find you interesting?

"Jesus," I muttered.

"Shep, you finding anything?" Garrett asked.

"Lots of pictures. And when I say lots, I mean thousands. These have to go back years and years." There was a menacing rumble in Shep's tone. A rumble I couldn't deny I liked a fuck of a lot. He was pissed and everything I'd heard about Shep indicated he was not a man you pissed off. He had the skill and the time to ruin a person. In other words, I was damn pleased he was on board with bringing this asshole down and quickly.

You find me interesting.

My hands balled into fists at my sides and my pulse throbbed in my neck.

"Come on, asshole, tell me something good," Kira mumbled under her breath and typed another message.

I do? What do I find interesting about you?

Everything, KG. You like everything about me. You always have.

"He's on my squad," Kira announced. "We shorten our screen names when we chat with each other."

"What do you know about the guys you play with?" I

asked, then clarified, "Personal stuff. What about the date on the tattoo? Does that mean anything to—"

Kira interrupted me in a breathy whisper, "Holy shit."

"What?"

She didn't answer me; instead, she sent a new message.

Do we have a lot in common?

You know we do.

Yeah, I know. Grief is the human condition, right? It's the universal tie that binds.

"Kira, talk to us," I demanded.

"The tattoo. November fourth. It's the day SorryNotSorry's mother died of a heart attack. I knew I knew that date. We've chatted about losing our mothers. Every November he goes into a funk. He was close to his mom. He misses her. And since I know what it's like to lose a mom and miss her every day, I talked to him about it."

"Do you have a name?" Garrett pushed.

"I don't know his real name."

Fuck.

Garrett turned to his computer and asked, "Do you know where he's from? Where his mother lived when she died? Age? Anything?"

There was a beat of silence, and I wasn't sure what had me more on edge: waiting for Kira to answer, waiting on the asshole's response, or waiting to hear what else Shep had found. All three had me grinding my molars.

"He was twenty when she died. Until her funeral, he'd never drank alcohol. His family was strict Mormons. He got plastered the day of the funeral. His father was furious with him. He told me they vacationed in Moab. Arches National Park was his mother's favorite place, they went there every year, and he still goes there on the anniversary of her death."

"How does he get there? Fly? Drive?" I asked.

"He drives." Kira paused to read the message SorryNot-Sorry sent back.

Took you long enough. I had higher expectations, Kira.

Sorry to disappoint you, SNS. As I said the last time we chatted I've been busy.

Busy? More like absent. You find yourself a legitimate job and boyfriend and suddenly you don't have time for your friends.

"Legitimate job," Shep grunted. "He knows about Patheon. The team, not the program."

"Is today break into Kira's terminal day?" Kira groused. "Come one, come all. By all means, Shepherd, poke around and have fun."

"Like you thought I wouldn't walk through the opening the asshole left," Shep huffed his excuse.

"Since you're in tell me; how'd he do it?"

"You don't wanna know."

"I do."

"Well, then, you're gonna have to wait because you have more important things to do than beat yourself up about downloading a game file with malware to a machine you also do work on."

"That's impossible. I virtual terminal the game; none of the files install on this machine."

"Will someone, please, for the love of God, just get me a name?" I growled.

I was totally useless standing around while three cyber geniuses worked. I needed something to do beyond running a background check on Toni Rea that was pretty damn pointless now. And the something I needed was to go out and hunt down this fuckwad and end this.

"I can't give you a name, but I can give you a location," Shep said.

"How'd you get his location?" There was a hint of disbelief mingled with respect.

"He's using a VPN, the internet dropped, and the IP tracker captured the public wi-fi he's using before the VPN kicked in and masked it again."

I was less interested in how Shep had found him and more interested in a location. "Where is he?"

"The Westin Annapolis on Westgate Circle."

I knew where the Westin was. It was three miles away from the office. About twenty miles away from the safehouse we were currently in.

Twenty fucking miles.

I pulled out my phone, tapped in my security code, and pulled up Zane's contact information. I was nearly out of the dining room when Garrett called my name and I looked over my shoulder.

"You don't know who you're looking for."

"Black Sentra."

"And if he's connected using his cell as a hotspot and that's at the hotel but he's not?"

"Is that possible?"

Garrett frowned and shook his head. "Yes, it's possible."

Well, fuck me sideways.

"Kira? What do you think?"

Without missing a beat, she launched in. "I think he's pissed at me because I stopped interacting with him and the squad daily. I don't think this is about the game or the championships, it's about all of us chatting *while* we were playing. Shep, does he have any files named HondaRebel, VDGeek, or WestSide213?"

I agreed with her assessment but it didn't answer my question.

"Baby, I'm asking about your take on what Garrett said. Do you think he's at the hotel or do you think he did the hotspot thing?"

Without looking at me she absentmindedly said, "It's possible to connect to a cell phone and use that to connect to the internet. But I don't think that's what he's doing. I think he's at the hotel waiting. I think he's using this time to find my location."

"Nothing with those names," Shep started. "I'll keep looking to see if it's buried, but his folders are organized. So neat, I'd bet he has OCD. There's nothing out of place. Do you know who designed End of War?"

I didn't need to know who designed the video game, I needed to call my boss and get him to call in my team. I had taken two steps when Kira's answer halted me in my tracks.

"Harry Reems."

"Come again?" Garrett choked.

"Harry Reems," Kira slowly repeated the name.

I heard Shep snicker and Garrett outright chuckled.

"What? Do you know him?"

"You don't?" Shep asked, but before Kira could answer Garrett went on to explain.

"Harry Reems is a nineteen-seventies porn star."

"So? There has to be more than one person named Harry Reems. And how in the hell would I know a seventies porn star's name?"

"*Deep Throat?*" Garrett helpfully supplied a movie title. "You know the film where Linda Lovelace's clitoris is located in the back of her throat, and she has—"

"You're done," I grunted.

"I'd hardly call *Deep Throat* a film," Shep argued. "Though the soundtrack was gold."

Kira's brows scrunched and she hilariously asked, "Porn movies in the seventies had soundtracks?"

Well, it would've been hilarious if I wasn't in danger of losing my goddamn mind.

"I'm calling Zane. I'd appreciate the golden age of porn lesson to be over."

"Damn, brother, when did you lose your sense of humor?"

I knew Garrett didn't mean anything by his comment, but I still felt my blood pressure rise.

"The day my woman was shot at."

With that, I left to go into the bedroom to call my boss and I hoped to hell when I told him the name of the video game designer, I didn't have to sit through ten minutes of him laughing his ass off.

Zane Lewis knew a great many things; porn star names was a topic he was well versed in. Not because he watched it but because as a way to fuck with the government, especially the CIA, anytime he accepted a contract he gave the mission the name of a porn star. It was his continued fuck you for them fucking him over. He'd happily take their money and laugh his ass all the way to the bank when the SITREP and AAR all had adult film star names neatly typed in the headers.

I'd give him three minutes to laugh, then I was hanging up and going to the Westin solo. It wasn't like I needed a full team to takedown a computer geek.

21

"IT'S BEEN TEN MINUTES," Shep reminded me.

But more importantly, it had been five minutes since Kevin had picked up Cooper. It had been five minutes since Cooper had dragged me into the bedroom and kissed the hell out of me and made me promise to listen to Garrett. I wasn't all that fond of being told to listen to anyone, but the firm set of Coop's jaw and his grim expression had me agreeing.

Now he was gone, and Myles was sitting out front in his old-school, cool-as-hell, beat-up Bronco.

There had been no time to discuss the plan, and even if there was, there wasn't much of a plan to discuss. Cooper and Kevin were going to the Westin to "scope it out"— Coop's words—and if we found the car SNS had replaced the Sentra with, he'd tag it.

It sounded easy, but I had a bad feeling. A horrible pinch in my stomach. A feeling of dread. There were too many variables. Too many unknowns.

Garrett was still trying to recover the footage from the last hotel SorryNotSorry had stayed in while at the same time pulling up cameras around the Capitol building in an attempt to find the car SNS was now driving. Shep was still going through his machine trying to find something we could use to identify him. And I was doing nothing. I was staring at my screen with SNS's last message staring back at me. I didn't know how to respond. It was like I was paralyzed with indecision. And Shep was correct; it had been ten minutes and counting since his last communication and I needed to engage.

Busy? More like absent. You find yourself a legitimate job and boyfriend and suddenly you don't have time for your friends.

He knew about my team. He knew about Cooper. He knew I now worked for Z Corps. He knew my name, where I lived, where I'd lived before I moved to Maryland, and he knew about my parents and my brother. Yet all I knew about him was his mother had died of a heart attack and he visited Moab every year.

"You have to keep him engaged," Garrett gently told me.

Right. I had to keep him occupied.

But now that Cooper and Kevin were on their way to the hotel my bravado had waned. In the years I worked with Patheon, I'd provided intel that had sent the guys out on dangerous missions. Missions that would have them going up against terrorists and warlords, yet sending Cooper to a ritzy hotel in downtown Annapolis felt different. Not that *I'd* sent Coop, that was Zane who'd agreed to Cooper's plan, but still, my heart felt like it was going to explode from my chest.

We didn't have enough intel. We didn't have a real name or a picture of SNS but he sure as hell knew what

Cooper looked like and it would be a good assumption he knew Kevin, too.

He had the upper hand.

We were at the disadvantage.

"This doesn't feel right," I grumbled. "We need to call them back. We don't have enough intel. They should at least wait until we have a name."

"KK, the team's gone out with less." Garrett was still using his calm, gentle tone. "This is what they do. You and I, we sit behind our keyboards, and sometimes it's easy for us to forget there's no substitute for fieldwork. If nothing else, Cooper and Kevin will be in place to tag the new car when we have a new make and model."

I wasn't stupid, I knew that eyes and ears and boots on the ground were critical but not when huge chunks of intel were missing.

We needed more and the fastest way to get it was to engage. The new question was: do I pull out the dead relative card and play up that connection or do I antagonize him? I finally typed:

I've always had time for you when you've needed me.

There was a brief wait before I watched the letters appear on my screen. It was odd watching someone type in real-time—a reminder he had remote access to my machine. Access to all my files.

Bullshit. You were using me because you were bored.

In the beginning, there was a kernel of truth to that statement. However as the months turned into years, my squad had become a lifeline of sorts, they became my friends.

That's not true and you know it.

I waited and waited and when that wait turned into two

minutes and I still hadn't gotten a response I went for it and asked the million-dollar question.

Why are you doing this? Why'd you try to kill me and Cooper? Why are you following me and sending me creepy pictures?

"Bold play," Garrett murmured.

"Call him Harry," Shep instructed.

"Harry? As in Harry Reems, the guy who designed End of World?"

"Yeah, I want to see his reaction. I think your guy is Harry. He's either coding a knock-off game or he's coding a new version."

"Is it called V-12?"

"Yes."

"Do you have access to my personal email?" I asked Shep.

"If I say yes, how pissed are you going to be?"

That was a yes.

I was beyond getting pissed. Further from that, I was beyond the embarrassment that not only SNS but also Shep had been able to breach my firewalls.

"Look back to January of this year. You'll find an email about the new End of World version twelve. There's no release date, it's just the announcement from the creator."

SNS still hadn't responded to my last message, which made the bad feeling only intensify.

Hey, Harry, let me ask you a question...

I let that hang for a moment before I sent another message.

If you wanted to talk to me, why didn't you just reach out? Obviously, you know everything about me so I'm assuming you know my phone number. You could've called me. You didn't need to follow me or try to KILL me.

Not even two seconds later my phone rang and the sick feeling in my tummy intensified. It was no coincidence my phone rang right after I'd told SNS-slash-Harry-slash-asshole he could've called me.

I reached to pick it up when Garrett's hand wrapped around my wrist.

"Speakerphone and keep him talking as long as possible." It was good to know Garrett and I were on the same page. "Shep, you ready?" Garrett finished.

"Yep. I'm muting myself."

"Answer it."

Garrett released my wrist and grabbed my phone. Sure enough, it was an unknown number. I turned the screen to Garrett hoping he could memorize the number quickly. He nodded and entered the number into an internet browser.

"Hello?" I chirped happily as if there wasn't a knot in my throat threatening to choke me to death.

"I've never met a woman who is as intelligent as you yet so goddamn dumb," a man said back.

Thank God Cooper was not there to hear that.

"I'm sorry, Harry, was that meant to be a compliment?"

"I had high hopes for you but just like the rest, you're a disappointment," he returned and didn't make a correction on the name.

"How did I disappoint you?"

Garrett tapped my arm and I looked over at his screen. He'd recovered the deleted data Harry had erased from the first hotel.

And there he was, face to the camera.

Ballcap on, but no sunglasses or fake beard.

Bam. Gotcha, asshole.

I gave Garrett two thumbs up and in return, he gave me a dazzling smile.

An honest-to-goodness smile that made the area around his eyes crinkle, and seeing that openness coming from Garrett had my heart squeezing. The sight of that smile served as a reminder this was not his norm. He joked and laughed with the team but there was always an essential part missing, and seeing him now, I understood what that was—joy. There was no joy in Garrett Davis's life.

"I thought you'd be a challenge," Harry said, pulling me back to the conversation.

"Funny, I could say the same about you."

"What's that mean?"

There was a whine in his tone that negated the snarl I was sure he was going for.

"It means it took me less than three days to track you. And here I thought you were worthy of my time. But it turns out you're easy."

Garrett nodded and motioned for me to continue pushing Harry's buttons.

"And *Deep Throat*? Seriously, how unoriginal," I chastised.

"Fuck you, Kira. That's my grandfather's name and *You* didn't do anything."

Well, damn, that sucked for him. Again, with the whiny snarl. He sounded like a child on the verge of a temper tantrum but he'd confirmed his name was Harry.

I ignored the accusation and continued to goad him.

"By the way, the Silver Team shirt? It was a nice touch. Much better than the boring white button-up you wore to check into your hotel. But thinking back, I guess that's how I always pictured you—a *boring* middle-aged man with no real-life friends and nothing better to do than play video games."

That was a lie; I'd never thought about how old he

was or what he was like in his personal life. And the thing that totally sucked was I actually liked SNS; that was when he was just another member of my squad. He'd always been funny, very chatty, and always up to play—day or night.

Now I knew why.

He'd developed the game.

"Fuck—"

I cut off his curse to ask, "Why'd you shoot at me, Harry?"

"I didn't."

"Bullshit. I saw your tattoo. November fourth, the day your mom died. I know it was you. And yesterday you followed me. Why?"

"I wasn't aiming at *you*," Harry spat.

In other words, Harry was aiming at Cooper.

A shiver of fear ticked up my spine until my shoulders tightened and my neck spasmed. After that my stomach flip-flopped reminding me that I had a bad feeling about Cooper heading to the hotel where Harry was currently holed up.

On the surface, it was laughable—a video game designer versus a former SWAT officer and current commando. There would be no competition; Cooper could squash Harry. Add in Kevin as backup and Harry didn't stand a chance.

But something was nagging at me.

"Why?" I asked again. "I don't understand any of this. I thought we were friends. You invaded my privacy, and you stole my program. I'm not sure which I find more offensive, you poking around in my private files or you stealing and recoding a program I worked on for years. The pictures you sent me are just textbook creepy and unimaginative. But you shooting Cooper makes no sense. If you're mad at me for not playing a stupid video..."

Fuck.

I realized my mistake too late.

I'd pushed too far calling the game he'd developed stupid.

"*Stupid*?" he rumbled. No whine in his tone this time, just fury and fire.

"I didn't mean—"

Shit. What have I done?

"I thought you were the one." Harry's voice had grown cold and clipped and hearing it scared the hell out of me.

"Harry—"

"I thought you were the perfect woman. Smart and funny and you enjoyed playing EOW just as much as I enjoyed creating it. We were *perfect* together. You're nearly as smart as I am. You test my every skill. For years I tried to get into your machine with no luck. I couldn't break in. So I had to outsmart you. Offer you something I knew you wouldn't refuse. I had to work extra hard. I knew you'd catch it if I didn't bury it deep. And it worked. I did it. You downloaded the new game pack and gave me access your own damn self. We had the perfect life until you moved."

"Please listen—"

Harry interrupted me again. "This is all your fault. We had everything and you ruined it."

Garrett tapped my shoulder and I jolted in my chair. I blinked away the haze I hadn't realized had crept into my vision and focused on his laptop. An image of Harry Reems's Utah driver's license was up on his screen.

I couldn't begin to digest SorryNotSorry, the guy I'd talked to for years, the guy who I'd spent countless hours chatting about grief and the loss of a parent with, the guy who had made me laugh at a time in my life when I was lonely, the guy who had kept me company on some of the scariest nights while I waited to hear from one of my teammates to report in after a mission, was the same man who had tried to kill Cooper.

He hadn't been aiming at me.

Garrett was firing off an email with the new intel and I was trembling.

"*You* ruined everything," he repeated. "Now you'll never forget me. Tomorrow and the next day and for the rest of your life, you'll remember me. Goodbye, Kira."

With that send-off, he disconnected.

The air grew heavy, and I fought to breathe. Each inhale felt laden with fear.

What did Harry mean by goodbye?

"How secure is your location?" Shep's voice boomed in the room.

"Myles is out front and no one's getting into this house without heavy artillery," Garrett returned.

"Have you heard from Cooper?"

"He and Kevin are in place."

I mutely listened to the two men with my heart beating uncontrollably and my mind racing.

Goodbye, Kira.

Trust your instincts.

"He's planning something," I rushed out and tossed my phone on the table with a little more force than necessary but not enough to qualify as a full-on throw. Which what I wanted to do. I wanted to chuck my phone at the wall, followed by my computer.

To Garrett's credit, he calmly stated, "He is."

"Pull up the Westin cameras," I told Garrett and went

to work crashing my computer. "Shep, get out of my terminal, I'm killing it."

"I'm out."

"Cameras are up."

We were missing something.

For the second time that afternoon, I activated a kill code, this time corrupting my own files and rendering the computer useless. I slammed the lid closed and turned to look at Garrett.

"What's his end game?"

Garrett didn't answer.

Shep was silent.

And my throat constricted.

Everything happened at once.

Like a train wreck or a ten-car pileup on an icy road. Once the chain reaction started there was no stopping it.

Cooper and Kevin were on-screen walking through the parking lot. Harry Reems was running full speed out the double sliding doors of the hotel, gun raised and pointed at Cooper.

Kevin sidestepped and drew his weapon from his holster. Cooper abruptly stopped and pulled his, lifting it up and taking aim. Harry kept running but I knew he'd pulled the trigger when his shoulder jerked. A nanosecond later Cooper returned fire.

Watching a shoot-out in real-time was not like the movies. Harry's body didn't fly backward from the impact of Cooper's bullet. He didn't even fall to the ground. He stumbled forward. And the blood took a moment to soak through his shirt. There was no sound, but I didn't need it to imagine the thud Harry's body made when it unceremoniously hit the pavement. Without the use of his hands to cushion his fall, Harry's head bounced as he crumpled.

Cooper's head whipped to the side, and Kevin adjusted his stance. My gaze followed to the edge of the screen, but the camera angle was wrong. I couldn't see what they saw. But I did see Cooper's big body jerk. And just like with Harry, it took a moment, but the blood appeared and soaked his t-shirt. The t-shirt that thirty minutes ago I'd snuggled against as he hugged me goodbye.

Goodbye, Kira.

Tomorrow and the next day and for the rest of your life, you'll remember me.

"No!"

I jumped up from the chair. I vaguely heard it crash onto the wood floor as I ran to the front door. Two steel bands wrapped around my waist before I could escape.

"Wait."

"Let me go."

"Wait."

"Goddamn it, Garrett, let me go."

"Honey, wait. I'll take you to him, but I have to make sure it's safe."

"Fuck safe. Let me go!" I screamed.

Garrett didn't let me go, but he did usher me to Myles's Bronco. Once there he scooped me up, opened the door, got in, held me in his lap, and told Myles to drive.

He might've explained the situation to Myles, he might've told him to drive fast, he might've said a lot of things, none of which I heard.

Harry's endgame.

Suicide by Cooper.

But we missed something.

I knew it.

I *fucking* knew it.

22

I HATED HOSPITALS.

I hated the smell, the sounds, the sadness that clung to the walls.

But none of that mattered. Not when Cooper was somewhere in the hospital. No, not somewhere—he was in an operating room.

When we arrived at the hotel the police had already blocked off the parking lot. Blue and red lights flashed but all I could see was blood. Garrett was on his phone talking to someone but all I could hear were Harry's last words to me.

You'll remember me.

How right he was. I would remember Harry until the day I died. I would forever remember how I'd ruined everything. Just like I knew I would.

My love would kill Cooper.

I knew it.

"Kira?" Zane's voice rang out like a shot. It zipped through the air and punctured my heart.

Since arriving at the hospital no one but Garrett had

dared to come near me. Not after I watched the stretcher holding Cooper's big, strong, motionless body yanked from the back of the ambulance. Not after I watched medical staff swarm. Not after I saw a woman in scrubs swing herself up onto the stretcher, straddle Cooper's hips, and take over chest compressions. Not after I unleashed an unholy scream in the hopes Cooper would hear me and jump up to tell me he was okay.

Garrett was the only one.

He'd grabbed my hand and pulled me through the emergency bay. I knew he did his best to get me to Cooper before he was wheeled behind the thick, double doors that stole him from me. But it was too late. I didn't get to see him. I didn't get to tell him I was sorry.

I didn't get to say *anything*.

"Kira," Zane repeated.

I closed my eyes to block out the sounds. The waiting room was full. Kevin, Myles, Gabe, Owen, Garrett, and Layla were all seated, softly talking amongst themselves. Jaxon and his parents were huddled together in the corner farthest from where I'd been staring out the window. I didn't blame them for staying away from me. I killed their son and brother. This was my fault. I ruined everything.

I warned Cooper to stay away from me. I told him this would happen.

Everyone told me to trust my instincts, but Cooper ignored them. He promised me he'd be okay. He promised it wasn't me.

"Sweetheart—"

My eyes shot open and rage unfurled.

So much fury I couldn't contain it.

"I hate you," I hissed. "You lied to me. You told me it wasn't me."

Zane took a step closer, and I snapped.

Totally cracked.

My soul shattered into a million pieces.

With no control over what I was doing, my hand came up. I didn't feel the sting on my palm when it connected with Zane's face, but I heard the echo bounce around the room.

"You told me to take a gamble!" I yelled. "You told me it was worth the risk. You *lied*."

This time when I hit Zane it was with a fist to his chest.

"You're a fucking liar, Zane Lewis! You said it wasn't me."

"It's not, Kira."

His denial tore through me. I hurt so bad; the pain was so huge I couldn't stop pounding on Zane's chest. I needed him to hurt with me. I needed someone else to feel the enormity of my anguish.

"I believed you," I sobbed. "I trusted you. I knew better. I knew this would happen. I knew I'd lose him. I ruin everything."

Zane lifted his hands and panic rose fast and furious. Panic and fear and pain—so much of all three, all mixed together into one gigantic knot of bitterness and agony I felt like my insides were on fire. I wanted to crawl out of my skin and run away. I wanted to be the one in the operating room. I wanted to be the one dying.

I won't survive this.

It was too much.

My parents. Finn. Now Cooper.

My past and present gone.

There would be no future for me if Cooper died.

Zane's palms cupped my face with shocking gentleness.

He lowered his face until all I could see were his startling blue eyes shimmering with unshed tears.

"Listen to me," he whispered. "It's *not* you. You didn't do this."

His words didn't penetrate.

"I hate you."

"I know you do, sweetheart."

I didn't know what came over me except that I was out of my mind. One second I was standing in front of Zane, the next I threw myself at him. He rocked back, wrapped his arms around me, and when my legs gave out, he followed me to the floor. Zane twisted and pulled me into his lap. He said nothing when I buried my face in his neck. He didn't utter a word when I saturated his skin with my tears. He didn't stop me when I fisted his shirt and cried harder.

Zane silently gave me what he could. I soaked in what I could, I tried to use the strength he was offering.

Unfortunately, it wasn't enough.

I still fell apart.

———

I SLOWLY CAME AWAKE. As I did, I heard Garrett's deep voice cut through the haze of exhaustion.

"Want me to take her?"

"No."

The one word vibrated under my cheek.

I didn't know how long I sobbed, but it was long enough I'd cried myself to sleep.

"You've been on the floor with her for two hours. I can take her."

Two hours?

My eyes popped open but before I could scramble to my feet and ask for an update, Zane continued.

"No one is taking her from me."

More rumbling under my cheek and I felt Zane's arms tighten around me.

I cracked open my eyes and looked around the empty waiting room.

I was afraid to ask but I had to.

"Where'd everyone go?"

"Jax took his parents to get some coffee. The others stepped out to take care of business," Garrett informed me.

"Business? Did the police find who shot Cooper?"

I felt Zane's body go from tense to rock hard.

After I saw Cooper get shot, I didn't wait to see if Kevin had returned fire, and in my daze, I didn't ask on the way to the hospital what had happened or who the shooter was.

"Yes."

Zane's angry growl took me by surprise. He didn't sound happy.

"Is he in custody?"

"No."

Before Zane could stop me, I scrambled off his lap and was on my knees next to him.

"What do you mean, no? Where is he?"

I didn't like the look on Zane's face, I didn't like the creases between his brow or the way his lips turned down into a grimace. But when Zane's head dropped forward, and his eyes went to the carpet I knew something was wrong. Very, very wrong.

My gaze swung up to Garrett.

"Where's Cooper?"

"Recovery."

"What?" I screeched and got to my feet. "How is he?"

"The doctor said the bullet missed all the important stuff and he'll make a full recovery."

There was a lot left to be desired with the vague answer but I wasn't of the mind to push for more detail so instead, I asked, "Why didn't you wake me up?"

Zane was slow to stand and when he was upright, he rolled his neck but still didn't answer.

I needed Layla. She'd give it to me straight.

I turned but Garrett's voice halted my progress.

"You needed to rest."

"That wasn't for you to decide," I spat.

"I made the decision not to wake you!" Zane boomed. "Coop got out of surgery thirty minutes ago. No one can go back for at least another hour. *I* made the call to let you rest."

There was a hint of remorse in Zane's tone, but I didn't think it had anything to do with not waking me up.

The door to the waiting room slowly creaked open and Linc silently appeared. He'd obviously been in the room previously and saw me sleeping and was trying to enter the room without waking me up.

Great.

I'd slept while everyone else was up and worried about Cooper.

"Detective Garcia wants to see you," Linc announced.

"Tell her, I don't want to see her," Zane returned.

I jolted at the vehemence in his reply.

"Brother—"

"Unless you want my children and wife to be visiting me behind bars for the next twenty years, handle the situation. I do not want to see Garcia or the goddamn chief. As far as I'm concerned, the relationship between Z Corps and the Annapolis Police Department has been irrevocably dissolved. I do not want their explanation and Kira sure as fuck doesn't want their apology. And if they get anywhere near Jaxon or the Cain family, I will personally find ways to fuck them in a way that is so lasting they'll feel me until their last breath."

"What's going on?"

Zane's angry eyes swiveled to me. I automatically braced but I'd find it wasn't enough.

"Sam Thompson shot Cooper."

What?

"Detective Sam Thompson?"

"Harry made a call to Thompson, told him that he had information on the shooting outside the office, but *I* threatened to send Cooper to kill him if he reported what he knew to the police. He asked Thompson to meet him at the hotel. Thompson got there as Harry was running out of the hotel. He saw Cooper shoot Harry, Thompson shot Cooper."

I was right.

Suicide by Cooper.

But I'd missed the rest.

Harry wanted Cooper dead, too—death by cop.

His plan had almost worked.

And that was the remorse I heard coming from Zane. Harry had used him as a way to get Detective Thompson to the hotel.

"Thompson shot Cooper," I stated.

"Because of me," Zane grunted.

"No—"

"Yes," Zane interrupted me. "That asshole's had a hard-on for me ever since he approached me about a job and I turned him down. The guy's got a chip on his shoulder. He sucks at his job, and he knows it because he keeps getting bounced around from partner to partner because no one wants to work with him. He's been itching to find a way to fuck with me. I bet when Harry called him, he thought he'd won the goddamn lottery. He hightailed his ass to that hotel hoping to get the dirt on *me*. What that stupid fuck didn't do was check in with Garcia and communicate. If he had, he would've known that I'd already given her the heads up with an ID on the shooter and I had Kevin and Cooper en route to the hotel. And if that stupid fuck would've answered his partner's call, he would've known all of this. But instead, he went off the reservation hoping he'd be the one to take me down. Instead of doing that he damn near killed Cooper and ripped you and his family apart."

Guilt assailed and I thought back to the conversation I had with Zane a few days ago, the same one when he told me to take a gamble and roll the dice. The same conversation where he told me he was exhausted and how his men put their lives at risk and in danger for him.

Keep on keeping on he'd said.

And knowing he carried the weight of the world on his shoulders I'd let my emotions get the better of me and I'd told him I hated him.

All the progress I'd made had gone out the window. I'd reverted right back to the lonely, scared Kira but I couldn't stay there. I *had* to pull my shit together. I had to get strong before I saw Cooper. I had to be brave.

And if I couldn't do it myself, I had to use my team—*my village*—to keep me upright.

"I shouldn't have—"

"Don't."

Alright.

I'd had enough of being interrupted.

"I have something to say, Zane Lewis, and you're damn

well going to listen to me," I snapped. "I shouldn't've told you I hated you. That wasn't cool. I was out of my mind but I still shouldn't have said it, especially in front of a room full of people that included Cooper's parents and brother. And I slapped you. That wasn't cool either and I'm sorry."

"I don't deserve an apology, Kira."

"You don't?"

"Fuck no. This is my fault."

Here we go.

"How is it your fault?"

"If Thompson—"

It was my turn to do the interrupting. My hands came up and I planted them on my hips and narrowed my eyes on my boss. I'd messed up and planted the seed, said things I didn't mean, and even after I was cruel and mean to Zane, he'd held me.

"We can stand around all day and debate who's more at fault. Me, for bringing Harry Reems into our lives. You, for pissing off Sam Thompson." I paused and transferred my scowl to Garrett. "You, for not being clairvoyant—*ten years ago*—and not knowing that the intel you received was fake. Me, blaming myself for my parents loving me and therefore dying. Or we can all grow the fuck up and let it go, blame the people who are truly responsible, and move on. Because I can't do this anymore. My mom and dad would be disappointed in me. They'd hate me closing myself off to Cooper, which is exactly what I want to do. I'm scared and I can either use this as confirmation that the people who love me are in danger or I can use this as an opportunity to prove I am brave. For me, for my parents, for Finn, for Cooper, but mostly for me. I'm gonna use this to show myself and the universe I will not break. I am not weak and I'm choosing to use today as validation. I love Cooper so damn much, my world would stop spinning without him. I'm not giving him up. I'm not letting him give up on me. He told me he wanted to marry me and have babies with me. He wants a future with me and I'm taking it. Now, it would suck if Cooper and I were blissfully happy while the two of you were stuck in the muck and sludge of life's shit."

I stopped again and gathered all my bravery before I held Garrett's eyes and continued. "My brother would hate you holding guilt. He was kind and fun and loved life. Please hear me, Garrett—he would *hate* this. He would be crushed if he knew all you gave up. He would be so fucking hurt you live half a life because of him. If you can't find a reason to let it go for you, I'm begging for you to do it for me. I need to move on. I need to go to Cooper free and clear and I cannot do that while I'm worried about you."

When I was done with my long-winded soliloquy Garrett looked like he was caught in a place that was both torture and serene.

Limbo.

He *wanted* to move on.

He wanted to be free of the guilt he logically knew wasn't his, but he needed permission.

"Please, for me," I whispered. "I need you to help me move on. I can't do it myself."

Garrett's jaw was clenched but he nodded.

I was taking that as a win.

"Zane?"

There was a long stretch of silence. And throughout the quiet Zane's piercing blue eyes held mine. He looked like a man torn. A man who could pile more blame and guilt on his shoulders and still stand tall. A man who singlehandedly kept three teams of alpha men and somehow (mostly) controlled the uncontrollable Jasmin Parker. A man so loyal he'd kill and die for his family. But he mostly looked like a man who loved deeply. In other words, he looked like his normal self.

That was Zane Lewis.

I could slap, punch, and yell at him and he'd still hold me. I could take my anger and fear out on him, and he'd still love me.

"Thank you," I whispered and stepped closer. "Thank you for having my back. Thank you for giving me some-place to rest my heart. I will always be grateful you gave me a safe place to close my eyes and settle my mind. I'd tell you how much I love you for doing that for me, but I'd prefer to see my man without vomit on my shoes."

That did it.

Zane's lips twitched and while I didn't get both dimples, I got the left one which in my opinion was the better of the two.

"You're learning," he grumbled with fake annoyance.

"Learning what?"

"The fine art of manipulation. Stick close, my young prodigy; you'll be a master in no time."

"Awesome," Linc huffed. "Just what the world needs— two Zanes."

"I already warned Cooper he was fucked. KK channels Zane like a pro. He says he can handle it which is great for him. But I'm not so sure the rest of us can."

Yeah, my man can handle me just fine.

"So is it too soon to talk about how my stalker had a king of porn's name?"

Lincoln groaned, Garrett smiled, and Zane's laughter rang out through the room.

"Goddamn but you're my favorite. It's like you're the female version of me."

I looked around the room with my stomach still in knots and my heart still in need of repair. Yet I'd latched onto something to hide behind so no one would see my pain. I felt no shame knowing the only person who could untie the knot of dread that filled me and fix the broken pieces of my heart was Cooper. And until I could get in to see for myself that he was going to be okay, I would do what Garrett accused me of doing and channel the great Zane Lewis.

I could fake being strong.

For a little while longer.

23

"COOPER, YOU SHOULD LISTEN TO KIRA," my mother told me with a scowl from her spot at the end of the table.

This was how my life had been for the last three months.

Kira and my mother bonded over bossing me around.

I caved most of the time.

But enough was enough.

I glanced across the dining room table hoping to rally my father or my brother. Jaxon was doing his best not to laugh, my father was doing a better job seeing as he had forty-some-odd years of practice dealing with my mom.

"Your mother's right, son. You should listen to Kira."

I felt Kira's hand land on my thigh, then the smartass patted it as if she'd won.

Silly girl.

I snatched her wrist before she could pick her hand up and slid mine down until I pinned her palm to my leg.

"I appreciate everyone's concern, but I'm fine."

"It's too soon," my mother argued.

"Too soon for what?" my sister-in-law Violet asked as she strolled back into the dining room after heating a bottle for my nephew.

Vi was handing Mason off to Jax to feed when my mom answered, "For Cooper to take Kira down to Virginia Beach."

"Why can't Coop go to Virginia Beach?" Vi asked the million-dollar question. "It's not like he's gonna take the motorcycle..." Vi's words died a slow painful death, and I knew she was about to side with my mother and Kira.

After listening to Kira go on and on about how much she loved riding with Jasmin and me not wanting her on the back of someone else's motorcycle last month I broke down and bought one, and next week I was taking my woman on a much-needed vacation to Virginia Beach. Two hundred and fifty miles away from my family, our teammates, and especially Zane, who was teaching my woman very bad habits.

"We're taking the bike," I confirmed. "It's been three months and I'm *fine*."

"Coop. We can take the new Mustang," Kira argued.

The Stang wasn't new, it was a 1969 boss 429 fastback and she was fucking sweet but in need of some TLC.

"Can't, baby, already took the heads off."

"Cooper Felix Cain," my mother admonished. "Your doctor said light activity for twelve to sixteen weeks."

I bit the inside of my cheek in an effort not to remind my mother it had been over twelve weeks since I'd been shot, and I was well aware of what my doctor's orders were.

Kira followed them to the letter; she was militant about my recovery. It started the day I was home from the hospital, which was four days after I had my gut stitched up. Kira announced that she had Theo and Garrett move all of her stuff into my house. I didn't mind this. It meant I didn't have to talk Kira into giving up her apartment to move in with me. The part that sucked was that all I could do to celebrate her moving in was kiss her. And by kiss, I mean a chaste peck.

Not until I was home two weeks did she deem a real kiss wouldn't be too taxing. Though it took me another week after that to convince her my hand hadn't been injured and my fingers still worked. Three weeks of kissing and fingering my woman to orgasm finally came to end when my doctor gave me the okay for light activity. I took a page out of Kira's playbook and used manipulation to get her so worked up and mindless she wasn't thinking straight when I pulled her up over my face and ate her. But it had been *over* twelve weeks since I'd been inside my woman.

It was torture.

So, I was taking her on vacation so I could fuck my woman without someone coming by to check on me. I was taking her four hours away and turning off our phones so she and my mother couldn't gang up on me and conspire.

"Abby," my father gently started. "If he says he's fine, he's fine. He wouldn't put Kira on the back of a motorcycle unless he knew he was a hundred percent."

Thank fuck.

"I'm just..." my mom trailed off and Kira squeezed my leg.

"You're my mom, you're worried about me. I get it. I know you love me. But Dad's right." I paused to slide my gaze to Kira. "I wouldn't put you on the bike unless I was sure you'd be safe."

Kira's lips pinched, then twisted, then puckered like she'd swallowed a lemon.

She wanted to argue but she wouldn't.

"I know you'd never put me in danger. I just..." she trailed off the same way my mother did.

"Love me and don't want me to overdo it," I supplied. "We're taking the bike and going down to the beach."

"Okay."

I heard my brother's exaggerated sigh and I flashed him a smile. I almost got away with it but got cocky and added a wink to rub in my good fortune.

Not that my brother hadn't found himself a good wife, he had. I knew instantly Violet was perfect for my brother; she brought out all the best parts of him.

Just then Kira leaned close and whispered, "You know just because I agreed to go with you to the beach doesn't mean I've agreed to anything else. You are still recovering."

Jaxon sputtered before he belted out a laugh.

Oh, yeah, Kira caught me.

"You know that me not getting any means you don't get any. How much longer do you think you can hold out?"

"Cooper!" my mom gasped. "You'd think I had no hand in raising these boys. It was like boys gone wild in my house when they were teenagers. My only hope was they'd grow out of it. Clearly, they haven't."

"I didn't say anything," Jax defended.

My mom didn't respond because of course Jax was right, he hadn't said anything, so she changed the subject.

"When are you two planning on getting married?"

"Yeah, little brother, when?"

There was a twinkle in my brother's eye that told me he'd been patiently waiting to pay me back because years ago, I called my mother to tell her that Jax had brought a woman to my house. That woman was Violet, and Jax was hoping for a quick visit to SoCal without introducing Vi to our mother. I'd called her for two reasons, Jax needed a push in the right direction, and Vi had been kidnapped and beaten up pretty badly. If there was ever a time a woman needed a woman's touch it had been then, and Abby Cain was good at taking care of those she cared about.

But the joke was on my big brother.

"As soon as Kira agrees to marry me."

"Um. You haven't asked."

I couldn't keep myself from smiling at her snappy comeback.

"Right. Wanna get married?"

"I'm not saying yes to that half-assed proposal."

I heard my mom snort and Violet giggle.

"Then it's a damn good thing you agreed to go to Virginia Beach with me so I can get on my knees, tell you I can't live without you, and hope you agree to be my wife."

"I think you're only supposed to get on one knee, Coop," my brother corrected.

"How would you know? You didn't get down on one or two," Violet huffed.

"Sunshine, you loved my proposal."

Violet's cheeks flamed red, and I could imagine my brother didn't propose as much as he slid a ring on her finger and told her she was going to be his wife. This likely happened while they were in bed. And the more I thought about it the more the idea held merit.

"You wanna marry me."

I wasn't sure if that was a question or if Kira was stating the obvious.

"I told you months ago I was going to make you my wife. And Mason needs some competition before my parents spoil him rotten, so we need to get on that, too."

"Please, I can multitask and spoil more than one grand-child at a time. But yes, I agree, Mason needs a cousin."

Kira went stiff beside me. Not just stiff, but it felt like she'd stopped breathing. I hadn't felt her tense like this in months. Not since she'd admitted to me she was afraid to love me. When I woke up from surgery I was fully prepared for the emotional fallout. I'd spent time planning for Kira's eventual setback since I had actually almost died, something that scared the fuck out of her. But the days went by and she never slipped. Those days turned into weeks, then months and she never showed any signs of fear. As a matter of fact, me getting shot seemed to wake her up. She was back to living life the way she did when I met her.

Therefore, I was unprepared for her turn.

"KK?"

She ignored me and bashfully looked at my mom from under her lashes.

"Will you help me plan?"

There were a great many things I loved about my mother, but seeing her face get soft was now at the top of the list. Of course, she wouldn't miss the enormity of Kira's request, she was Abby Cain after all—the best mom in the world.

"It would be my honor."

"I don't...I mean..." Kira paused and sucked in a breath before she went on, "Thank you."

"We'll get started as soon as my son gives you a proper proposal. We can do it up big or do something small and intimate. Whatever you want, it's yours." My mom's nose scrunched, and I knew what was coming next. "Howard, help me clear these dishes and start coffee. It's getting late and the kids need to get home soon."

Translation: I'm getting ready to cry so I need to leave the table.

"Yes, dear."

My father stood and watched his wife disappear into the kitchen without picking up a single plate on her way. Not that my father would allow her to clear the table after she'd cooked and served.

"Two sons I couldn't be prouder of," my dad weirdly started. "Two beautiful, intelligent daughters. A grandson that is perfect in every way. My blessings are embarrassingly abundant."

With that, he left the room, leaving my brother and me staring at each other. Both of us doing our best to look casual but feeling anything but.

24

IT TOOK THREE RINGS, but he answered.

Not that I doubted he would.

"Someone better be bleeding, or you need me to help you hide a body."

"I'm marrying Cooper."

"So, with that I take it you don't need me to murder somebody."

"I want you to walk me down the aisle."

Silence.

All I could hear was deep breathing.

Finally, someone had rendered the great Dimple King speechless.

"Be my pleasure."

I heard the gruffness in his voice but ignored it.

"Love you, Zane Lewis."

I got dead air in return.

I tossed my phone on the bathroom counter and finished getting ready for bed.

I didn't need the words. I knew he loved me back.

After all, I was his favorite.

———

"KIRA."

Cooper's hands in my hair fisted on a downward glide.

"Pull me out, baby."

I ignored his request and continued to work his big, beautiful cock. But I did open my eyes and glanced up to find him watching me.

That was hot.

Cooper had two pillows against the headboard. His shoulders and head were propped up, his chin tipped down, one leg bent to the side, and I was straddling the other. My eyes ate up the sight of him laid out before me. All of him amazing—well-defined pecs, broad shoulders, all that hard muscle covered in warm, smooth skin that just minutes ago I'd kissed and trailed my tongue over on my way to his cock. It didn't matter my mouth had taken that route before, every time felt new, like a discovery. Each time I touched Cooper it felt like I was unearthing a treasure chest of riches—a trove of pleasure that was mine to unlock.

All mine.

One of his hands left my hair, glided over my cheek. His thumb paused at the corner of my mouth and he groaned.

"Love your mouth, baby. Love watching you suck me off. Love the way you get off having my cock down your throat. But I want your pussy. Pull off."

It had been a long three months. It had been pure torture not to give in to Cooper's requests, but I was determined that he make a full recovery. And as much as he promised to go slow and gentle, I knew my man. He could go slow when he had a mind to do so. He could do gentle but that was after he fucked me hard.

"Kira." Cooper's growled warning had my nipples pebbling and the hair on my arms standing up.

It wouldn't take much more for his control to snap, and I had every intention of making him do just that.

I dragged my tongue up his shaft and circled his broad head before I teased the tip.

I got no further.

Cooper knifed up and I ignored the urge to reprimand the fast jerky movement. If Cooper said he was back to a hundred percent, then I believed him.

Suddenly I was flat on my back and Cooper's hips were cradled in mine. I felt the head of his cock circling my opening but that wasn't what had my attention. It was his eyes that held me captive. Dark hunger and gentle adoration. The man loved me beyond all reason. And right then he was at war; he wanted to fuck me and make love to me at the same time, and he was trying to work out how to do both.

Silly man.

Hard and rough, slow and sweet, it didn't matter.

I was no longer afraid.

I had it all.

Everything I could imagine and more. I kept my parents and my brother tucked in my heart—I felt their love every day. I cherished it. I no longer fought the memories. They'd want me happy. They'd want me to have Cooper. They'd want me to be a wife and a mother.

"Love me, Coop."

He lowered his head and murmured against my lips, "Until my dying breath."

With that, he drove inside.

My arms wrapped around his shoulders, my back arched, and I dug my heels into the small of his back.

"Jesus," he grunted and held his body still.

I felt his muscles bunch under my palms. He was working hard to keep his control, but I wanted him unleashed. I wanted my Cooper.

"Coop," I whimpered and lifted my hips.

"Do. Not. Move. It's been three very long months. Three excruciating months since I've been inside of you. Three months of sleeping next to you, wanting to feel this..." To punctuate his meaning, he swiveled his hips. "Make no mistake I missed your pussy, but I missed this more. I missed the feel of you wrapped around me. I missed the feel of your bare skin against mine. I missed the closeness that only comes when I'm buried inside you. I missed hearing you whisper my name when you're taking me. I missed the tightness I feel in my chest, like my heart's gonna explode when you kiss me. So, I need a minute to soak it in. Remind myself: this is my future. I can go three days, three weeks, three months but I'll always get it back. You'll always be mine."

"Yes, Cooper, I'll always be yours."

"Hold on tight, baby, I'm gonna love you."

I held on tight.

I let my hands roam over his back. I whispered his name between kisses. I made sure every inch of my body was pressed close to his. And when my orgasm broke, he loved me through it, slow and gentle.

———

"KIRA."

My eyes slowly came open, the early morning light bathing the bedroom registered in a vague way, however it was Cooper's lips on my shoulder and the distinct, resulting shiver that woke me up. I started to roll to my back when his hand went to the middle of my back.

"Like this."

I knew what that meant.

Cooper was feeling bossy.

That sent another shiver through me, this one waking up all my girly parts.

I'd take Cooper any way he came, but bossy and rough Cooper was my favorite.

I felt him shift, his lips moved over my shoulder blade to the center of my back, then down until he reached my lower back. He stopped to yank the covers off. I only felt the chill in the air for a moment before his big hands covered my ass and squeezed.

"Love your ass, KK."

"I love that you love my ass, Coop."

I heard him chuckle, and since I loved seeing him smile, I turned my head as far as I could and looked back at Cooper. He was on his knees behind me, straddling my closed legs, chin tipped down, eyes on what his hands were doing on my booty. I liked him watching himself touch me. I liked the way his eyes followed his hands. I liked the way he clenched his jaw as if he liked what he was doing so much he had to fight his urges. I loved knowing I could reduce Cooper, a strong, driven, powerful man, to the brink of recklessness. Knowing I had that kind of power over Cooper sent a surge of wetness between my legs. Cooper could boss me in bed and I'd totally get off on it. But I knew I was the one in control, he would do anything I wanted. He'd stop, he'd go harder, faster, slower, whatever I commanded, he'd do.

"You want my mouth, baby?"

"No."

"My fingers?"

He didn't wait for my response. The tips of his fingers traveled down and dipped between my legs.

"No."

"Wet."

I was hauled up to my knees, my back pressed tight against Coop's chest. One of his arms went up and diagonal and that hand cupped my breast. The other went low and cupped my sex.

His face went into my neck and there he growled, "Gonna fuck you just like this."

A full-body tremble tore through me as his words hit and his teeth sank into my flesh. With my legs still closed it was a tight fit, and by the time Coop had worked the first inch in I was panting. His fingers pulled and rolled my nipple while his other hand toyed with my clit. There was a reason I called Cooper's cock beautiful—it was long and thick and perfectly formed. He was big, from behind he felt bigger, like this he felt huge.

"Cooper, honey," I whimpered. "I'm gonna come."

"Not inside you yet, KK, wait."

That was not going to happen. It was building too fast.

"Can't."

With a savage twist of my nipple that sent an electrical current straight to my clit I bucked and cried out.

"Don't come without me," he roughly commanded.

"You...I can't..."

"Not until I'm inside you."

I screwed my eyes shut, held my breath, and thought about kittens.

That worked for men, right?

I breathed out a sigh of relief when Cooper's fingers released my nipple, which seemed to be hard-wired to my clit. That relief was short-lived when he used that hand to fist my hair. My scalp tingled and my pussy convulsed.

Kittens. Kittens. Tiny baby kittens.

Arousal flooded me as Coop worked his cock in deeper.

"Good fuck, your pussy is so goddamn sweet."

Oh, no. It was gonna happen.

Ten...nine...puppies...AR-15...eight...*kitties.*

"Cooper, honey, I'm there."

"Not yet."

Dead baby puppies.... *whoa, too far*...Baseball, think about baseball.

Sweat beaded on my forehead and my muscles clenched trying to ward off a monumental orgasm that was so close to the surface I could feel tiny contractions forewarning me of the impending climax I was beginning to fear.

"You feel too good," I whimpered. "Please, Cooper. I can't hold on."

Cooper's hand twisted in my hair, forcing my neck to arch. His lips went to my throat, he pressed a wet kiss there, then finally growled, "Come with me."

Thank God.

Cooper drove deep, slowly dragged out to the tip, then slammed back in. The pad of his finger rolled over my clit and that was all it took for white-hot pleasure to roll through me. Throughout this, I moaned nonsense. I chanted his name. Coined him a God among men and took a pounding that left me gasping for oxygen.

I was coming undone but still speaking in tongues when Cooper released my hair and his arm sliced around me like a steel band.

I felt Cooper's rough voice at my neck. "Fuck, you feel beautiful." When he was done rumbling that out, some of the gravel slid out of his tone when he rasped, "Want your mouth when I come, baby."

Our kiss started deep and wild with lots of tongue. It was the kind of kiss that overwhelmed the senses and since I was still half-delirious from an earth-shattering orgasm, I got lost in the kiss.

What could I say? It was a really freaking awesome kiss. So, I groaned when Coop slowed the kiss. My disappointment was short-lived when his body tensed and he growled down my throat. When he tore his mouth from mine, he didn't move far but he did speak—two words.

"Marry me?"

"Yes."

What else could I say? I didn't care about the proposal or the ceremony. I just wanted to be Cooper's wife.

25

"KIRA? Do you have anything to add?" Garrett asked from his spot next to Zane at the head of the conference room table.

"Two things," Kira started. "Someone needs to give Bridget Keller an award for the most patient woman that ever lived. The trial was pushed back *again*. She's been under federal protection for like five years now living in a safehouse."

"More like six months," Theo corrected.

"I'm gonna second that award," Easton joined in. "Last night when I got to the safehouse, Theo looked fit to be tied and Little Miss Bridget was cool, calm, and collected."

My gaze caught on Cash smiling at Theo. I knew that kind of smile; it was the same one my teammates gave each other when they were getting ready to dish out shit.

"Two weeks ago, when we were moving her to a new place, she wasn't calm. She looked like she was ready to take Theo's balls off," Jonas put in.

I glanced from Jonas to Zane. His eyes were open and he was absentmindedly coloring in that damn adult coloring book Layla had bought him, but I was fairly certain the man was sleeping. Or he was so used to team meetings going off the reservation he'd tuned everyone out. Technically I wasn't supposed to be in the meeting, but my team was off training and since I still wasn't cleared for full duty, I was missing a day of sky diving. Strictly speaking, it wasn't so much training as it was the guys going out for a day of fun and expensing it to Zane, but the guy was loaded and since none of us were using what Zane called the Prophylactic Fund we figured why let the money go to waste?

"That's because Theo has no finesse with the ladies. He thinks he can pound his chest and throw a slab of wooly mammoth into the cave and she'll drop to her knees...in gratitude," Smith quickly rushed out the PG version of the end of his statement.

"Actually," Cash rapped out. "Theo's caveman routine worked a little too well and Miss Keller wanted a little action. Theo turned her down flat. And that's not to be mistaken with her being flat on her back and Theo turning her out. I mean he turned her away when she tried to kiss him. Now the sexual tension is so thick it's like trudging through honey anytime you're in the same room with the two of them."

Theo's face turned to stone.

Cash smiled wide.

Those two are going to be trouble.

That thought made me look over at Layla. It would be her job to keep the new team in line. Her frown spoke volumes. She needed lessons from Zane *stat*.

"She tried to kiss you?" Kira chirped. "Why didn't you kiss her back? I've seen pictures of her, she's totally hot."

"Kira," Theo grunted.

"Ignore him, KK." Cash chuckled. "His plumbing's backed up and he's grumpy."

"No banging the clients," Zane said at the same time Layla snapped, "No fun on ops."

"What's the second thing?" Garrett asked in an attempt to steer the conversation back to work.

"Since we all agreed on Silver Team, I had shirts made. You'll find them on your desks. I expect everyone to were them every Friday."

"Not happening."

"No."

"Not a chance."

"Hell no."

After that assortment of rapid-fire denials finished, Cash put in his answer, "I'll wear it any time you ask."

"If you'd stop watching kinky porn from unknown sites you wouldn't have to suck up to KK every other week and have her get the virus off," Easton rightly informed Cash.

"Cover your stump before you hump," Zane muttered.

The room went silent, and all eyes went to Zane.

"Is he awake?" Theo asked.

Garrett leaned forward for a better look before he answered, "No."

"So he just mumbles condom edicts in his sleep?" Theo went on for clarification.

"Pretty much," Garrett confirmed and pushed back from the table. "Since we're done here I have work to do. Kira, did you look over the new case?"

"Yep. I already sent you my notes. If you're free after lunch, we can strategize."

"I'll make time."

With that, Garrett left the room.

He didn't make a big deal about Kira meeting with him

to devise a plan of action. He was used to it, we all were. Kira was no longer an island unto herself. She understood the meaning of teamwork; not that she couldn't solve a case on her own, but the value in having people who cared at your back.

I pushed back and swiveled my chair to face Kira and asked, "Ready?"

"Yeah, you?"

"Taco truck?" I asked.

I saw the corners of Kira's lips tip up into a devilish grin that had me pushing away from her.

But I was too late.

I watched her yank a Nerf gun out from under the table, then I was up and running out the door as darts pelted me in the back.

"You gotta be quicker than that, Cain!" she shouted from behind me.

I looked around the office. Not seeing an extra gun anywhere I changed tactics and doubled back, running full speed at her. The crazy woman kept her gun up and rapid-fired darts, hitting my chest before bouncing off and landing on the floor. When she was within reaching distance I tagged her around the waist and pulled her flush against my body.

"You think you're sneaky."

"It's not my fault you're unprepared."

I wouldn't be making that mistake again though I denied my oversight. "I'm not unprepared."

A cute pout played on her lips as she whispered, "You keep promising me we'll put those..." She paused to glance around the room before she leaned closer and whispered, "butt plugs to use but you don't have lube."

Another oversight that needed to be rectified immediately. But in my defense recovering from a gunshot wound to the gut hurt like a motherfucker and it was just last night she'd lifted the sex ban.

"We'll get some on our way home."

"Can I use one on you?"

"No."

"*Please.*"

"No."

"What if I promise never to tell anyone your middle name is Felix?"

"Are you blackmailing me so you can take my ass?"

"Yes."

Straight out.

No denial.

My head tipped to the side and I belted out a laugh that echoed through the office.

Jesus, I needed to keep her away from Zane.

When I got control of my hilarity, I looked down and found her smiling.

I'd promised myself I'd never again take any of her smiles for granted, and since that day, I hadn't. Thus I took a moment to take it in and let it settle over me.

"You're not taking my ass, baby."

"Fine," she huffed.

"Love you, KK."

"I know you do, Cooper Fe—"

I leaned forward and kissed that silly name off my fiancée's lips.

26

Garrett Davis

My ass had barely hit my chair when Cash walked into my office.

"Ever heard of a filing cabinet? Or better yet, save some trees and go digital."

Yeah, I'd heard that a time or ten before.

I fought the urge to roll my eyes and told him, "Don't touch anything."

"If you tell me you know where everything is, I'm calling bullshit."

He'd be wrong, except after Kira had blown through and rearranged my shit for no other reason than to screw with me.

"Did you come in here just to bust my balls, or did you need something?"

"*All-Work One*. Nothing's changed."

I felt my gut knot before I remembered I was turning over a new leaf.

I'd promised Kira I'd let the past go, so hearing Cash call

me an old nickname shouldn't make my heart pound in my chest.

"Lot's changed," I semi-lied.

I now had the beginnings of gray in my sideburns and I was ten years older with a fuckton more regrets.

Cash smirked but didn't comment.

"We're going out tonight, sushi, you game?"

A few months ago I would've come up with an excuse—any excuse not to go out with my old team.

But now...

New leaf and all that shit I told Kira I'd work on.

"Yeah. What time?"

Cash blinked but recovered quickly. However, not quick enough.

My ringing phone on my desk flashed my mother's name. I reached out and grabbed it, pressed my thumb on the screen to unlock it, then answered the call.

"Hey, Mom."

"Garrett," she cried.

At the sound of my mother's voice, my heart dropped into my stomach and I stood.

"Where are you? What's wrong?"

"It's...your...father."

Her broken statement slammed into my chest and her words burned straight through me.

"What's wrong with Dad?"

She didn't answer. Instead, she wailed into the phone. I grabbed my keys off my desk and started for the door.

"Mom, I need you to calm down and tell me where you are. I'm coming, but you gotta tell me what's going on."

I heard footsteps pounding on the carpeted floor behind me and when I stopped at the elevator Cash was on my ass.

"Tell Zane something's wrong with my dad. I gotta go

home for a few days. Kira can handle everything while I'm gone."

"Do you need me to come with you?"

Jesus Christ.

Ten years ago, I'd turned my back on Cash and the rest of the guys, yet there he stood, loyal, offering to go home with me into an unknown situation—no questions asked.

Fuck, yeah, I had to pull my head out of my ass and stop acting like Finn's death only affected me.

"No, but thanks." Then I quickly added, "Appreciate the offer, Cash. I'll call you as soon as I have details."

The elevator doors opened, and I stepped in.

"Mom. Tell me what happened?"

"Your dad's been in an accident. It's bad. They don't think he's gonna make it."

Fuck.

I reached out to brace myself on the wall as a wave of nausea hit.

When was the last time I'd seen my father? Two years ago in Wyoming on a fishing trip. When was the last time I'd been home to Blackhawk? I shoved that unhappy thought away before I could summon up a picture of her in my mind.

"I'm headed to the airport right now. I'll be there as soon as I can."

"Okay, son. I love you."

"Love you, too, Mama. I'll call you when I have my flight."

I disconnected and stared unseeing at the metal doors in front of me.

They don't think he's gonna make it.

Fuck.

I love you with all my heart, Garrett.

Christ.

I closed my eyes and without permission, her sweet smile filled my mind.

I could face my past with my old team, I might even be able to let go of some of the guilt, but what I couldn't do was face the woman I'd loved for most of my life.

This was gonna hurt.

Can Garrett forgive himself and move on,
or will he lose the woman he loves
forever...

Garrett book 6 coming soon.

ALSO BY RILEY EDWARDS

Riley Edwards

www.RileyEdwardsRomance.com

Takeback

Dangerous Love

Dangerous Rescue

Dangerous Games

Dangerous Encounter

Gemini Group

Nixon's Promise

Jameson's Salvation

Weston's Treasure

Alec's Dream

Chasin's Surrender

Holden's Resurrection

Jonny's Redemption

Red Team - Susan Stoker Universe

Nightstalker

Protecting Olivia

Redeeming Violet

Recovering Ivy

Rescuing Erin

The Gold Team - Susan Stoker Universe

Brooks

Thaddeus

Kyle

Maximus

Declan

Blue Team - Susan Stoker Universe

Owen

Gabe

Myles

Kevin

Cooper

Garrett

The 707 Freedom Series

Free

Freeing Jasper

Finally Free

Freedom

The Next Generation (707 spinoff)

Saving Meadow

Chasing Honor

Finding Mercy

Claiming Tuesday

Adoring Delaney

Keeping Quinn

Taking Liberty

Triple Canopy

Damaged

Flawed

Imperfect

Tarnished

Tainted

Conquered

Shattered

The Collective

Unbroken

Trust

Standalones

Romancing Rayne

Falling for the Delta Co-written with Susan Stoker

AUDIO

Are you an Audio Fan?

Check out Riley's titles in Audio on Audible and iTunes

Gemini Group

Narrated by: Joe Arden and Erin Mallon

Red Team

Narrated by: Jason Clarke and Carly Robins

Gold Team

Narrated by: Lee Samuels and Maxine Mitchell

The 707 Series

Narrated by: Troy Duran and C. J. Bloom

More audio coming soon!

BE A REBEL

Riley Edwards is a USA Today and WSJ bestselling author, wife, and military mom. Riley was born and raised in Los Angeles but now resides on the east coast with her fantastic husband and children.

Riley writes heart-stopping romance with sexy alpha heroes and even stronger heroines. Riley's favorite genres to write are romantic suspense and military romance.

Don't forget to sign up for Riley's newsletter and never miss another release, sale, or exclusive bonus material.

Rebels Newsletter

Facebook Fan Group

www.rileyedwardsromance.com

facebook.com/Novelist.Riley.Edwards

instagram.com/rileyedwardsromance

bookbub.com/authors/riley-edwards

amazon.com/author/rileyedwards

ACKNOWLEDGMENTS

To all of you – the readers: Thank you for picking up this book and giving me a few hours of your time. Whether this is the first book of mine you've read or you've been with me from the beginning, thank you for your support. It is because of you I have the coolest job in the world.

Made in the USA
Columbia, SC
23 September 2022

67852882R00161